Artscape

Books by Frederick Ramsay

The Ike Schwartz Mysteries
Artscape
Secrets
Buffalo Mountain
Stranger Room
Choker
The Eye of the Virgin
Rogue
Scone Island

The Botswana Mysteries
Predators
Reapers

The Jerusalem Mysteries
Judas
The Eighth Veil
Holy Smoke

Other Novels
Impulse

Artscape

An Ike Schwartz Mystery

Frederick Ramsay

Poisoned Pen Press

Poisoned Pen Press
6962 E. First Ave., Ste. 103
Scottsdale, AZ 85251
www.poisonedpenpress.com
info@poisonedpenpress.com

Printed in the United States of America

For Susan

This book began with a dare. My wife heard the story and my wistful idea of someday writing a mystery and asked, "Why not write it now?" Why not indeed? So we did—several times. She it was who put me on the path to writing. I need to thank my critique group, Bette, Nancy, and John for the twice monthly dose of encouragement and good advice. A special thanks to my daughter Eleanor and her husband Mick for teaching me about root kits and keyboard loggers, to Poisoned Pen Press Barbara, Robert and Jennifer, for their patience. And to the many friends I made at the Southern California Writer's Conference, Michael Steven Gregory, Betty Abel Juris, Jean Jenkins, and especially Raymond Strait, whose public assessment of my writing skills still makes me blush.

Frederick Ramsay, 2004

Chapter 1

The sun, still low in the east, heated the morning air and sent it shimmering off the asphalt. The humidity, which had hovered around sixty percent all night, began its gradual ascent into the nineties, and people who had started their day an hour or two earlier showered and crisp acquired the wilted look that comes with summer in southwest Virginia. And summer in southwest Virginia begins in May.

It is an area blessed with mild winters, pleasant autumns, and breathtaking, beautiful springs, all compressed into seven months. The remaining five make summer. The procession of the seasons, thus compressed and distorted, characterizes the area and shapes the personalities of those who live there.

Ike Schwartz grew up in Picketsville, a town tucked away in the southwest corner of the Old Dominion. For all of his boyhood, Ike took it as a natural course of events that God intended life to be this way. It wasn't until he went to school in Massachusetts and experienced the splendor of New England's weather, deep snow in winter, gentle springs, summers which were warm by day, cool by night, and those blazing golden and red falls, that he realized there might be something better to look forward to from May through September than a shirt permanently sweat-plastered to his back and the inevitable lethargy that overtook everyone by three in the afternoon.

He had been in Boston no more than a week when he experienced the difference climate created in the lives of people. He, like the natives, found himself immersed in its frenetic pace—a pace that seemed never to slow irrespective of the hour. Back home, folks worked slowly and carefully, conserving their energy against the afternoon's heat. By three o'clock, almost everyone was off the streets, out of the sun. There was a tacit understanding that mid-afternoon was a time not suited for work. Employer, employee, and customer all recognized that little, if anything, was going to be accomplished.

To the occasional traveler from up north, this behavior was a source of wonderment, frustration, and anger. To have to sit in the waiting room of Cardwell's Gasateria, alternately cooled and ignored by a rattling, old-fashioned oscillating fan, and to watch, helplessly, while the mechanic, one's only hope to get back on the road to Wisconsin or Pennsylvania or wherever, sat and sipped root beer for an hour or more, qualified as punishment bordering on the cruel and inhumane. These purposeful people, Ike soon learned, had no comprehension, no experience, and therefore no reason to falter in their daily activity. Early in his collegiate years he discovered a number of reasons for not going home again, and summer topped the list.

Yet here he stood in the sweltering Shenandoah Valley, his shirt already damp at nine-thirty in the morning and a whole day ahead of him. *Sheriff* Ike Schwartz, duly elected by the people and sworn to enforce the laws of the United States, the State of Virginia, the County of Rockbridge and the incorporated town of Picketsville. He was also expected to bend those laws here and there, overlook the kids with a keg in Craddock's woods, the incestuous family of Craddock himself, and turn a blind eye to the broken speed limits, parking violations, and certain cash transactions entered into by members of the town council. An easy life, all in all.

He reckoned (as negligible) the number of serious crimes, difficult cases, or dangerous situations he experienced. The only time anyone shot at him was when Chester Duncan came home to find his wife in bed with his brother, Darryl. Chester shot them both, and vowed to take the whole of the town with them. After he pumped two barrels of his twelve-gauge into the bushes six yards to Ike's right, he sat down on the porch and cried like a baby. Ike only had to gentle him into the police cruiser and take him away. A jury of his peers, small towns being one of the few places on earth where juries are truly composed of one's peers, acquitted Chester of the murder charges, declaring any reasonable man would have done the same. The judge, being of a somewhat less lenient disposition, found him guilty of disturbing the peace, discharging a firearm within the corporate limits of the town, and disorderly conduct, and remanded him into the custody of the state mental institution, where, it is reported, Chester is making excellent progress.

"At least I don't have to deal with terrorists down here," Ike muttered to himself. He hoped it would make him feel better. It did not.

He stepped off the porch and headed toward his black and white. The eighty feet he had to walk to the car was enough for the heat to break a light sweat on his forehead. As he heaved his two-hundred-pound, six-foot two-inch frame behind the wheel, he wondered for the first time that day, and the hundredth time that year, why he had ever decided to come home, and having done so, why he had allowed himself to be talked into running for sheriff of this Godforsaken crossroads. But he did know why, thanks to the expensive psychiatrist at the Phipps Clinic.

"You can't run forever, Isaac."

No one but his mother ever called him Isaac.

"Sooner or later, you have got to go home, face your father, those other people, and when you're ready, talk. Talk about your wife, your life, what you can of it, of course, and make peace with yourself. I cannot convince you, and you will not accept the therapy that would allow you to do it yourself, so go home, touch base, and start again. It is like hide and seek. You remember when you were a kid? You'd hide from another kid who was 'It', and you'd be half-frightened behind some bush or tree, not knowing if 'It' was close to you or after some other kid. You would peep out and if his back was turned, you would make a dash for base . . . all-ee, all-ee outs in free. Right? So go home, touch base, when you're ready, if you need to, but only when you're ready, we'll talk again."

One hundred and eighty-five dollars an hour and all Herbert Rosenberg, M.D., board-certified psychiatrist, tenured professor at the Johns Hopkins University School of Medicine, and author of three books and fifty juried articles, could give him was hide-and-seek. All-ee, all-ee outs in free, for God's sake. But Ike knew that sooner or later, he must remember Zurich, and Eloise, but not now, not today, no, definitely not today.

He rolled down the windows, started the engine, turned the air-conditioning on high, and switched on his radio. After a moment, he punched the transmit button and called in.

"One to base...."

Essie Falcao's voice crackled back, "Base to One. That you, Ike?"

"Now who else would be calling you on the radio, Essie? Garth Brooks? Of course, it's me."

"Right. Sorry, Ike."

"Okay, Essie, listen. I'm driving out to the college this morning and I'm going to turn this radio off because I don't want to have to listen to you gabbing with everybody in town on the police frequency."

"Ike, how do I contact you if anything comes up?"

"Essie, the possibility of anything coming up in the next forty-five minutes is so unlikely that I reckon we'll chance it. Hell, Essie, the way this town works, it would take somebody an hour to even recognize anything was going on, and another half hour before they would get around to calling it in. But on the off chance a Boeing 747 makes an emergency landing on Main Street, or the phantom rapist shows up at Mrs. Cardwell's coffee klatch, or worse yet, the mayor makes a decision, you call Whaite or Billy, then call me at the college on my cell phone."

"Right, Boss."

"And Essie, the next time you see Billy, you tell him for me that one, he's to stay out of this cruiser. This bucket of bolts is about to conk out as it is and I don't need him yahooing around the country scaring old ladies and impressing young girls in it. And two, if he does use it, he is to keep his smoking to an absolute minimum, especially the funny cigarettes he rolls himself with stuff that should be in the evidence locker. And three, if he does use the car and does smoke in it, he should clean up the mess afterward. Got it?"

"Okay, Boss, Yes, sir. I got it."

"And, Essie, since you're the one with him when he does that crap, the message is for you, too."

"Now, Ike, I never...."

"Essie, are you missing anything, a bit of personal attire maybe? A little red, frilly—what is this thing? It looks like it belongs on a slingshot. You don't have to answer, but you might check the glove box next time you find yourself in this car. Really, Essie."

He snapped off the set before she could answer and, grinning, put the car in gear. He opted for a quick detour and breakfast at the Crossroads Diner. He hoped food would fortify him against the appointment he dreaded keeping.

The regulars had already arrived at the diner when he pushed through the door and took his usual stool near the back. Flora brought him his coffee, already creamed and sugared. He nodded his thanks and spent thirty seconds staring at the tiny yellow blobs of butter fat circling his cup. Nothing changed. His eggs over easy, toast, limp bacon, and the mandatory dollop of grits would come next. Flora served grits thick and gelatinous. "Can't stand them city grits," she declared. "Look like soup—can't do a body no good that way."

He sighed and turned his attention to the antique television in the corner. He forced himself to watch a scene which, played incessantly over the last two months, had been indelibly etched into his brain.

‹›‹›‹›

The steady thump of bullets hitting the side of the house and the whine of ricochets all but drowned out the orders he screamed at the three men crouched behind tables, sofas, and anything that might offer some measure of cover.

"Set your bombs to go off as soon as you release," he shouted. Just then the firing stopped. They waited in the eerie silence that followed—guns off safety, explosives strapped to their bodies.

"I am sorry, Rascheed," one rasped.

"It is all right. You tried. The guard was not supposed to be there. Our information was bad. The Italian will pay."

"He should die for that," a third said and shook his fist.

"Yes," the one called Rascheed said. "But we will not be the ones to see to that."

A bullhorn shattered the silence.

"This is Captain L. P. Davis of the New York Police Department. Come out with your hands in the air. You are surrounded, you cannot escape."

"Shhhh," Rascheed whispered. "Do not say anything."

"Can you hear me in there? You are surrounded. Give yourselves up."

"Abdul, show the nice policeman what we think about giving up."

Abdul scuttled across the floor to the window, stood, and snapped off three shots, killing one policeman and wounding another. He fell backward as a hailstorm of government-issue bullets tore through the window and him. For the next five minutes the noise was deafening. Bullets, shotgun pellets, and balls slammed into the house from all sides. Windows shattered. The siding was reduced to slabs, to splinters, to toothpicks. Their meager cover of furniture could not protect them from the rain of ordinance that shredded the room around them. The shooting stopped again.

"They will ask us to surrender again, Rascheed?"

"Not this time. We have killed one of theirs. They will not stop now until we are all dead."

"Allah be praised."

"Yes. You know what to do next?"

The two others nodded.

There was a thump and hiss as a teargas canister arced into the room.

The assault resumed, only this time the shots were high and off to either side of the door.

"Be ready, they are coming," Rascheed choked. They heard the footsteps on the porch and then in the room. They lay still, faces close to the floor and the little breathable air it afforded, bandannas over their mouths. When he was sure there were at least a half dozen police within range, Rascheed, with his last breath, screamed, "Now." And three bombs went off, the concussion detonating the fourth on the lifeless body of Abdul.

The house exploded in a ball of fire. Debris and body parts flew upward and as far away as the next block. Eight of New York's finest were killed in the blast. A dozen others were hurt. Houses on either side were flattened. Two across the street had their fronts caved in and windows blown out. There was no trace of the bombers. The NYPD had been victimized by yet another terrorist tragedy, another sad day in a city already burdened with more than its share of senseless deaths.

By midnight the awful work of cleaning up and identifying victims began. DNA samples were taken and matched to scraps of humanity, dental records collected and checked, and, in the end, a fair amount of guesswork employed as the death toll was totted up. It would be weeks before the investigating team left the scene and three months before the shattered buildings were razed and hauled away.

Ike, his coffee now cold in its cup, watched in fascinated horror, as the scene was run and rerun. He barely heard the running commentary from the talking heads, safe in their studio or blocks away with camera crews.

"This bizarre set of events began early one Friday morning when four men attempted to break into the rare book room of the New York City Public Library. Sources in the Antiterrorism Task Force now report they believe the men planned to seal themselves in with thousands of precious volumes and, in effect, hold them hostage. The bombs which blew up the house in Brooklyn were to be detonated in the library if their demands for millions of dollars were not met.

"A suspicious guard attempted to detain them and was shot. Another guard's quick thinking locked down the rooms and the men had no choice but to flee, leading New York police on a high-speed chase across Manhattan and into Brooklyn, where as you just saw, they barricaded themselves in the house, then—the terrible explosion. Two months ago, we witnessed these terrible events. Today, a spokesperson for Homeland Security reports they have identified the group responsible, the New Jihad. The question every American is asking today: Where will the terrorists strike next? Now this...."

The coifed and polished newsreaders were replaced by a commercial.

"Shut it off, Flora," Ike said.

Flora Blevins stubbed out her cigarette in a fried egg and snapped off the television.

Ike stared at his eggs, congealed with the bacon in a puddle of whitish grease. His toast, never hot in the first place, lay limp and cold next to them. His grits remained at attention, awaiting orders to do a body some good. He turned and stared at the parking lot through the double glass doors and sighed, pushed his breakfast away, and walked to the cash register. Monday morning in the Crossroads Diner—the beginning of another day, another week, a lifetime. A little past nine o'clock in the morning, but becoming clear it was going to be one of those days. He pushed through the doors and strode toward his patrol car. He turned the air-conditioning on high and headed out of town toward the low hills that shielded Callend College from the untutored eyes of the townsfolk.

Chapter 2

"Can we come to order?"

It was not a command, barely a request. Just a bit after nine o'clock and Charles Dillon's head pounded from the effects of the bottle of expensive scotch he had consumed the night before.

"Order please," he said again, only louder. Charles Dillon was affectionately known, by the few who held any affection for him at all, as Charlie Two. His son, the bright young archeologist and the apple of his grandfather's eye, answered to Charlie Three.

"I have before me the report from the Foundation and I will read it. After that we will discuss its contents and then I will call for the Board to vote on an issue of some importance to us all." He cleared his throat and began to read.

Four men and two women sat at the conference table—the Board of Trustees of the DCS, the Dillon Collection South, a euphemism which described the half billion dollars' worth of paintings, statuary, and rare prints stored in an air-conditioned building constructed to house them on the Callend College campus. The building was a product of the 1950s, when people believed they could avoid a nuclear holocaust by going underground for a few months. Bomb shelters were as popular as hoola-hoops. Charles C. Dillon, inventor, entrepreneur, philanthropist, eclectic art collector, and confidant to then President Eisenhower, Charlie One were he still alive, did his part to forward the administration's civil defense policy by building what had to be the country's biggest bomb shelter, not to house people, but to safeguard evidence of Western culture, something people would need when civilization was rebuilt, after the smoke cleared—his art collection.

He selected Callend College for Women as the site for this marvel because it was far removed from any target Russia might consider worthwhile. Thus, one half of the Dillon collection sat safe in an underground vault, the bunker it came to be called, surrounded with enough reinforced concrete to build an impressive highway. Every six months or so, tractor trailers arrived, and as guards watched, a ton or so of art works was unloaded and stored, and an equal amount removed to be carried back to Cleveland for display.

The college benefited in a number of ways. The collection generated additional annual revenues of one million dollars and subsidized the salaries of the college's larger than normal security force, a sum in the neighborhood of two hundred and fifty thousand dollars. The collection enabled the college to have an excellent History of Art Department that attracted a number of distinguished scholars to the campus. They, in turn, helped attract students and thereby maintain the college's competitive position in the enrollment sweepstakes.

It also enabled the college to solicit other gifts from the Dillon Family Foundation: the Dillon library, the Martha Denby (née Dillon) professorship in Modern Dance, the Charles C. Dillon Audio-Visual Laboratory, not to mention a number of unnamed, but useful additions to its physical plant, including a substantial grant to overhaul the school's communications and information processing capacity. A gift, the senior Dillon had declared, to honor the inauguration of Ruth Sydney Harris as the school's thirty-fifth president. Computers, information management systems, arrived in boxes and crates. "Modern times call for new leadership and the equipment to support it," Dillon wrote at the time.

Ruth Harris had been named president of Callend College eighteen months previously. She arrived with hopes high and the confidence needed to tackle the problems endemic to small colleges across the country. An annual deficit of a million dollars did not dismay her. The threats of faculty unionization left her unmoved, and the task of maintaining a single-sex school in an era of declining interest in that remnant of early Americana was, to her, just another challenge

What she had not counted on was the crushing boredom of administration, the inertia that permeates bureaucracies, even in the smallest and most informal organizations, and the pettiness of college politics. It was not that she was unfamiliar with all these things. She had been professor and chairman of the history department at the University of Chicago and was the only child of the distinguished Barton M. Harris, former dean of the Yale School of Law. Yet it was one thing to be a child-observer and, later, a player on the other side, and quite another to be the establishment. And that is what, she ruefully admitted, she had become. The student radical gone to seed, espousing the procedures, behaviors, and values she had once so vehemently opposed.

She was six in the summer of 1968. Her father served on the Northwestern School of Law faculty the year Chicago exploded in a swirling, screaming mass of student radicals, tear gas, and police. Barton Harris spent weeks defending himself and the battered young people the police dragged into lockups all over the city. Ruth heard and absorbed her parents' outrage. Later she marched with them in Washington as the Viet Nam War wound down. By the time she entered Wellesley, she, like many of her generation, had adopted the behaviors and attitudes of older brothers and sisters but not their causes. The war ended. Nixon crushed George McGovern in a landslide. The country was about to embark on its experiment with conservatism.

Without a quintessential cause like the war, students became radical generalists. They deplored toxic waste, hugged trees, and marched for the ratification of the Equal Rights Amendment. They were suspicious of the government and most of its institutions. They believed in conspiracies and despised, in no particular order, the Office of the President, capitalism, the FBI, the CIA, the OMB, and the whole alphabet soup of bureaucracies. Bereft of a focus for their disdain, many, including Ruth, drifted into Marxism, the radical *chic* of the day. The campuses of America offered the one place where to be a Marxist was not viewed as a negative. Quite the contrary, it was often seen as a positive, the mark of an independent thinker. That so many adopted this stance reduced somewhat, the appellation *independent*. However, it served Ruth well and she advanced through the ranks to become a department chair, a dean, and, now, the president of Callend. When the Berlin Wall collapsed, so did her devotion to Karl Marx. Instead, she became addicted to chocolate, thereby joining millions of her sisters in the single solidarity that cut across ethnic, economic, racial, and sociological lines.

She gazed at the others around the table. Charlie Two droned on. Ruth listened for the words she knew were coming, words she was helpless to prevent—words which would tip Callend's precarious economic scales into the red, and spell its eventual doom.

To Dillon's right was Sergei Bialzac, chairman of the history of art department. To his left was the wife of the president of Picketsville Bank, Marge Tice. Her membership on the board was a mystery to some. But those who knew her, knew she had the brains and the blunt honesty to run her husband's bank and the good sense to pretend she did not. Ruth sat across from these three, flanked by Ben Stewart, owner of Stewart Galleries, New York and Philadelphia, and Dan Clough, president emeritus of the college.

Ruth tried one more time to grapple with the problem she had so far been unable to solve: how to stop the board from voting to terminate the lease and remove the collection. She had just begun to erase the chronic deficits thought by her predecessor as permanent. Another year, two at the most, and the college would be in the black and the annual raids on the endowment at an end. She had done it. Almost.

Dan Clough would be pleased to see her fail. His retirement and the consequent appointment of Ruth to the presidency were occasioned because of the economic problems the college had developed. His position had been, and remained, that there was no solution to the deficits. The money would have to come from elsewhere, a merger with one of the men's colleges in the area. His insistence on that point brought him into conflict with the alumnae and the Board of Trustees. He was asked to step down and, as a final blow to his already damaged ego, a thirty-five-year-old woman was named to replace him.

Stewart's recent opposition to "burying the world's treasures" puzzled Ruth. Always in the past, Ben acted as a rubber stamp for the college, but no longer. She and Sergei would vote against, and that left Marge the swing vote. A vote for would end it; a vote against would create a tie that would defeat. And then there was Senator Rutledge's proxy. The senator was a member of the Board but as yet had not attended any meetings. However, he did send lengthy and detailed comments, doubtless prepared by his staff, to be read into the record on each agenda item before the meeting and a beautiful letter of apology afterward. Never before had he sent a proxy vote, nor had there ever been a need to.

Dillon's sonorous voice took on the tone speakers have when they are nearing completion. The timbre improved and the volume increased, his words resonated against the rosewood paneling and buried themselves in the two fifteenth-century tapestries on the walls. Eyes once glazed returned to alertness.

"In conclusion," he read, "the Foundation's position is as follows: Whereas the lease expires in three weeks and, Whereas there is no realistic reason to renew it, the Dillon Collection South shall be removed from storage to be displayed in a new gallery in New York which the foundation has just leased with the able assistance of our friend, Ben Stewart."

A bombshell! She expected the termination, but not in three weeks. Three weeks…and Ben—the quisling.

"The corporate bylaws require a majority vote of the members of this board; therefore, I move the following: the lease not be renewed at its termination date three weeks hence, arrangements be made to remove all the contents from the Art Storage Compound and the practice of storing the collection at Callend be ended forthwith."

So there it was. Stewart seconded the motion.

"President Harris, I am sorry to have to put this to you this way, especially on such short notice, but you see, times change. And, of course, the vault itself remains the property of the college. No way we can take that back, is there?" Dillon chuckled.

Maybe it was the heat or maybe just hearing the words. Whatever the reason, Ruth lost the cool detachment on which she had built her reputation at the college.

"Mr. Dillon, under the circumstances, I can't bring myself to see the humor in that. The fact is if the collection goes, you might as well take the building with you. The hole you would leave behind would be far more useful. We could bury our hopes, our future, and one hundred and fifty years of educational traditions in it. A four-story underground, air-conditioned bomb shelter is of no use to us whatever." Ruth's eyes glittered, partly from anger, partly from disappointment.

"The question, Mister Chairman."

"Not so fast, Ben. You'll get your super gallery soon enough," Ruth snapped.

"The motion has been made and seconded. Is there any debate?"

Ruth waited for what seemed to be an eternity. Stewart whistled through his teeth; Clough drummed his fingers, eyes fixed in space, dreaming of his triumphal return, the Douglas MacArthur of Callend—back to an embattled academic Corregidor. He would turn the school over to the democracy of merger, or sub-merger, with…whom? There were no more all-male colleges left in the area.

Ruth championed all-women institutions. It was not that she was old fashioned. Her friends could not believe she would bury herself and her career in what they considered an academic dinosaur. But she believed that women performed better without the distraction of men. In a single-sex environment, women could assume leadership positions and build confidence. She saw in her teaching years that when the testosterone titer in the immediate area rose, women sometimes became deferential and even silly, and would let any moronic position formulated by a man override their own, no matter how much better it might be. In an all-female environment, women excelled. Their natural sensitivity and intuitive understanding of human relations came to the fore. There was time enough in the real world that awaited her graduates to go head to head with men. Now they needed to grow in both knowledge and confidence.

"Dr. Bialzac?" Ruth needed some help, some time. "You were about to say?"

The little professor blinked, paused, and then unleashed a virtual torrent of words. They poured out of him in spurts, gushers, and streams, rolling together, and cresting into a tidal wave of protest. His eyes glittered behind his wire-rimmed spectacles. His Van Dyke pointed, punctuated, and launched paragraphs of polemic. He discoursed on the tragedy about to be visited on the college, the department which he had the rare privilege—no, honor—to head, the academic community, even the State of Virginia. He pleaded. He threatened. The entire gamut of human emotions crossed his moon-like face as he contemplated certain destruction. It was an incredible performance, even for Bialzac.

"This will not be forgotten, sir," he spat at Stewart. "No, sir, Judas was paid his thirty pieces of silver and got a cemetery and himself as the first customer. This is betrayal, this is blasphemy, and you are the Philistines who have delivered up Callend to be crucified."

Bialzac stopped his tirade in mid mixed metaphor as abruptly as he had started and slumped back into his chair. He looked rumpled, exhausted, and distraught.

"Thank you, Dr. Bialzac," Ruth inserted. "Are there any more comments for the record?"

Dillon was on the thin edge of losing his temper. The others were too nonplussed or amazed to speak. Ruth turned to Dillon and with all the patience she could manage, tried one last time to salvage the collection. She spoke to him as the mover, but her words were for…whom? Marge Tice? Stewart?

"Mr. Chairman, Mr. Dillon, I can understand the foundation's position, and your concern for and generosity to the college attest to your long commitment to it. I ask only that you consider the impact this decision will have on us, not just in the long run, but particularly, in the short run. I suppose we all knew that sooner or later this could happen, would happen…but three weeks.

"Mr. Dillon, we have only one month left of the spring term. A new class of first-year students is to be registered in the fall and our faculty is under contract. Many of the students on campus, and those coming in the fall, chose Callend on the promise that the collection will be part of the college's educational resources. We are known throughout the country for our departments of art history and fine arts studies. This precipitous decision will require us to inform our current and incoming students as well. It is much too late for us to recruit new students to replace those who will now elect to transfer or enroll elsewhere. Think of the faculty scheduled to teach courses in a curriculum contingent on the collection, Mr. Dillon. Three weeks. Sir, please give us some time. We might make a transition in a year or two. The collection has been here for fifty years; twenty-four months more will not make that much difference."

"President Harris, I appreciate your position, indeed we all do, but it is quite out of the question. My instructions are to remove the collection with all due haste and that is what I must do. I am sorry," Dillon replied, his aquiline face arranged in a sympathetic expression.

Ruth wracked her brains for a wedge. She had anticipated the decision. The idea of storing art works in an underground bunker in this day and age was, she conceded, ridiculous. But she could not understand the rapidity of the move. There must be something she could do, something to make it all come out right. If only she could buy some time, just a little time.

"Mr. Dillon, I wonder if I might ask one favor?"

"Certainly, if it's within reason. We don't want to be rigid about this and ah—"

"Fine. Could we split the motion? Could we first vote on terminating the lease and agreements, yes or no, and then, second, move and debate the time of termination? I don't want to prolong this if the answer is no, but at the same time, there may be a way we can salvage something here."

"Well, I suppose that will be all right, if the Seconder agrees. Mr. Stewart, you will agree, will you not?" Stewart agreed.

It took Senator Rutledge's proxy to pass the first part of the motion. Dillon then moved the time be three weeks. Stewart again seconded and both looked at Ruth.

"Excuse me, Mr. Dillon. I have, I think, an amendment, but if you will indulge me for a moment. Sergei?" She turned to Bialzac who still ashen-faced, looked like he had been handed a death sentence.

"Sergei?"

Bialzac's eyes came back into focus.

"President Harris? Sorry, you were saying?"

"Sergei, we must try to make the best of a bad situation. I need to know something and you are the only one who can tell me. How long would it take to photograph the collection—what is in the vault and, with Mr. Dillon's permission, the items in Cleveland, all of it?" She glanced in Dillon's direction. He would not dare refuse, not if Bialzac gave the right answer.

Bialzac thought a moment, ticking off the number of paintings and other items he would have to photograph, the equipment, lights, film, time.

"We'd need two, at least two, pictures of each painting…the sculpture and artifacts, perhaps three or four…then we have to be sure of the exposures, develop them, mount them. Eight to ten weeks would be fair. If we began with the items here and all goes well, we might be finished with that portion in say six weeks. The other items because they are wall mounted or free standing in the museum in Cleveland, in another four. Yes, ten weeks should do it."

"Thank you, Sergei." Thank you, indeed. Time—it would buy some time—not too much, but enough. Dillon should go along. It was too reasonable a request to refuse. Now, to sweeten the pot just a little.

"I move the following amendment: the removal be made after the collection has been photographed, and that to be completed as quickly as possible, but no longer than ten weeks and," here came the sweeteners for Dillon and Bialzac, "we will produce, under Dr. Bialzac's editorship, the first complete color catalog of the Dillon Collection, to be sold by the foundation and the profits split equally between them and the history of art department."

That ought to do it—something for everyone. Ruth glanced around the table. Stewart's face remained blank. Marge Tice winked. Clough's expression was bleak. His return to the islands, delayed. And Bialzac relaxed.

"That is quite out of the question, Dr. Harris," Dillon intoned.

"But on what objection?" Ruth asked. "What difference will seven or eight weeks make?"

"Our move to New York includes photographing the collection and the production of a new catalog. Mr. Stewart has arranged for that. We will, of course, make these catalogs available to you when they are ready."

She had lost. With as much grace as she could muster, Ruth sat back in her chair and listened as the financial underpinnings of her college collapsed around her. Dillon ended the meeting and dismissed the Board with thanks.

Chapter 3

In an age of mass architecture and design, it has become difficult to distinguish one venue from another. Malls in the suburbs of most cities are so much alike that once inside there is no way to tell where you are. Hotels and lobbies blend into one long, carpeted sameness. Ike recalled Charlie Garland's story about the time he was running late to catch a flight to Columbus and got on his plane just as the door closed. He arrived at the end of the flight, booked into his room at the hotel, ate dinner and it was not until the following morning that he discovered that he was in Toledo.

Waiting rooms, however, are different. Doctor's offices have year-old *Time* magazines, *The Reader's Digest*, and two-day-old newspapers, set off by a faint scent of disinfectant. They differed from dentists' in that they had a different smell. Ike could not recall what the difference was, but he was sure that if he were led blindfolded into a dentist's office he would know it.

Callend College offered *The Smithsonian*, alumnae magazines, well-designed four-color brochures noting Callend's academic programs, and coffee-table prospectuses of the college showing the beauties of the Shenandoah Valley. No question about where you were.

Ike tossed the pamphlet describing the college's annual art festival, Artscape, on the table and stood as the conference room door swung open. Six people filed out. He inspected them as they emerged, judging their state of mind by their expression, sorting and classifying them. A tall stooped man exited looking satisfied, perhaps smug. Next, an agitated, bespectacled, bearded man Ike could not place. He recognized Marge Tice, who flashed him a smile. A beaming Doctor Clough followed, and behind him a willowy young man in a plum-colored velvet jacket.

Ike focused his attention on Ruth Harris—Sydney Harris in another lifetime. Some people, he thought, improve with age. A striking girl years ago—she had grown into a beautiful woman—and at this moment, a very angry woman. If she shared her father's personality, he guessed his meeting would go badly.

As her secretary ushered him into the office, he rehearsed what he wanted to say, wishing all the while that he had arranged the meeting yesterday or the next day or any day but today. She sat ramrod straight in her swivel chair and glared at Ike. Her left hand toyed with the letter opener.

"Yes, Sheriff, what can I do for you?" she growled.

Ike launched into his speech. There were complaints from some of the merchants in town about some bad checks. They believed they were mostly, perhaps all, being written by area citizens passing themselves off as college students. The merchants wished to continue the tradition of honoring Callend girls', excuse me, women's, checks without question, but times change. They wanted to establish some means of ensuring that the young women writing checks, without question, were Callend students and proposed that the college issue each student a picture ID. That would help them and the sheriff's office because lately, there had been incidents involving these…young women…he might have handled more diplomatically had he, Ike, ah, been able to make the connection.

"What incidents, Sheriff?" Ruth Harris asked, her voice like ice.

"Dr. Harris, we've had a couple of arrests involving your… women and their dates. Trespass, public drunkenness, a little pot, which I think needn't have made the police blotter if we could have established their connection here sooner, called someone, and let you handle them. It's embarrassing to them to have to call parents…or whomever.…"

"Let me get this straight, Sheriff, you correct me if I'm wrong. Lord knows I do not want to overburden the sheriff's office, or its mental capacity. You want Callend to provide picture identification for its students so you can keep them separate from the townies that have been bilking the local shopkeepers. Am I right so far? We have eight hundred students here plus two hundred and fifty faculty, staff and support personnel, who will also be branded, I assume, and this is so your people, who have lived in this social backwash all their lives, can separate perfect strangers from the college from local residents and their children. Have I got it so far?"

"Well, not quite, you see—"

"What did you have in mind? Nice plastic card or would you prefer a tattoo? I am told that you can get a bar code tattoo now. That would do it, don't you think? Folks down at the local Piggly Wiggly can run the student through the checkout scanner. You can't lose a tattoo, Sheriff, no chance of it falling into the wrong hands."

"Dr. Harris, please, it's a real problem and not as simple as you seem to think."

"Sheriff, the whole idea of carrying identification, of proving you are, or are not, who you pretend to be, is hateful. I will not contribute to some kind of a fascist police state. If your merchants can't tell who's a townie and who isn't, then you issue IDs to the townies—the ones without them are mine."

"Dr. Harris, I hoped we could come to some simple solution that would not produce a…" Ike paused, drew a breath, and plunged on.

"I understand that you do issue cards to your students so that they can access the books in your libraries. I assume you have a problem with books and access—I don't know. But since you don't seem to have any objection to issuing some form of ID, it seemed reasonable to me to suggest its scope be expanded. In every school in the country, every governmental agency, business, everywhere, people are issued IDs."

"Nonsense, Sheriff. In the first place, the cards you refer to are to allow our computer to keep inventory in the library. It has nothing to do with thefts or lack of trust. Second, what every other institution does to its employees, students, and whomever, is of no interest to me. This is an institution of higher education. We try to teach independence, free thinking, and a healthy skepticism for the lemming-like behavior that characterizes our society as a whole."

"Oh, I'm mistaken. I was led to believe that computers were going to be used to manage card access door locks on your buildings, dormitory rooms and—"

"You understood wrong."

"I see. Look, Dr. Harris, I've come on a bad day. Why don't I just arrange to talk about this with you some other time?"

"There is nothing more to talk about, Sheriff, now or any other time. In the future, you will discuss these matters with my chief of security, Captain Parker, not me. Now, if you will excuse me, I have some phone calls to make."

Ruth Harris picked up the phone, swiveled around so that her back was to Ike.

"Millie, I can't make this idiot phone work. Can you…what? Oh sorry…well, as soon as you can."

‹›‹›‹›

Loyal Parker waited in the outer office. He greeted Ike with a smirk.

"How are they hanging, Ikey?"

Ike ignored him and retraced his steps down the long corridor to the main entrance. He waved to Millie Tompkins at the reception desk. Millie had been enthroned at that desk for longer than anyone could remember. She had mastered the art of knitting the cables on the old-fashioned PBX into spaghetti. Now she was trying to master her third phone system. She squinted at the manual in front of her through half glasses, perched on the end of her nose. The headset wrapped around her like a fallen halo.

"Here it is. I can get you your New Jersey number now," she said into the microphone. She waggled her fingers and smiled a goodbye at Ike.

He let himself out through the double doors into the sun and headed to his car. Once in its privacy, motor running, and air-conditioner on full, he allowed himself two good minutes of uninterrupted profanity.

Loyal Parker stood across the desk from Ruth Harris at the closest approximation of attention he could manage. He was not ex-military, so he did not manage very well, more like a Klingon than a Marine. There was an air of insolence about his manner that always irritated Ruth. Cops were, she decided, all alike—good, bad, successful, or, like this one, failed—they were all alike.

"Captain Parker," she began, without looking at him, "the board has voted to remove the Dillon Collection from the Art Storage Compound in three weeks. I must tell you, with the collection gone, we can no longer justify retaining our large security staff. By Monday, I want you to provide me with the names of everyone in your department and rank order them as to effectiveness, one through whatever number there are. I will dismiss them in reverse order. I do not know how many that will be yet.

"Also, there will be a lot of strangers in and around the building for the next three weeks. All will have letters of identification. Instruct your men to ask to see them if there's any question. Have you got that?"

"Yes, sir, Ma'am," he replied.

"Good. That's all."

Chapter 4

He heard the telephone ringing. Anyone else would have rushed to the door, fumbled for keys, dashed to the phone, and more often than not, been greeted by a dial tone. But Vito was a deliberate man whose continued survival depended on caution, careful planning, and a habit of trusting no one. He let the phone ring as he inspected the door for any traces that would indicate someone might have attempted to open it in his absence. Satisfied, he opened the door and pushed it in while moving to his right so that he was out of the line of sight of anyone who might be inside waiting for him. At the same time, he glanced at the mirror hung inside the foyer to give him a clear view of most of the living room.

He stepped into the apartment and went to the phone. As he had with the door, he checked its polished black surface to see that the thumbprint he placed on it after he polished the hand set was undisturbed. Then he picked up the phone.

"Yes."

"This is Artscape," the voice on the other end said. "We have a problem. You will have to do the job early."

"How early?"

"In the next two weeks."

"Impossible. What happened?"

"They're moving the collection to New York in three weeks. One week will be packing and inventory. We've only got two weeks."

"I am sorry about that, but our contract says July the fourth. If we go now, the risks change."

"We have no choice. It has to be now."

"How did this happen? You told me you were in charge, that you could do anything you wanted with those pictures. You could get my people in to check the alarms, the number and size of the pictures—all of it."

"I couldn't do anything. The votes weren't there."

"What votes? What is this? Are you in charge or not?"

"Look, it doesn't matter. The board wanted to bring the collection to New York and before anyone knew it, they voted to move the collection. Bang. Just like that."

"Bang? You didn't tell me anything about votes or boards. We picked July because nobody would be around and the risks would be small. The contract price assumed those risks as part of the pricing. You understand then, that if I do this—"

"*If* you do this…we have a contract. You've got to do it."

"We have a contract. I always honor my contracts. Mine says July four. I will, if you insist, break in on that date, and remove everything I find. Then your bosses can see what sort of ransom they can extract from Dillon with it. That is my contract. Are you are suggesting a new one?"

There was silence on the other end of the line. Vito waited. Finally, the voice said, "What do you want?"

"The same, but because the risks are greater and because I will not have time to put together the team and backup I need, you will have to come up with a whole lot more cash. Up front."

Vito Donati loved moments like these. His client could do nothing—no time to find someone else, even if it were possible. He had them over a barrel. Vito made a mental note to step up his protection after this job. He knew these people well enough to know that the squeeze he was putting on them now would result in an attempt on him later. But that was the nature of the business—all in a day's work.

"Here's the deal. First, none of your people will be part of this. I don't have the time to train them, and after what happened at the library two months ago, I don't want to be within a hundred miles of them. Second, the price is now ten million plus expenses, one-half up front, the remainder on delivery. And three, your people will pick up the ransom, and then deliver the goods. Agreed?"

Vito waited again while his caller thought, calculating the effect this new deal would have on the men in Damascus or Yemen or wherever they lurked at the moment. They would not be happy, certainly not with Donati. But they had no other viable choices.

"We pay the second half when we have the ransom, not on delivery. I'll go along with the rest."

Vito smiled. It had been easier than he had expected. He liked working with ideological people. They were so obsessed with their causes they did not take time to drive a good bargain.

"Fine," he said. "We'll go next Thursday." He hung up, picked up the phone, and dialed area code 704 and the number. The phone rang fifteen times before an angry Red Burnham answered.

"Whatcha want?"

"The plan's changed. We go next Thursday. Get the trucks and trailers to the Shenandoah Truck Park by Monday and check into the Dogwood Motel west of Picketsville. They are expecting someone named Michaels or Dolan. You are Dolan. Got it?"

"I got it, but what's the rush?"

"I'll explain later. It is a sweeter deal so be happy. You get bumped to fifty thousand for a week's work."

Vito hung up. The change in plans made some things more difficult, but he could manage. And since the business with Giacomo, he felt squeezed and unsafe in his part of New Jersey. Spending two weeks out of town could be very convenient, not to mention necessary. In two weeks his problems would blow over. Martelli promised he would see to that. It just needed a word to a few people, maybe the application of some muscle, and money. He could fix it.

But right now, he needed his man, the locksmith. With more time, he could play this man like a fish, reel him in, let him run, and boat him. But he did not have the time. He would have to go in hard and offer lots of money, maybe even lean on his man through his kids. And he would have to be lucky. Grafton drank. He might be too broken up. Either way he would be no good, even if he decided to do the job.

Vito left the apartment, but not before he had reestablished his checkpoints and replaced the hair on the doorsill. He would not return for several weeks. By then this new phone would be tapped, too, and he would have to make other arrangements.

He walked through the doors and signaled for Angelo to bring the car up. The black Cadillac whispered to the curb. Vito got in, gave Angelo an address, and settled himself back into the cushions to think.

⟨⟩⟨⟩⟨⟩

The drive back to town had not afforded Ike any relief. He threw the door to the sheriff's office open with such force, it bounced against the booking counter and upset a coffee cup filled with pencils. A startled Essie Falcao sat at the dispatch desk, phone in her left hand, her right covering the mouthpiece.

Ike glared at her and then at Whaite Billingsly, who busied himself picking up the pencils.

"Do I look like a fascist?" Ike yelled to no one in particular. "Am I some kind of rube cop who enjoys pushing people around? I go out there, nice as pie, a pussycat—that's what I was. I go out there and suggest—suggest—a simple solution to a problem and that woman calls me a...says I want to start a police state."

"Ike?" Essie said, and then ducked as Ike turned and continued.

"Let me tell you something, Essie. I never, ever got into the town and gown crap that most of the people hereabouts did. I never took the Callend girls or faculty for granted or as something special, different, or anything, but now...."

"Ike?"

"I'm going to lean on that arrogant, self-righteous, over-educated b...whatever, until she starts wishing she was back in Connecticut, or wherever she came from, getting her rear-end kicked at a faculty meeting."

"Ike?"

"I'm going to watch her car and—"

"Ike."

"What, Essie. What the hell is it?"

"Ike, it's your father on the phone."

"Tell him I'm not here."

"He said to tell you that if you said you weren't here, that he's across the street in the barbershop and he saw you come in and—"

Ike's fist hit the counter, the pencils jumped. If he had been a character in an animated cartoon, smoke would have come out of his ears. When the color in his face ebbed from maroon to just red, he said, "I'll take it in my office."

"He'll be with you right away, Mr. Schwartz," Essie murmured into the phone. "What? Oh, thank you. And God bless you-all real good, too."

Ike went into the eight by ten, glassed-in cubicle that served as his office. He kicked the door shut and took perverse delight when the vibration knocked the cup of pencils over again. He picked up the phone and stood staring at the blinking button. He thought about leaving his father on hold for five or ten minutes. He thought about hanging up. Instead, he punched the blinking button.

"Hello."

"Isaac, this is your Poppa speaking."

"I know who you are, Pop."

"Well, I couldn't be sure. It's been such a long time since your Momma and I have seen you. I was thinking maybe you forgot," Abe Schwartz said sweetly.

"Will you cut out the *yiddisher momma* routine, Pop? You can't even do the accent right. It's, 'I vas t'inking you maybe forgot.'"

Abe Schwartz chuckled, "You're not so hot at it yourself, Ike, and you've had the benefit of hearing it on television, living in the big city, and going to Ivy League schools. Us poor ole country boys are educationally disadvantaged when it comes to trotting out a nice, clean, lower Eastside accent. Maybe I should go to Berlitz and take a course."

"Two weeks in the Catskills, Pop, be just as effective and lots more fun. What do you want? I'm kind of busy and I've had a bad day."

"A bad day? Ike, it is only eleven-thirty, you ain't even had a morning yet, good, bad or indifferent, much less a whole day. What I want is for you to come out to the farm this weekend. Your mother and I haven't seen you since March and Ike, she isn't any better."

"Okay, Pop, I know, I know. I would have come out before, but—I don't know. Every time you and I get together, we start arguing politics and my future and I think that upsets Mom more than my staying away."

"Ike, you and I have been arguing that way for twenty years. If we stopped now, your mother would want to know what was wrong. She'd worry."

"Maybe in the past, Pop, but not now. I don't think she can manage the noise level anymore. And even if she can, I can't."

"Okay, Ike, we won't talk politics or anything else. We'll talk about the Baltimore Orioles, old times, anything you want, but come, please."

"You promise—no politics or careers?"

"I promise. Come out Friday for dinner. Stay the weekend."

"I'll be out Saturday."

"For breakfast?"

"Too early. Saturday is the only time I have free. I need sleep. I'll be out for lunch."

"Good. Your mother will be pleased. Oh, yes, I forgot to tell you, your mother asked Barbara Rubenstein out for the weekend, too. Good-bye."

"What? Wait a minute. I am not...." Ike slammed the phone back into its cradle. "I've been set up."

Chapter 5

Even in death, Harry thought, Ellen managed to make things unpleasant. He chided himself for the thought. She was dead, after all, and that was the end to it. He needed a drink. He stood in the rain staring at the fresh earth piled beside the grave. Brown rivulets of muddy water formed on its surface and ran into the fake grass covering the raw earth left by the backhoe. No one else in sight. There hadn't been that many there in the first place, when you got right down to it—a couple of people from the hospital, some friends from the old neighborhood, maybe eight or ten people in all, and Ellen's parents, of course. They glanced at him with a look as cold as Duluth in December. It was their funeral, bought and paid for. Harry hadn't even been invited. If the funeral director hadn't called him about an item of clothing, he'd never have known about it. As it turned out, he'd trudged up the hill through the sodden grass, rain dripping from his hair and down his neck, just as the priest finished.

Now, he was alone. Five years of dying, and it ends here. All gone, house, savings, job, wife, and God only knew how or when he was going to get the children back. He fought the growing anger and despair.

He had worked for twenty years, good at what he did, maybe the best. But he could not sell his skills anywhere now. He glanced at the men hunched down in their slickers next to the backhoe and nodded. No sense in everyone being miserable. He turned and headed down the knoll to the road that led back to the street. Behind him he heard the backhoe cough and start and then whine as it dumped the earth that would separate Ellen Grafton from the world of the living.

He'd walked several yards before he saw the limousine. Damn, he thought, I asked them to leave me alone. Can't anyone do what they are told? He'd brushed off the funeral director's offer for a ride, telling him to take the hearse and limousine away. He'd declined rides from others as well. They lingered for a while, uncomfortable and embarrassed, and then left him.

He walked toward the road, ignoring the car, heading for the gate. The limousine rolled abreast. He heard the hum of the electric window. Irritated, he turned and spoke through the open window.

"Please, I told you people to go. I do not need or want your services anymore today."

"Mr. Grafton, let me offer you a ride. We need to talk."

The voice did not sound like that of any of the funeral parlor people. Grafton squinted into the gloom of the back seat. He did not recognize its occupant. His heart began to race. So this is how it begins. The Bureau listed him as a liability. He knew too much and since they let him go, he could not be allowed to wander about. He stepped off the road and turned toward the forest of headstones. He would have some protection there, but for how long? If they wanted him, they would get him sooner or later. He stopped and his shoulders sagged. He turned back to the car.

"Okay, okay, let's get this over with," he muttered as the door opened. Harry got in. The window slid up, and the car accelerated. Harry waited, feeling the man's eyes, calculating, measuring him.

"Grafton, I think you have mistaken me for someone else. I am not with your former employer. I am here because I believe I can help you, and you can help me."

"Who are you, then, and what makes you think I need or want your help?"

"I am a contractor, Mr. Grafton, and I have a job to do, a very complicated job. It requires someone with your special skills, and at the moment, you are the only person with those skills available. I am taking a risk even talking to you because you can always put your old friends in the FBI on to me. That would be very embarrassing. I am taking that risk because I believe you will not do that. You will not because I have something you need, and I am the only person in the world who is willing to give it to you."

"And what is that? What are you talking about? Who are you, anyway?"

"My name is Donati, Vito Donati, and what I'm talking about is money, Grafton, lots of money."

"Why would I care about you and money, Donati, if that's who you are? What makes you think I need or want money?"

"Oh, you need money because you owe money. You owe the hospital one hundred and forty-seven thousand, three hundred dollars and ah, thirty-seven cents. Can you imagine that, a hospital bill that big? Says a lot about the state of medical care in the country, don't you think? And you owe four, no, five doctors a total of fifty-two thousand three hundred eighty-three dollars. There are also an assortment of medical laboratories and service people who expect some serious money from you. You owe your landlady three months' back rent. You will need money to hire lawyers to get custody of your kids. You have no job and no insurance, because the Bureau let you go three months ago. They said you had lost your nerve or your touch or whatever nice way they describe someone who needs Jack Daniels for breakfast. You have no assets worth mentioning. You cashed out your 401k, sold your house, car, sound system, television, and furniture to pay bills. Your in-laws have an Illinois court order giving them temporary custody of your children. The grounds are not important, but I will cite them if you wish. You just buried your wife. I would tell you I am sorry, but I never knew her, and I am not a sentimental man. In short, Grafton, your back is against the wall. You are unemployed and unemployable.

You cannot even tell people what you did for a living, at least not right now. In a year or so, you could get a job with a company selling or manufacturing security systems, but if, and only if, the FBI decides you're safe and lets you.

"Oh, you need me, Grafton, you need me big time. Lucky for you, I need you, too, so I want to offer you a deal."

Harry sat speechless. Donati had access to information that could only come from someone deep inside the Bureau. And Donati was right. Harry needed money.

"I am hoping," Donati added, "that I have estimated your financial problems and your level of, shall we say, disenchantment with the Bureau and all it represents."

"All right, you've got your facts right. Tell me what you want and then I'll tell you whether I'm interested."

Donati stared straight ahead without speaking for a moment. "Grafton, your outstanding debts come to something over two hundred thousand dollars. Throw the lawyers in there and you are looking at a quarter of a million shortfall. That includes your landlord but not your credit cards, which are also maxed out. I will pay you one hundred thousand dollars for a week's work, work you have done before. When we are finished, we are finished. You get fifty thousand up front, the remainder when I collect my money after the job."

"Just what do I do for one hundred K?"

"You go to a little town in Virginia and inspect a building for burglar alarms. When I say so, you go back to the building, deactivate them, and then help me and my associates remove several hundred paintings from the building. That's all."

"Sorry, I need to know more. I need to weigh the risks. I can't work without that."

"Fair enough. I have been employed by a group of people who specialize in political, shall we say, manipulation. They are funded by one of those groups in the Middle East that you know more about than I do. They want me to steal some paintings and hide them. They will then ransom them for a great deal of money. When that has been done, I collect my fee, I pay you and the others, and we all separate."

"What's to prevent me from blowing the whistle on you and your friends?"

"I hoped you wouldn't ask that. Well, I believe I have your price and I am correct about your anger at the FBI. If that is not enough, there are your children. I do not like getting at people through their families, you see, but I am a businessman in a business with no margin for error. Do you understand?"

Harry weighed the man's words. Donati had done the math—he stopped counting months ago but guessed he owed at least that much. He weighed the risks. He thought of a career spanning twenty years devoted to, for the most part, the prevention of crime. There were times when it was not clear which side he was on—Waco and Ruby Ridge, for example. And now, he was about to cross the line, become a thief. He was the best, even now, at breaking alarm systems, and as Donati said, he would work or not work when the Bureau let him, and they were not about to turn him loose. Not yet.

"Okay, you don't need to threaten me. If I work, I work. That means you buy the whole package. But...."

Harry paused, trying to guess how far he could go, what sort of price he could squeeze from this man, wondering what he was worth in this world. "I'll need more money. The price is two fifty, one hundred up front and equipment and expenses are extra."

Donati raised his eyebrows. Harry thought he saw a ghost of a smile flicker across the man's lips.

"You may be down, Grafton, but you're not out. One seventy-five, you pay the expenses."

"Two fifty, fifty up front, and you pay expenses."

"Two fifty, twenty up front, we split expenses."

Harry guessed he'd squeezed as much as he was going to get. He nodded.

"We'll drop you here."

Harry looked out of the window. The car had transported them across the width of New York and pulled to the curb a block from his apartment.

"You hang around a couple of days, and then tell your land-lady you're going away for a while, up north to the mountains or something. Fly out to Roanoke, rent a car, and go to Picketsville, Virginia. Book into the motel there, the Dogwood Motel. They are expecting Dolan and Michaels. You are Michaels. I will have more information for you there, where to go, what to look for. You got it?"

Harry opened the door and stepped onto the sidewalk. "Got it."

Donati handed Harry an envelope, nodded, and settled himself back in the seat.

"One more thing, Grafton," he said. Harry waited.

"No booze 'til this is over." The car door clicked shut and the Cadillac rolled away.

Chapter 6

A week had slipped by and Ike could not remember a single thing that happened, well almost. He had had the run-in with the Ice Queen at the college, had gone to the farm, been called to two domestic disturbance scuffles, both at the Craddocks', and issued twelve speeding tickets. Exciting. Now he had the opportunity to repeat it or, who knew, top it.

Monday mornings, Ike decided, were the pits. It was not an original thought. It had been the second or third thing to occur to Adam. Except for people who hated to go home and lived for their work, Mondays with their excruciating distance until Friday had a depressing effect on body and soul. Everyone in the Crossroads Diner wore the same "here we go again" expression. The regulars were there, stretching breakfast into the previous weekend, reluctant to let it go.

Ike surveyed their faces, greeted some, and waved to others. He knew them all, all except the travelers and truckers who left the interstate five miles to the east and were, for one reason or another, passing through Picketsville. Two men sat in the back booth. One, burly and red-haired, attacked what appeared to be two or three breakfasts spread out in front of him. The other, darker with craggy regular features, nursed a cup of coffee. Ike paused. Years of practice taught him to notice people, to catalog and remember them. This man seemed familiar somehow. They'd never met, but something about him struck Ike as familiar and caused him to pause and consider. Agency? Were they still keeping tabs on him? No one, he was sure, had been in the area since Charlie Garland had come down two years ago.

"Ike, we're all sorry as hell," he'd said, "and I don't want you to have to go through anything, but I've got to talk to you. You've got to tell me what happened."

Dependable Charlie, whose job at the Agency seemed to be as nondescript as his clothes. Charlie was related to a whole battalion of Garlands and Radfords, and God only knew whom else. One of those old Baltimore families that retain their style and connections long after the money is gone. They send their children to prep schools and Ivy League colleges on money scraped together by selling the family farm, silverware, and dipping into whatever is left in trust funds and modest inheritances, doing what was necessary to maintain their continuity with the past inviolate. Somewhere in that heritage, there would be merchants, mayors, bishops, owners of clipper ships and mills, and perhaps a U.S. senator. Those male offspring who could, traveled west to marry the homely heiresses of automobile manufacturers, or seed companies, or brokerage houses. And with family fortunes thus replenished, brought their brides back to the Chesapeake Bay to keep tradition alive.

Charlie was one of those whose heiress had never materialized. He ended up in the Agency as the special assistant to the director. He had no job description and no duties. Most people believed he occupied a sinecure created for him by his politically connected relatives. In that capacity, he brought his prep school manners, Princeton education, rumpled tweed sport coat, khaki slacks and blue, frayed oxford shirts to work every week, sat in an office in the basement and, as nearly as anyone could tell, devoted his day to the *New York Times* crossword puzzle.

Occasionally, Charlie appeared in public, in those rare instances when something of a public relations effort needed doing, and then Charlie would grin and trot out his beautiful manners and charm everyone in the room. He could tell stories, knew everybody, and in his own disorganized way, managed to divert anyone or anything, the epitome of the superannuated preppie. Ike once asked him if Brooks Brothers had a special department where they sold only rumpled tweed coats and pre-frayed shirts. Charlie had grinned owlishly through his old-fashioned horn-rimmed glasses, run his hand through the curly disarray of his hair, and replied, "No one, Ike, no one buys from Brooks Brothers except rich Texans. We," he added archly, "buy only from Jos. A. Banks."

Ike liked Charlie. He was the closest thing he had to a friend all those years he'd worked in Washington and Europe, but he didn't want to talk to him or anyone else after Zurich, and told Charlie he'd have him arrested for vagrancy if he ever showed up in town again. Ike added, somewhat more kindly, that the way Charlie dressed, he would have no trouble making the charges stick.

His thoughts returned to Monday at the diner. He shelved his curiosity, took one last look at the two men, and slid onto the stool at the counter.

"Usual, Sheriff?"

"Thanks, Flora, coffee first."

Ike sensed the change in the two men behind him. He could almost feel their eyes on him. Now that's interesting, Ike thought, and he glanced at the glass surface of the refrigeration unit opposite him. He could see the two men exchange looks. The red-haired one said something to the other. The second drained his coffee and got up. The first wolfed down the last of his pancakes, stuffed four blueberry muffins in his pocket, and rose as well. Ike followed their reflection to the cash register, then pivoted on his stool and stared at them as they paid their bill, pushed out through the glass doors, and disappeared. Flora brought his bacon and eggs.

"Ever seen those two before, Flora?" Ike asked.

"Can't say that I have, Ike, but you know we get truckers and such in here all the time, I reckon that's what they are."

"One of them, yes, the other one, I don't know…maybe."

Ike turned his attention to his breakfast and newspaper.

‹›‹›‹›

Harry and Red crossed the parking lot.

"I don't like it," Harry said.

"Don't like what?" Red replied, picking his teeth with a broken kitchen match. They got into the rental car. Harry took the wheel.

"I don't like being made by the police," he replied.

"Made," Red snorted. "Son, this is the backest of the back woods. They do not have police in these little towns; they have the otherwise unemployable sons, nephews, or cousins of county politicians running their sheriff's offices. These country dicks couldn't find the prize in a box of Cracker Jacks."

"Maybe so," Harry mused, "but—"

"No buts, Grafton. I was born and raised in towns like this. The only thing on that sheriff's mind this morning is how to get enough money together to make the payment on his house trailer."

"You may be right, Burnham," Harry said. "I hope so. But that one is different. I don't know how or why, but I'd bet the farm he's not just another local cop."

"Horse hockey," Red grunted as he leaned back in the seat and fished a muffin from his pocket. "You're as jumpy as a girl in an asparagus patch. You can take it from me. The locals ain't going to be a problem." Harry was not reassured. He put the car in gear and drove off. He had work to do.

It took an hour and a half to make the round trip to Roanoke and the truck leasing company where he dropped off Red. It was a little after eleven when he parked outside the Art Storage Compound. The little plaque on the building's corner read *ARTSCp* and had a number under it. Funny name, he thought. Usually colleges name their buildings Something Hall, but there it was, in neat stainless steel letters affixed to the wall: *Art Storage Compound.*

Harry got out of the car, stretched, and mopped his forehead. He scanned the area and spotted the camera. He entered the building. Harry shivered and slipped on his jacket. The guard sat behind a desk on the far side of a deep lobby. He looked at Harry.

"Brand, Jason Brand," Harry said, handing the guard a letter of introduction, "from the Titan Company. We're moving all this stuff in a couple of weeks. I've got to look at the building, measure doors, passageways, and estimate the time we'll need."

The guard glanced at Harry, the letter, and handed it back. "Help yourself," he said, and turned his attention back to a dog-eared copy of *Sports Illustrated*. Harry saw himself and the guard on one of the monitors behind the desk as the camera swept the room. The other showed the parking lot.

"Thanks," said Harry, "I won't be long."

He finished before lunch.

Chapter 7

Four of them gathered in the room and even though it was large by motel standards, Harry felt confined, crowded. He supposed his discomfort measured an inner uneasiness more than the environment. He would soon become a thief. At one time or another he'd fantasized what it might be like to be on the other side of the law. His colleagues at the Bureau used to say that those fantasies were a necessary part of the business. "If you can't think like one, you can't appreciate how it must be, you can't catch them," his old chief used to say.

Harry wondered how he'd feel if he cracked a safe or broke into an office and then kept what he liberated instead of tagging it and putting it in envelopes or bags, or more usually, photographing it and putting it back. Well, now he was going to get his chance.

He glanced at the other three men. Donati looked exactly as he had the day they had met, down to the black suit, black silk shirt and black tie, and impassive, aquiline face. Angelo, Donati's beefy factotum, flanked him. Harry recalled he had chauffeured them from the cemetery. Red, the player Harry had met two days before, lounged against the wall, lighting and stubbing out an endless chain of filter cigarettes.

Donati looked at Harry, his face expressionless, his hand resting in his lap. Harry squirmed under the scrutiny and wondered if he should speak or continue to wait. Silence made Harry uncomfortable. He remembered the sensitivity group he and his wife joined years ago in an attempt to improve, or was it salvage, their marriage. A favorite maneuver in those sessions was a silence that built tension until someone in the circle felt compelled to speak. Steeling himself, he returned Donati's gaze.

"Okay, Grafton," Donati said, "what have you got?"

Harry breathed a sigh of relief. He could talk now. He had a job to do and irrespective of whom he was working for or why, a job was a job. Harry, even in the bad days, took pride in his work, delighted in the challenge each new job provided. This one was no exception.

"It's complicated, but not impossible," Harry began. "There are two or three systems that have to be dealt with: first, we have the television surveillance—one camera outside sweeps the parking lot. It has a forty-five-second cycle one way—a minute and a half to return to the starting point.

"During the day there is one guard at the main desk. He used to be replaced after eight hours, but now, the guard tells me, there is an economy program on and so there is only one eight-hour shift—nine to five."

"Except holidays and weekends. We all know that, Grafton."

"Okay. The guard leaves at five and the whole system is switched up to the main security office. It will stay that way until nine in the morning. Inside, a second camera covers the lobby and reception desk on the first floor. There are none beyond that point.

"To put them out of commission, I will tap the lines carrying the transmission to the monitors at the security office. I'll tape three minutes of surveillance, then cut the tapes into the lines, and transmit the same three minutes over and over again for the rest of the night.

"Getting inside the building is another matter. The system or systems are partly connected, partly freestanding. The report you gave me only described one set—the new one. The door is protected by a standard contact alarm, the kind you see all over the place—little boxes side-by-side on the door or windows.

When the system is on, separating the boxes trips the alarm. That one is easy. The problem is the motion detector set up inside. Any movement and it triggers either a silent alarm through the house current or a siren, buzzer—something like that, which may, in turn, set off a sound-sensitive alarm.

"Like the door, once I get to it, it's easy enough to deactivate, just pull the plug. Getting to it may take some doing. It and the door alarms are easy. After I get them turned off, I've got a series of things that have to be shut down. Whoever put the system in built it to last. It's as good as I've seen. Better than they need."

Harry paused and searched the faces of his listeners for comprehension. Donati's eyes remained impassive. Red exhaled smoke toward the ceiling where it mixed with the already heavy haze he had created. Angelo watched Donati.

"Anyway, I've got to get to the main panel and disarm thirty or forty separate trips before anyone can come in, and I've got that piece of science fiction to get by before I can do that."

"What do you mean science fiction?" Donati murmured.

"The photoelectric alarm—but one with real class," Harry replied.

"Photoelectric—invisible eye, something like that?" Donati replied.

"Yeah, but these are lasers and tricky. You know in big beam units you just have to set a couple mirrors at ninety-degree perpendiculars and bounce the beam around or back, depending on how it works. In this one, the tolerances are very tight and the transmission angles are a fraction off ninety degrees and no two alike. I can't make a mirror box because I don't know the angles and I can't get them until I see the beams on."

"You mean there's more than one?" Donati asked.

"Oh yes."

"How many?"

"Forty-seven, one every foot or so in the floor and ceiling, and five horizontal, every two feet on the walls. The whole makes an irregular grid with one by two foot intervals. Since they used lasers, you can't see the beams—just ruby dots on the floor, ceiling, and walls. And, as I said, the angles are off a degree here, three or four there. It's tough."

"Can you get through?" Donati asked.

"I think so."

"You think so. I am not interested in what you think. What do you know?"

"I think so, yes. You ever go to the beach, Donati?"

"Huh?" Donati looked startled.

"The beach. You ever swim in the ocean?"

"Sometimes, when I was a kid…what's the beach got to do with this?"

"People drown at the beach, Donati, and you know why? Because they know. You swim in the ocean. It's always the same—waves come in, break, roll up the sand, wash back, and in comes another. You swim in the ocean a hundred times and it's always the same. So you figure you know how to swim in the ocean. One day, you go to the beach and it's the same—same sand, same sun, same umbrellas, and same surf. You decide to take a dip in this same ocean, only this time it's not the same. There's an undertow, never felt it before, or maybe there's an icy current ten, fifteen feet off shore, a rip tide. It feels like the Arctic Ocean. Before you know it you're under, cramped, or washing out to sea. People drown at the beach, Donati, because they know. Been to the beach a hundred times and they know.

"Now, the guy who doesn't know, the guy who's afraid of the ocean…respects it. He won't drown. Nothing surprises him because he figures the worst could happen, so he's careful. He checks everything—not once, but several times. He prepares. He thinks he knows but then, you never know, do you?

"I've seen every alarm system there is, Donati, a hundred times—and every time I work on one, I'm scared. See, I don't know, Donati—I think." Harry sat back, the challenge still in his eyes.

"Okay, you've made your point. How long will it take, all of it?"

"Maybe two and a half, three hours."

"That's too long, Grafton. We got four floors of pictures to put into the trailers. It gets light around five, and we can't start until after midnight. You take two and a half hours and that leaves us two and a half hours for the rest. No good, you get one hour."

"Two."

"One."

"Look, Donati, I can't work any faster and be sure. There are a lot of steps that have to be taken and systems to get around before I can even begin to work on the box. I can cut some time by rigging the TV early—say eleven o'clock. It shouldn't make much difference when that happens. You can save some time by pulling the trailers close to the site and not putting the pictures in the racks. Why not just stack them flat—floor to ceiling. Leave out the spacers too."

"It'll ruin the pictures, they said. When we move, they'll rub and mess up the paint."

"What do you care about that? Look, if you are going to pack them right, you'll need more than five hours—you'll need five days. If you just toss them in the trailer, you can get all of it done by five thirty or six at the latest. That is at least three, three and a half hours. If one of you does nothing but pull frames and make bundles of say, thirty pounds each, and the rest of us just haul and stack, it could be done."

Donati thought a moment and then agreed. "Okay, Grafton, two hours—one and a half would be better. You shoot for one and a half. Two is a maximum."

Donati turned to Red, dismissing Harry from his thoughts.

"You got what you need?" Red scratched and nodded.

"Two trailers, one big Peterbilt tractor. They are painted to look like Titan Van Lines, like you said."

The room became silent again. Harry felt more uncomfortable. He allowed his mind to assemble a shopping list—magnets of different and standard strengths, induction coils, the video recorders, and switching boxes....

Donati's velvet smooth voice cut through Harry's calculations.

"The plan is simple. We're calling it Artscape—don't ask why, I don't know, it's what they want. So, Thursday night, we go to the building and get into position. Red will have one trailer ready. As soon as Grafton starts, Red, you bring it into the lot and park by the door, unhook, and go get the other one. When the alarms are off, we go in and start pulling the pictures from the frames and loading. When the first trailer is filled, Red pulls out and we fill the second one. When we are done with that one, Red hauls it away and we all split.

"Grafton, you and Red go to the Dogwood Motel, out on the highway, and wait. Angelo and I will go to the Old Dominion, south of here. We will move around, one motel to the other until we are paid. Then, we all go our separate ways.

"I don't like hanging around the area," Red said. "Why can't we all get out, go down to Roanoke and get lost in the crowd? Small-town motels are as private as army showers."

"We stay around," Donati explained, "because we have the goods and they have to be kept hidden. To do that, they have to be moved, from one truck stop to another. That's your job. I need to keep an eye on you, so I stay. Angelo won't leave me, so he stays. That leaves Grafton here, who's new to the business." Donati's green eyes swept across Harry's face. "I think he might need some support as he begins his new career, don't you agree?"

"Okay," Red complained, "but I still don't like the motels."

"These places are as safe as you'll find," Donati said. "There are five of them we will use—one near Lexington, one just south of Natural Bridge, this one, the Lee Jackson, and one just south of here. We have two rooms available to us for as long as we need them and whenever we need them."

"You booked rooms in five motels for what, a week, two weeks? Donati, you're crazy. The cops will be checking motels within hours. They'll pick that up in no time. Even the bozos they have down here will figure that out," Red fumed.

Donati remained calm; his voice never rose or varied. "We are not booked anywhere, Red. I said we have some rooms. They will be very private because no one will know we're here—or care. All of the motels are owned by, ah, a former business associate. He was having some domestic problems that I was able to alleviate. He bought up a string of motels in the area with the insurance money. He has visions of becoming a redneck Conrad Hilton. Right now, he owns about a dozen. This is one of them. They're all fixed up with what passes for comfort and convenience, for a cracker. As far as anyone knows, we are not here. There will be no names on the register. The help will not be in and out. That means no room service, no fresh towels, no one to make your bed. Feel better?"

"Yeah, I guess, but how long? When is this business over?"

"Monday night, our employers get a yes or no on the TV. We turn over the pictures to them, and they pay us the money. That part will be Tuesday or Wednesday. The drop is arranged so all Dillon has to do is get his fifty million together, say yes and then pay."

"How do we know we'll get paid?" Red asked.

"Because we have the paintings and I have their names. If they don't pay, I approach them as I would any client who'd welch on a deal. You understand?"

Red shuddered and grinned, "What happens if Dillon won't pay?"

"He'll pay," said Donati. "We don't just have five hundred million dollars' worth of paintings—we have part of the cultural heritage of the Western world. He may not want to, but he will pay. He won't stand by and let all that culture go up in smoke."

"Smoke?" asked Harry. "What do you mean, smoke?"

"I mean, Grafton, that Dillon will be told to pay or the paintings will be burned—incinerated. He can get them back for fifty million dollars. He will have to pay. There is no way he, or anyone else, for that matter, could take the heat from the press, if he let them go. You see?"

"But...." Harry was going to ask a question, and then decided not to. He had enough of his money up front and did not care about problems in that area. Once the job was done, he was out of it.

"But," Donati said, picking up on Harry's unspoken thought, "how do we know he'll believe it? Because he will be sent one picture already burned. That's it. Our employer will take the risks after the robbery. They will contact Dillon and make the exchange. If there is a screw-up, they get nailed for the whole job and we are clean. Okay, you people lie low. Stay out of town and out of sight. Grafton, you go get your gear together, and all of you be ready by nine o'clock. We will move into the area at ten forty-five, and we should be out by five the next morning. Let's go, Angelo."

Donati and his sidekick-shadow-bodyguard oiled their way out the door and into the night. Red lit another cigarette and sighed.

"I'm going out, just as soon as those guys clear the area."

"Out. Are you crazy? That is the last thing you need to do."

"Sorry, but I need a drink. I'll just drop down to the bar and get me a six-pack. You want one?"

More than anything in the world, Harry wanted a six-pack. A dozen—enough to numb the fear and the sordid sense of personal betrayal he was fighting. A drink. He licked his lips.

"No, I guess not, got to do some more planning. Thanks anyway."

"See ya in a coupla."

Chapter 8

Harry crouched in the bushes east of the building. He'd worked his way to that point from the access road through the woods and into the dark side of the building. Avoiding the surveillance cameras had been simple enough, but he did not know if there were trip alarms in the approaches or not. At last, he decided he was overcautious and moved through the trees. Everything looked pretty much as he expected—no activity at the building, no sound, nothing out of the ordinary. Then a car crossed the parking lot and nosed into the trees. He could make out two heads in the front seat. The headlights extinguished and the motor went silent.

He glanced at his watch. Donati would contact him soon. There was nothing to do now but wait.

"Anything on the tube, boys?" Loyal Parker stuck his head in the campus police center. The eleven to seven shift had just come on duty. Jake Tarbull hunched over the television monitors displaying various walkways, corridors, and buildings on campus.

"Naw, Chief, one of them quiet nights. Wait a minute, there's a car pulling into Paradise."

Two screens monitored the Art Storage Compound. One covered the interior, the other the parking lot and the short lover's lane that adjoined the facility's parking lot—Paradise.

"Do you want me to ask Hank to go down and chase them kids away?"

Parker shook his head. "No, don't think so. I'm about to go off duty. I'll slip down there and do it myself on the way home."

He left the building and went to his car, picked up the large flashlight he kept there, and struck out through the boxwoods toward the ravine next to the lane. He had made the trip many times. Chasing, or more accurately catching kids in the act was a duty he reserved for himself.

<>‹>‹>

Harry watched the car for a few more minutes, then made his way to the east wall of the building where he had left his equipment, and waited for Donati's call. He worried about the car. A car meant people, and people meant complications. If it did not leave soon, it would be there for the night, at least as far as the guards up at the main building were concerned. That might provoke one of them to come down to check. Donati had not allowed for enough people to watch the car and everything else. He waited another minute, and then Donati's voice crackled in his earphone.

"Grafton, what's the holdup?"

"There's a car parked about one hundred yards from the building. It's been down there for ten minutes."

"I'll send Red down to look. Listen, I don't care, go ahead. We'll just have to risk it."

Harry decided to wait another five minutes. When the car did not move, he went ahead with interrupting the closed circuit television surveillance.

The system was not an integral part of the alarm system. It had been added only recently and not very expertly. All of the cables and power lines were exposed and exited from a simple junction box attached to the back of the building. Surprisingly, it was just out of range of the exterior camera. Harry wondered about that. No reputable company would leave their system unguarded like that. It looked like someone had changed the angle of the camera after the system had been installed. The area covered now included a view of a small dirt road leading into the woods but which, Harry knew from his earlier survey, was blocked by a tree trunk ten yards in. The car parked there now.

Harry moved to the junction box, backed out its retaining bolts, and lifted off the waterproofed covering. He put it aside and took the battery-operated recorders from their cases. He checked the cassettes and made sure everything was in order. He scraped the insulation away from the coaxial cables, cleared a bit of the sheathing away from the core, and fastened alligator clips. He turned the recorders on and watched as the cassettes completed their loops—three minutes. He then punched the playback buttons and at the same instant cut the cables behind the clips. Now the guards would see the same three minutes for the rest of the night. The batteries were good for nine hours. After that, it would not make any difference.

〈〉〈〉〈〉

Loyal Parker slipped into the clump of bushes beside the car. He had set the lane up years ago, dropping the tree to block it so cars parked there could be approached unseen from the passenger's side. He listened to the girl's muffled cries and protests. He licked his lips in anticipation, unaware of the saliva that dribbled down his chin.

Little tart, he thought. Get what she deserves. They all do. He thought how this one would look when he snapped on the torch—naked and afraid. It was the last thought he had on this earth. The tire iron caught him behind his right ear, crushing most of his occipital bone. The force of the blow drove one piece into his brain stem. For all practical purposes, he was dead before he hit the ground.

〈〉〈〉〈〉

Jennifer Ames was angry. She was angry with herself for having listened to her roommate.

"You'll love him, Jen. He's Jack Trask, you know, the big lacrosse player from UVA and he just doesn't date anyone."

Betsy Mae Billups had one of those honeyed accents that only come from the depths of Alabama or Mississippi—the kind of accent that can distract the most rational men and even other women. Jennifer nicknamed her Magnolia Mouth.

"And besides," she went on, "you'd be doing me a huge favor. My boyfriend is just dying to get a bid to St. Elmo's and Jack Trask can help him. It's really important, Jen."

"Why me?" Jennifer had asked. "Why not Laurie or one of the Marys in fourteen B or someone who wants a date and knows what the hell lacrosse is?" Jennifer grew up in Chicago and, until she came east to go to school, Lacrosse was just a town in Wisconsin.

"Magnolia, you know I don't like to go out much, and I hate jocks." It was true. She had gotten a reputation in her years at Callend as a loner. She didn't date much, content to spend her free time in the library and weekends in Washington, New York, and Boston, cities where her parents and their respective spouses had houses or apartments or connections. She discovered early in her freshman year that the boys who attended the mixers and the few she had dated were boring and juvenile. She gave up, deciding there was something wrong with her because she could not get into the whole scene.

"Jen, they already have dates, and besides, you're the one he wants to go out with. He said, 'How about Betsy Mae's good-looking roommate?' That's what he said and…oh, come on, Jen, he won't bite."

<><><>

Like hell he won't, thought Jennifer. And now here she was, in the woods, fighting for her—what? Her life? Her honor? Not her virginity. Her second cousin, Danny, had taken care of that three summers ago.

"Stop it, Jack."

Jack Trask was an octopus. His hands seemed to be every-where, unbuttoning, unhooking, squeezing, and clumsy. Jennifer tried to stop the assault and repair the damage, all the while pleading, cajoling, and insisting he stop. But as fast as she got one part of her dress repaired, Jack's hands found another target and she would feel her blouse being unbuttoned and her bra unsnapped. When she would try to redo that, the hands went to work somewhere else.

Jack's body had her pinned against the door and his weight was pressing her down on the seat.

"Damn it, stop." No hope. He wasn't going to stop. She felt the elastic go somewhere, she guessed she knew where, and heard the thin cotton fabric tear. "That's it," she thought, as she twisted back and forth trying to get a purchase, a foothold—anything to get her back into a position where she'd have some room to maneuver or open the door and get out.

She felt her skirt being pulled up around her hips. Why am I doing this, she wondered. Why not give in and get it over with? For one thing, she did not want to be date-raped, and by God, she was not going to have some arrogant, oversexed adolescent push her around.

"If I want to get laid, I'll decide when and where." This last comment she delivered aloud, and to make sure she had her assailant's attention, bit his ear—hard.

The counterattack had not been expected, nor the initial resistance. Jack Trask, like most pampered athletes, expected easy conquests, and he found Jennifer's reluctance to keep his uninterrupted string intact annoying.

The stabbing pain on his ear caused him to rear back and raise his fist, ready to strike.

As he jerked back, Jennifer realized just how near to his goal Jack was. She was aware of his raised arm, but in the split second his weight lifted from her hips, she twisted, drew on what strength she had left, and sent her right knee to his groin.

Light, bright as noon, flooded the car. In that moment Jennifer saw it all. She sprawled across the seat, practically naked, blouse pushed back, underwear in a shambles. In a brief, irrational moment the words to a Tom Lehrer song her father used to play on an old vinyl record came to her…*revealing for all of the others to see, just what it was that endeared you to me.* Jack screamed in pain as the shock of her knee rocketed to his brain.

"Nicely done, honey. Before he recovers, give him a quick poke in both eyes with your fingers. That will keep him out for at least another fifteen minutes."

The voice was male and accented, but Jennifer could not see anyone. The light shone in her eyes. She shoved Jack away, scrabbled to the side of the seat, and attempted to put her clothes back in order.

"What the hell we got here?" Another voice. There were two of them, maybe more, Jennifer thought.

"Okay, lady, you too, sport. Put your duds on and get out."

Jennifer did not know whether to laugh or cry. Now what? She did as she was told and managed to pull her clothes into some sort of order. She got out of the car. Jack still moaned in pain.

"I guess I hit him pretty hard," Jennifer said to the voices.

"I guess you did, honey. Okay, sport, suck it up and get out."

She saw a burly arm emerge from the shadows, grab Jack by his collar, and drag him from the car.

"Walk," commanded the first voice, "that way," and the light described an arc pointing the way to the parking lot and the bunker.

As Jennifer walked, she felt what was left of her underpants slide down her right leg. She let them fall and kicked them away as they reached her ankle. She was aware of voices, other voices, four voices, discussing her. She wondered who they were. Her first thought—she and Jack had gotten mixed up with a motorcycle gang. The thought terrified her. But now, with the realization that there were only four, she decided she'd been wrong. Besides, she would have heard the roar of the motors. Even Jack's heavy breathing wouldn't have drowned that out.

"Bring them over here," one voice said, and they were steered toward the bunker. "Sit."

She sat and felt the cold steel of the handcuffs circle her wrists, heard its ratchet-clatter as they were closed. Jack, recovered from her kick, decided to be a hero. He jerked his arm away from the cuffs and demanded to know who these people were.

"Shut up, kid," a voice said.

Jack danced back and forth like a boxer and told them in no uncertain terms the consequences that would come if they messed with him.

"I said, shut up, kid."

Then, Jack dropped into a martial arts crouch and signaled them to come on. There was a sigh and then one of the biggest, ugliest red-haired men Jennifer had ever seen stepped into the circle of light. Jack swallowed, raised his fists, and was about to speak, when the red-haired man's fist caught him flat on the nose, mouth, and forehead. It was a big fist. Jack dropped to his knees like a sack of trash, spitting blood and teeth, and making funny whistling noises. They handcuffed him beside her.

The light and the men moved away. Jennifer looked around. Her back was to the building, its low profile barely visible, even with the parking lot lights on. She wriggled around so that she could watch.

Two men stood in front of the door. One held a heavy rucksack. The other wore a black suit, hat, and tie. He seemed overdressed, she thought. Then she heard the rumble of a truck and watched in fascination as it stopped, air brakes whistling, and backed its trailer up to the door. The trailer unhitched, the tractor drove off again.

I don't believe this, she thought. They're going to break into the bunker.

Jack started to whimper.

"Shut up, kid," she said.

Chapter 9

Harry studied the door, oblivious to Donati's presence and the activity around him. It was his show now. Whether the job would go off as planned depended on his skill. It also depended on his willingness to go through with it. He could not refuse, not and live. But he could trip one of the several silent alarms without anyone knowing it, and within minutes the area would be crawling with police. He'd considered that possibility several times during the previous week. It might get him his job back at the Bureau. But he'd rejected the plan as too risky. He would be the first to go, once the double-cross was discovered, and even if he survived that, the chances of the Bureau being impressed were slim. Then there were Donati's frank references to his children. So now he had to shut out the world and do the only thing he knew how to do—disarm alarms and let his new employers get at the treasure the system protected.

Concentration. It's about concentration. He took a power drill from his bag, fitted it with a quarter-inch diamond bit, selected his spot in the upper right-hand corner of the door, and drilled a hole through its face. The steel sheathing was thin and soft. The bit cut into the door's wooden core, solid oak by the look of the curl emerging from the hole. He felt the bit grab metal again and adjusted the drill's speed to its lowest setting. He gentled the bit through the inner steel sheath, felt it give way, and stopped the drill, leaving it suspended in the hole.

Harry reached into his bag again and removed a tissue-thin diaphragm. He backed the drill out and, as the bit cleared, slid the diaphragm over the hole. Fingers, placed V-like, held it in place. Nothing moved. He waited thirty seconds and studied the diaphragm. There was no ballooning outward, no movement inward. The building had not been equipped with a positive or negative air pressure alarm. Thank God for that. He had not allowed time for fitting an air lock, and doubted he could have done it had it been necessary.

He tossed the diaphragm in the direction of the bag and mounted a cutting device on the door using the hole he just drilled as a fixture point. A self-tapping screw locked in the base plate. He fitted a threaded shaft to the plate, locked a tripod to the shaft, and pressed its suction-cup feet to the door. Next, he attached a four-inch arm to the shaft and fastened a hand crank to that. Finally, he locked the diamond-bitted cutting tool to the arm and began rotating it with the crank. The tip incised an eight-inch circle in the door. When the inner face was breached, he stopped. Now came the hard part. He backed the arm out, removed the tool, and replaced it with a toothed clamp, drawing the clamp tight to hold the new circle to the arm. He advanced the arm again, a millimeter at a time, allowing the cutout to protrude into the room, but so that the movement could not be detected by motion alarm inside. When he had three inches clear, he stopped.

He reached into the bag for the magnets that would bypass the contact alarms on the door. With the same painstaking slowness, he reached through the hole he had just made, holding the wafer-thin magnetized plates between his thumb and index fingers. His second and third fingers felt for the contacts. He found them. Harry removed his hand and cranked the cutout back into place. Twelve minutes. Well ahead of schedule.

Now, he thought, we come to the first make-or-break. He had to swing the door open far enough to slide his deflector panel and himself through, and he had to account for the difference in movement caused by the fact the door was hinged and its outer edge would move more rapidly than its hinged edge. Because the door, no matter how slowly opened, would create an angle that would deflect the sonic beam and trip the alarm, he wasn't sure how far he dared open it—one inch, two, three—enough.

He slipped the six-foot three-inch transparent Teflon-coated clear plastic screen through the gap, positioned it in front of the door and parallel to the wall. He eased the door open until there was enough room for him to slip through. Harry shouldered his bag, stepped out of his shoes, and entered the building. Once in, he closed the door and surveyed his surroundings. The motion detector was eight feet in front of him, its cord running to an outlet just to his left, beyond the edge of the door—his first break. Plugged in anywhere else, he would have had to inch his way to the device itself and cut the line. This way, he could slide left sixteen feet and just pull the plug. Thank God for slow security guards unable to clear the distance from the back wall to the door within the fifteen-second delay built into the system.

It took Harry five minutes of slow lateral movement to get to the plug and pull it from the outlet.

He laid the panel down and padded over to where the laser grid was located. He had to look hard to find the red glowing dots on the floor, ceiling, and walls. He assembled a shallow trough from snap-together sections, filled it half full with water from the canteen strapped to his waist. Returning to his bag he removed a brick of dry ice. Placed in the trough, the dry ice boiled, and within minutes the room was filled with a dense fog. Now the grid was visible, its bright red beams crisscrossing in front of him

Harry lay on his back, tied the bag to his left foot, and using the palms of his hands and his shoulder blades slithered between two vertical beams and the lowest horizontal. Like doing the limbo, he thought. Once on the other side, he dragged his bag through, stood up, and walked to the master panel.

Disconnecting the remainder of the alarms at their source came next. The panel was mounted flush to the wall and its contents protected by a locked door. Harry reached for his lock picks and then paused. The lock looked different somehow. The key slot seemed normal, but something....He looked closer, and then ran his fingernail over its face. It was plastic. The face, the key slot, the whole lock assembly was plastic. Harry studied the lock. He had not noticed it two days ago. He had inspected the panel, but from where he stood, the lock's metallic face looked just like any other. Good news and bad news. The good news is that the door was probably not rigged, just the lock; the bad news was he had no idea why it was plastic. There was only one way to find out—open it. He guessed that it must work on a plastic key and be wired so that any metal inserted into it would close an electrical circuit and trip an alarm. He decided it could not work any other way. He put his picks away and rummaged in his pockets until he found the toothpicks he carried to make wedges to jam trip switches. They did not work as well as his lock picks, but they did work, and he was able to pick the lock and swing the door open.

Harry gaped at the interior. He shook his head in disbelief. There must be forty different alarms in this building. Donati would have been better off stealing the alarm system than the paintings. It was worth more.

There were two rows of lights, each marking the location of the trip in the building. To the right was the master switch. Throw it and the whole lot was killed. Harry reached for the switch, paused, and then squinted at it. Too easy, he thought. There has got to be one more trip here somewhere behind the switch. Throw the switch and they know up at the main building that the system is deactivated. He would have to remove the whole plate from the recessed box and get at each trip separately. It was bolted at the corners.

Harry removed a palette knife from his bag and slipped it behind the plate at the top. It slid freely across the width of the plate, bolt to bolt. On the right side, it caught halfway down. He tilted the blade and worked it past the obstacle, heard the light click as the trip switch snapped back when the blade passed by. He worked it back over the switch and taped the knife to the wall. With another blade, he repeated the maneuver at the bottom—no switch—and left side—one more.

With the two knives taped in place, he backed out the bolts, removed the plate, taped the knives more securely, and turned his attention to the dozens of cables coiled spaghetti-like in the box.

Harry's hands moved like spiders through the delicate, complicated electronic web, capturing each alarm system like a fly, immobilizing and rendering it useless. His concentration was absolute as his mind sifted through his options. Options developed in equal part from his years of experience and his intuitive grasp of the system. Even in the bad days, when he would often work in an alcoholic haze, his instincts never failed him, had in fact often saved him where someone else, even someone with complete faculties, might have failed. His old boss had once admitted that Harry Grafton drunk operated better than almost anyone else sober. But that was a long time ago—a life that belonged to another Harry Grafton, the one with a wife and family and a job on the right side of the law.

He saved the lasers for last. He watched the beams wink out in the last wisps of water vapor. He was done. He glanced at his watch and then looked again. He had done the job in an hour and fifteen minutes. He guessed there was something to be said for sobriety.

He packed his bag and walked to the door. It had been cool in the building. The designers had included a constant temperature and humidity ventilating system. In spite of its sixty-eight degrees, Harry was soaking wet. He stepped outside, nodded to Donati, and walked to the edge of the woods where he gave in to the nausea. He retched, caught his breath, and retched again.

Red backed one trailer to the main door. He climbed out of the cab and gave Harry a thumbs-up sign, which he changed to a single finger salute. He swung the rear doors open and went into the building. Harry caught his breath and let the sweat cool his forehead. The two kids, now blindfolded, sat handcuffed together, right wrists to the other's left, encircling the bole of an oak tree. A little late for that, he thought.

Donati appeared at the door and motioned to Grafton. "We got work to do, pal, and we don't have no union men here, so help haul these pictures up and into the truck. We don't have all night."

Grafton swallowed and went into the building to join the others.

It took three and a half hours to remove the paintings and load them into the trailers.

‹›‹›‹›

Jake was relieved at half past three by Henry Tompkins. Henry was late as usual. They shared the eleven to seven shift and took turns walking the grounds or watching the two television monitors. In the winter, watching the monitors became the better job, in the summer, walking the grounds.

"Anything doing?" he asked. Burt shook his head.

"Nope. There's a car parked down in Paradise. Parker said he'd chase them out before he went home, but I didn't see him or the car move so I shut her off."

"Maybe he's still sitting and watching. That's what he does, you know. Don't seem to be able to make it with the ladies, but I hear he likes to watch."

"I'd be careful, if I was you, Henry. Last person talked like that was Darlene Thigpen. And you know what happened to her."

"Yep, damned shame, she was a right smart-looking female up until then, even if she was a whore."

"Yeah, well there was talk. Some say he had her worked over and arrested after she started talking about him."

Henry fell silent and thought about Lee. "Shoot, I don't care how he gets off, long as he don't start watching me." He burst into guffaws and Burt snorted.

‹›‹›‹›

The sky had begun to lighten in the east when they finished. Red closed and latched the doors of the second trailer and turned to Donati. "What about the kids? We can't let them go and we can't leave them. You want me to take care of them?"

"We'll take them with us," said Donati. "We might find them useful later. If not, we can decide what to do then. Right now, we've got to get out of here. Grafton, put them in the back seat of the car. Here." He handed Harry a snubbed-nosed thirty-eight. "You watch them and," he raised his voice so that the girl and boy would be sure to hear him, "if they make any move at all, shoot them."

The boy groaned and slumped. The girl's back stiffened. She's tough, Harry thought, a tough cookie. He unlocked one set of handcuffs and herded them stumbling into the car.

"You heard the man," Harry muttered with what he hoped was a convincing degree of menace. "Nobody move." Straight out of the movies. Grafton, you missed your calling. Maybe there is a place for you in Hollywood.

The truck rolled up the road. Angelo started the parked car, backed, braked, and followed the truck. Donati slipped behind the wheel and started the rental car. They followed it out to the highway. Donati turned left. Harry, who was facing the two hostages, saw through the rear window that the truck was headed in the opposite direction.

Donati drove through town and west, away from the inter-state. Ten minutes later, they were at the motel. The hostages were ordered out of the car and into one of the rooms. Donati told them to lie down on one of the beds. He re-cuffed them to the footboard and headboard.

"There you are, sonny," he said, "you wanted to get her into the sack—you got her." Then to Grafton, "Watch them. I have to pick up Red and Angelo." And he slipped out the door. Harry heard the car start up again and drive off—east this time.

He was exhausted. He wanted nothing more than a shower and six or seven hours of sleep. Then, he wanted to run, as far as and as fast as he could. The whole operation had gone sour. He could feel it more than he could define it. First, Red had to knock out the guard. Harry wondered what became of him. If they took these two, why not take the guard as well? Harry shuddered at the thoughts trying to surface in his mind. And then there were these two. They had seen too much, heard too much. Unless Donati believed they could not identify any of them, he would have them killed. And that, thought Harry, is what he could not allow to happen. He could accept becoming a thief, but not a killer. God, what a mess.

Her voice startled him. She spoke, calm, conversational, a pleasant voice.

"Can I ask you something?"

"Sure."

"Well, first I want to know if I can use the john. It's been almost seven hours and my back teeth are floating. Another minute and I'll wet my pants—that is, if I had any. Thanks to Mister America here, I can't even do that."

Harry grinned. He liked this girl.

"Jennifer," the boy whined, "don't make them angry."

"Oh, shut up, Jack. What can they do to us? I mean, whether I am nice or nasty isn't going to make any difference now, is it, whoever you are?"

"No, Miss," replied Grafton, "probably not." He unlocked her cuffs and led her to the bathroom. He stood in the door and indicated that she should go ahead.

"Do you mind? I would like a little privacy. I know there isn't much of me that you people haven't seen, but I would like to, you know—alone."

"I'm sorry...Jennifer? That's your name? I'm sorry, Jennifer, but I can't. This is one of those motels where they install a lot of useless extras, like instant coffee makers and telephones in the john, so you don't notice how rundown and tacky the place really is."

The girl glanced at the wall to her right and saw the phone that was an integral part of the paper dispenser.

She sighed and started to lift her skirt.

"Hold it a minute," Harry said. He went to the phone, bent down, and disconnected the modular clips at both ends of the cord, removed it, and shoved it in his pocket. He turned, checked the window over the tub, painted shut, and then waved.

"Enjoy," he said, and left the room, pulling the door closed behind him.

She showed him a lopsided grin. "Thanks."

Chapter 10

Somehow, Ike realized, he had managed to get through another week without incident. Except for the usual traffic accidents and violations, the loud parties and occasional D and D, the week passed quietly, uneventfully. He congratulated himself for having buried another one hundred sixty-eight hours of his life. Now it was Friday noon, and in five hours or so, he could begin the weekend, one that was his, not a repeat of the previous one.

He sighed. Was it just a week ago he had been conned by his father into going out to the farm? It had passed pleasantly enough. His father kept his promise and not talked politics, career, or Ike's future. That left little they could talk about, but they shared some hours reminiscing. Ike's fears about having to fend off the advances of the eligible Miss Rubenstein turned out to be groundless. To his delight and his parent's consternation, she showed no interest in Ike as a marital prospect at all. She had, it turned out, a "gentleman" in Richmond whose virtues she described in great detail and at great length all day Saturday and Sunday. Ike heard about Dr. Milton Rappeport, the eminent orthodontist, at breakfast, at the swimming pool, in the library, at every turn. Milty, she declaimed, was kind and considerate. He escorted Barbara to only the best restaurants, purchased nice presents for her, and danced attendance on her every wish and whim. He was expert in the inner workings of the New York Stock Exchange and people's malocclusions. He knew the difference between Bordeaux and Burgundy, which years were good or excellent. He read books, went to plays, vacationed in Stowe and Miami Beach. "He skis on water and snow, Ike, did you ever..." Barbara gushed, eyes aglow, hands clasped Madonna-like over her heart.

Ike had been impressed. He hoped she would find real happiness in this new relationship. Indeed, the only thing standing between Barbara and certain connubial bliss was the disconcerting fact that Milton was, if not happily, permanently married to the mother of his five children.

All in all, it had been a quiet time and fulfilled his filial duties for a month or two. He could now feel free to spend his weekends as he pleased. And this one, he decided, would be at the cabin, a retreat he purchased years ago as a place to hide. He had an idea a dozen years before that he would like to write. Except for the yellow-lined legal pads and the computer with its high-powered word processing software he bought when he purchased the cabin, he'd made no progress on that career. But the cabin played an important part in his life, anyway. He ran to it three years ago, like a hare from a fox, after Zurich, after the funeral. Without phone, television, or radio, he reveled in his privacy, cut off from any intrusions from the rest of the world.

Maybe this weekend, Ike thought, maybe this weekend I'll write it down...put the whole mess on paper, but he knew he would not, could not.

He stared at his desk and shook his head at its clutter. Not by nature a disorderly man, his survival in the past depended on a methodical way of working. But desks were an unsolvable mystery to him. Somehow, no matter what system he devised, papers, memos, reports, letters, and reminders piled up in untidy stacks with coffee cups, parts of ballpoint pens, rubber bands, and paper clips. His desk, he decided, looked like a sanitary landfill.

The department secretary, Rita Joyce, learned to copy everything that went into Ike's inbox, because the likelihood of its ever coming out again was nil. Periodically, Ike would clean, sort, annotate, and discard paper in a frenzy of neatness. His desk would be clear for perhaps two days and then the mess miraculously reappeared.

Ike pulled a trashcan over to his chair and began sorting. Urgent/important items he piled on the floor at his feet. Letters to be answered went into his lap. Items which were completed, or whose deadlines for completion had long since passed, went into the outbox for filing. Everything else went into the trash.

After an hour, the trashcan was filled and its overage spilled into the urgent pile at his feet. When he reached to separate the two, the pile in his lap slipped down to join them. It was almost three o'clock and Ike decided he had enough. He scooped up all the papers at his feet and returned them to his desk. Even though a substantial number of documents had ended in either the trash can or the outbox, the pile on his desk looked as large as when he started. There must be a law, he thought—one of Murphy's, perhaps—that covered this. The depth of the pile on the desk is inversely proportional to the occupant's importance. Not bad. The phone rang. Essie wigwagged to Ike from the outer office that he should pick up.

"Sheriff's office, Schwartz."

"Sheriff, this is Dr. Harris' secretary…out at the college." The last word was pronounced with a rise in inflection, making a verbal question mark.

"Yes?"

"Well, Sheriff, we've got a problem here."

"What sort of problem?" Ike said, wondering why people never seemed to be able to get to the point in the first exchange on the telephone.

"Well, we've had a robbery," she said.

"I'm sorry to hear that, Miss, Mrs.…."

"Ewalt, Agnes Ewalt. I'm President Harris' personal secretary," she said, barely disguising the pride she felt for holding such an exalted position.

"Well, Agnes, pardon, Ms. Ewalt, I'll send someone out right away."

"I don't think 'someone' will do, Sheriff. President Harris said you'd better come yourself."

"Me? Just what happened?" Ike said. Now he was getting impatient.

"Well, someone seems to have broken into the Art Storage Compound. Are you acquainted with the Art Storage Compound, Sheriff?" she asked. Ike was close to losing his temper.

"Ms. Ewalt, will you please get to the point? Yes, of course I know the facility, everybody in town knows about the bunker. What was taken?"

"All of it, Sheriff."

"All? All of what?" Ike shouted.

"Why, the paintings, Sheriff. They've stolen the Dillon Art Collection, that's what all."

"Good God, Agnes, why didn't you say so in the first place. I'll be right out," he shouted.

He hung up the handset and bolted out the door.

"I've called Billy and Whaite. They're on their way," Essie announced.

"Thanks, Essie. Tell one of them to come by here on the way and pick up a kit. We'll want to dust for prints and collect whatever we can find."

‹›‹›‹›

Ike pulled into the parking lot next to the Art Storage Compound and climbed out of the car. A knot of people stood around its open door. He recognized Ruth Harris, Colonel Scarlett of the state police, and two of Callend's security people. A few paces away, Whaite Billingsly was talking to the little moon-faced, bearded man Ike had seen the week before outside President Harris' office, the day she'd called him a fascist. This ought to be fun, he thought.

As he drew closer, he was struck by the expression on each of their faces. Ruth Harris was angry, exasperated. Colonel Scarlett, who had the rugged outdoor look one associates with cigarette ads or country music singers, at least before they all started growing beards, a look he accentuated by wearing tooled cowboy boots and his service revolver low on his hip, stared off into the woods, impassive. The security people looked uneasy.

Whaite wore the look of strained patience which seems to be the exclusive property of police officers. His companion was agitated.

"Good afternoon, President Harris, Colonel," Ike said and nodded to the others. "You've had a robbery. Your secretary, Ms. Ewalt, says someone cleaned this place out. Is that right?"

"Yes, Sheriff, that's right," Ruth Harris snapped. "We are in the process of getting on with the business at hand. Colonel Scarlett here said we had to notify you. Something about jurisdiction, he said. So, you have been notified, thank you."

"Appreciate that," Ike said, turning to Scarlett. "What happened?"

"Well," Scarlett drawled, "I got a call at dinner time, 'bout noon, I reckon, from somebody up at the capitol saying I should get my butt out here pronto because some pictures got ripped off last night. So here I am. When I found out you ain't been called, I told them to call you. I haven't done anything else."

"Thanks, Colonel," said Ike. Scarlett was as phony as a three-dollar bill. Except for three years on the highway patrol, where he was an efficient, but not noteworthy writer of speeding tickets, Scarlett had served his entire career, before making regional commander, as one of the governor's series of bodyguards and chauffeurs. Nevertheless, he was not stupid and he knew his limits. Right now, he was off limits and he had called in Ike.

"You said 'last night'? The robbery was last night?"

Scarlett opened his mouth to answer, but Ruth Harris cut through whatever he was about to say.

"That's right, Sheriff, last night someone or some people broke in here and removed almost all the paintings."

"I see. When was the robbery discovered, Ms....Doctor Harris?" Ike asked, feeling the anger beginning to build. He knew what the answer might be, and he was trying to get his temper under control before his suspicions were confirmed. He did not want another go-round with this woman. Keep cool, he thought.

"Nine this morning," said Ruth.

"Nine," Ike exploded. "You knew at nine this morning and you waited until three this afternoon to report it? What in God's name—"

"You are mistaken, Sheriff," Ruth interrupted icily. "We reported it almost immediately."

"To whom?"

"Well, we called—"

"We? Who's we, Ms. Harris?" Ike was angry. There was no hope for it. He and this insufferable woman were going to go at it now.

"We, is me, if you must know. I called—"

"Thank you, that's what I thought."

"And what is that supposed to mean?"

"Skip it. You called whom, President Harris?"

"I called the Dillon people. After all, it's their art and their building. I thought they should know. And of course, I wanted their guidance. They, that is, Mr. Dillon himself, said he'd arrange for the state police and the FBI to be notified. So then I called the insurance company to alert them. That's it," Ruth said.

"That's it?" Ike asked in amazement. "Didn't it occur to you to call the police?"

"We did, Sheriff. Colonel Scarlett is here. The FBI's on the way, I'm told."

"No, no, Ms. Harris. Not the state police, not the Federal Bureau, the *police*—me. Don't you know that you call the local police first, that the state troopers and the feds have no jurisdiction here—can do nothing for you unless I ask them to?"

"What?" Ruth exclaimed. "You mean to tell me that you are going to decide how to investigate the theft of a half a billion dollars' worth of the world's art heritage—you?"

"Sorry, lady, but that's the way it is—my rural police force and me. Isn't that right, Colonel?"

"That's the size of it," Scarlett said, "and you know you can call anytime, Sheriff. Well, I'm off. Keep in touch." Scarlett ambled off with a wave of his hand.

"Colonel Scarlett?" Ruth was near panic. "You can't leave. Mr. Dillon expects you to take charge here. He...."

"I'll be in touch, Colonel," Ike said and turned to Ruth Harris.

Chapter 11

"Let me get this straight. This robbery was pulled off last night. It's now three in the afternoon. You have known since nine o'clock this morning and nothing has been done? Your bungling gave the thieves a six-hour advantage they shouldn't have. Do you have any idea how far you can go—I suppose in trucks for this job—in six hours? Do you have any idea what your screw-up gave them?"

"Bungling? Screw-up?" Ruth shouted, "Now look here, Mister—"

"Screw-up. In six hours, they could have gone three hundred, three hundred fifty miles. Figure they pulled out of here at dawn, say, five-thirty. They've had nine hours to get lost. They could be in New York or Pittsburgh by now. What in hell were you thinking about? I am fifteen minutes away. You call your police. They start the investigation. If the state police or the FBI or the U.S. Army is needed, we call them in—not you," Ike shouted back, outraged at this smug, arrogant woman.

"You? You and your fumble-fingered cowboys are the last people in the world I want to handle this. We are talking about five hundred million dollars in art, Sheriff. This is not a holdup at the local Taco Bell. We need experts—"

"You get me, lady. Until I say otherwise, you don't get a choice." Ike turned his attention to the two embarrassed security police.

"Nine o'clock you discovered this?" Ike asked, fixing them with eyes that by now had taken on the characteristics of a ninety-mile-an-hour wind off the South Pole.

"Yes, sir, nine," one answered. He swallowed, his eyes gazing out of focus at a tree behind Ike's right shoulder.

"I thought this building had the most elaborate alarm system and television surveillance in the state," Ike shot at him.

"Sheriff, I don't believe I want my people to be interrogated by—"

"Dr. Harris," Ike snarled, "you will go over there to that bench and sit down. You will stay there until I say so. If you don't, so help me, I will arrest you on suspicion of grand theft larceny, obstruction of justice, assaulting a police officer, jay walking or anything else I can think of. Is that clear?"

Sparks flashed from Ruth's eyes. She was about to reply when something in Ike's manner convinced her she was not hearing an idle threat. She turned and did as she was told, settling for a frosty, "You haven't heard the last of this, Sheriff."

Ike turned back to the guard.

"Well?"

"Well, Sir, them alarms got broken into somehow and the television worked all right, but they fixed it so we seen the same picture all night." The guard shuffled his feet and looked at the ground like a small boy caught sneaking into the movies.

"Fixed? What do you mean fixed? What picture all night?" Ike said.

"Ike," Whaite Billingsly broke in, "they got a pair of video tape decks back there." He gestured toward the back of the building. "They must have tapped the line, recorded a couple of minutes for each of the cameras, then cut the tapes in on a loop playback and cut the live transmission out. These guys looked at the same sequence all night."

Ike thought a minute and turned back to the guard again. "The interior scene, I can understand, but the exterior camera… it was a night scene, right?"

"Yeah, that's right, I guess," the guard mumbled.

"And the sun comes up around five-thirty, six o'clock, this time of year, right?"

The guard nodded.

"So by six-thirty at the latest, someone should have noticed that the sun was shining on the whole State of Virginia, everywhere except on this parking lot. Didn't it occur to you that something was wrong?"

"Well, yeah, I guess, only—"

"Only what?"

"Well, I come on at seven o'clock and the monitor for the lot was off," he replied.

"Off. Why off?"

"Well, Jake, he had the eleven to seven shift, said that on account of the car...see, we didn't want to make no trouble for old Parker, you know, and so we generally turn it off when there's a car down there."

"What the hell are you talking about? What car?" Ike shot back. He was getting angry again. His whole day seemed to be filling up with circumlocutions.

"Well, Sheriff, we got this rule, see, that nobody's supposed to park down there, so if someone does, Captain Parker he slips down and shoos them away. Sometimes he makes the kids walk out and hitch back to town and then they have to come back next day and get their machine. Parker calls it impounding. He says it teaches them a lesson."

"If no one's supposed to come down here at night, why don't you all just lock the damned gate at the end of the lane at the main road?"

"Well, generally we do, but—"

"But what?" Ike waited, watched the man's eyes turn from apprehensive to fearful.

"Well, see...listen, you won't tell him I told you, will you? He can be mean as hell sometimes, and I need this job," the guard stammered.

"Tell? Tell whom? Who's mean as hell? What in God's name are you talking about?" Ike was shouting again.

"Parker. See, he leaves the gate unlocked sometimes when he's on duty at night, you know? He hopes kids will come so he can go after them. You won't tell, will you?"

"No, I won't tell. So, because you didn't want to know about the car, you or your buddy turned off the monitor. Where is Parker, by the way?" Ike asked, looking around,

"Don't rightly know," the second guard said. "When I came down here this morning to open up and seen this mess, I right away called and…Well, nobody can find him."

"Whaite." Ike turned to his deputy. "You seen or heard anything of Loyal Parker?"

"Not a thing, Ike. You want me to look?"

"No, not you. I need you here. Get a bulletin out. Have one of the boys start looking for him. Get on the radio and tell Essie to pull everyone back on duty. Get one group to go through town and locate Parker, and ask for anything you can get on two men." Ike described the two men he had seen Monday in the Crossroads Diner.

"Get another group out here and see if they can find anything. Start inside, then out here. We will want footprints, tire tracks…anything. Then move out a hundred yards or so—have Billy do that.

"I want you to get those TV tapes and get what you can on the car. Find it. And Whaite…" Ike paused. "Fingerprint the whole lot here, including her." He jerked his head in Ruth's direction.

"You're sure?"

"Oh, yeah—her particularly." He turned back to the guards. "You two stay here, and, I'm sorry, I don't know who you are," he said to the bearded man who sidled up.

"Bialzac, Sergei Bialzac. I am the head of the history of art department here at Callend. Shocking, positively shocking," the man said.

"Yes, well," Ike muttered, "you've been inside, Dr. Bialzac?"

"Yes, I have. It is awful. It is just dreadful. They have gone through there like vandals, like Huns. Even if you find the paintings, it will be months, perhaps years, before they can be displayed again," Bialzac groaned.

"How's that?" Ike asked.

"Look, I'll show you, Sheriff," said Bialzac, and indicated that they should enter the building.

Ike paused at the door and noted the hole inscribed in its face. He inspected the magnet on the contact alarm and stared at the screen lying against the wall, the trough of water in the corner. He walked to the alarm panel and whistled at the lace-work of wires, clips, and jumpers that had been constructed. He peeled away the tape that held one of the palette knives in place and stared in admiration. Good work, Ike said to himself, better than good—damned near perfect.

"Sheriff?" Bialzac ventured.

"Coming, Doctor. I was just admiring a little artwork they left behind." Ike shook his head, and turned to join Bialzac.

Ike and Bialzac surveyed the wreckage on all four floors of the building. All but twenty or thirty paintings had been removed from the racks that held them vertically. Their progress was slow because they had to step over the hundreds of frames scattered all over the floor.

"Tell me," Ike said, "what's the collection worth?"

"Well, that's hard to say, Sheriff. It's insured for five hun-dred million dollars. That's its appraised value—the amount they might get for it if Dillon decided to sell. If they don't sell, they're worthless."

"How's that again? What do you mean, worthless?"

"Well, Sheriff, this is a well-known collection. It has been cataloged, studied, and described by hundreds of scholars and collectors over the years. Everything in it is as well-known in art circles as *La Giaconda*, um, the Mona Lisa. It is, for all practi-cal purposes, unsellable. No reputable art collector would buy any part of it. He would know right away where the item came from. I do not understand this at all.

"There are some people, of course, who even knowing it was stolen, might buy a piece—rich collectors, Arabs, people like that, who would put the painting aside for ten or twenty years, then bring it out. But there aren't many of those." Bialzac paused, deep in thought.

"There are pieces in the collection which are not well-known which Dillon bought later and which, while valuable, haven't the sort of recognition the bulk of the collection has, but...."

"But what, Doctor?"

"Well, they seemed to be the ones they left behind. They took the most important pieces, the least saleable. It's strange."

Ike studied the little man and tried to read his thoughts. Then he said, "You wanted to show me something, Doctor."

"I beg your pardon, what?" Bialzac came out of his reverie.

"You said before, outside, something like vandals, it would be months or years before the paintings could be displayed again when they are recovered," Ike replied.

"Oh yes." Bialzac's mood shifted again. He became agitated, angry once more. "Look here, Sheriff." He picked up a dozen or so frames and discarded them. "You see, the pictures are held in place by clips or a retainer of some sort. To extract the paintings from the frames properly, they must be removed. But look here, and here, and here; they have just yanked the pictures out. They must have torn or damaged them. Scandalous, they had no right—they knew how important...."

Bialzac retreated into the professor's cluttered world again.

"No time, I suppose," Ike said. "If they'd removed all the paintings like you're supposed to, they'd still be here."

"But it's monstrous, the work of thugs, people who know nothing about art, crazies," Bialzac expostulated.

"No, I don't think so," Ike said.

"What do you mean, Sheriff?"

"Well, the work on the alarms has a master's touch. And they only took the good stuff. You said so yourself, they left the less valuable pieces. No, these people were professionals, and professionals never pull a job without knowing what they're stealing."

"But the damage..." Bialzac said, concern in his eyes.

"Oh, that. Well, that confirms your guess, Doctor. They do not care about the paintings as paintings. They have something else in mind for them. Now, if we only knew what."

They were back at the door. Ike turned to the little professor and extended his hand, which, after a brief hesitation, Bialzac shook.

"Thank you for your help, Doctor. Would you do me a favor and join the others, and tell Dr. Harris I would like to meet with her in her office later, say, six o'clock. I'll be tied up here until then." Bialzac's hand was dry.

Ike watched him make his way over to the bench and speak to Ruth Harris. He was amused to see her back stiffen and smiled at the angry glare she flashed at him. If looks could kill, Ike thought. He looked at the door and let his eye run over its surface, down to the sill. He bent, looked again, and picked up the wafer-thin diaphragm. Very good, he thought, very good indeed.

Police cars began to arrive. Ike made his assignments and told Billy to call the county.

"We haven't the time to do all of this, Billy. See if they will send out a crime unit to dust inside. You stay with them, look for things that might be useful. Start inside, and then do the outside. Take your time. I don't want to miss anything. Whaite will join you when he gets done up at the college."

Ike got on the radio and was patched through to the state police frequency. Colonel Scarlett was as laconic as ever.

"Can I do for you, Sheriff?"

"I've had a chance to look around, Colonel. I think we're looking for trailers, one tractor and two trailers. That means unless they've got another tractor somewhere, they're hop-scotching the paintings out of the area, or they're parked. If your people notice anything would you let us know?"

"Will do, Sheriff. Anything else?"

"Not right now, thanks. I'll be in touch," Ike said, and signed off.

The afternoon submerged into the orderly confusion of police work. Ike moved through the ever-growing cadre of people arriving on the scene. He had cordoned off the area, but still had to deal with the media, local papers, a stringer from the *New York Times*, a television crew, and the editor of *Callend Comments*. He shooed away self-appointed assistants and people with theories from the college faculty and the town. He moved in and out of the bunker a dozen times. Billy joined him outside the building a few minutes before six.

"Ike, I reckon we got one or two hours of good light left. You want me to get the floodlights?"

Ike considered a moment and then said, "No, I guess not, Billy. We've lost so much time already. We're better off being careful than quick. Wait until tomorrow if you have to. We can't afford to miss anything. Tape this place off and put a couple of the boys on the line to keep folks out before you go."

"Oh, I don't know if it means anything, but I found this piece of paper over by that tree there. Somebody tossed their cookies and this might of fell out of their pocket."

Ike scanned the scrap. The word *Artscape* had been scrawled at the top and there was a series of figures and what could be serial numbers in a neat column below.

"Bag this and give it to Whaite."

Ike stretched and glanced around him. He was startled to see Ruth Harris still seated on the bench. She could not have been there all the time, or could she? He walked over to her.

"You been here all this time, Ms. Harris?"

"Most of it, Sheriff, all except when your Boy Scouts took my fingerprints." She looked at her fingers, which still showed the smudges of ink on their tips. "Do you think any of us would—?"

"I don't think anything, Ma'am. I just do police work. You were in there. There may be prints left by the thieves. I have to know which belong to whom, if you follow me. Frankly, I don't think we'll find any prints in there. They were pros, and pros make few mistakes. Certainly, they won't leave their fingerprints."

"Then, why in Heaven's name were we subjected to this harassment?" she retorted.

"Routine, Ms. Harris, just routine. Could we finish this somewhere else—say, your office?"

"Of course, Sheriff, my office will be fine. By the way, I have reported your behavior to Mr. Dillon. I thought you ought to know. We take a dim view of the kind of inept—"

"Your office, please. You can skewer me there."

Chapter 12

Ruth ushered Ike into her office and gestured toward one of the two large wing chairs opposite her desk. Ike sat with a sigh. Ruth sat behind the ornately carved library table she used for a desk. She placed her hands palms down on its glass surface and faced him. Her back was ramrod straight, masking the bone weariness she felt.

"All right, Sheriff, what do we do now?" she said, a trifle too loud, a trifle too patronizing.

Ike slouched back in the chair and extended his feet straight out, eyes closed. His hands, thumbs hooked into his belt, lay idle in his lap. Ruth felt edgy and tired, and Ike's calm grated on her nerves. Nothing he did or said all afternoon was anything but correct. He moved through the confusion, fended off offers of help from a variety of well-intentioned but useless people, others who wanted to exploit the publicity implications or the political consequences. He took notes, made endless phone calls and, she had to admit, deported himself as a competent police officer—confident, in charge, and able. Damn, she thought, I ought to be grateful. But the habits of youth still held her fast. Schwartz represented authority and stood at the other end of the span that ran from right thinking to unthinking. He was the cops—the Jackie Gleason to her Burt Reynolds. All the years of demonstrating, posturing, and commitment to a doctrine of distrust of authority had left her no place to go except to dismiss

Ike and all that he stood for. Every year, she found it harder to hold on to those convictions, and tonight she realized the struggle might well be lost. In addition, something about this particular cop did not resonate with her biases.

"Dr. Harris," Ike responded, eyes still closed, "*we* do nothing. *I* put people to work. *I* make phone calls. *I* go back over the building with a fine-toothed comb, the whole area, in fact, interview and ask endless questions. I guess. I sort through information. I start all over again and I wait. I wait for whatever it is that comes next. *I* do that…not *we*.

"You, on the other hand, should go home, pour yourself a stiff drink, climb into a hot tub, and call your boyfriend."

Ruth bridled. Her eyes flickered and sent invisible poisoned darts at Ike's forehead.

"I don't have a boyfriend, Sheriff, and I don't need you playing drug store psychiatrist for me."

Ike opened his eyes, surprised. "Sorry, I didn't mean to offend. It's just that, well, there is nothing for you to do. Just go about your business. If you notice something, remember something, anything—no matter how trivial, that you haven't told us, let me know."

Ruth studied him, dispassionately.

"That is not good enough, Sheriff," she said. "I am worried about this investigation. You have dismissed the state police. You have refused to even talk to the FBI. Do you think you and the rest of your rural constabulary are up to something as important, as big as this? Face it, Sheriff, neither you nor your people have the experience, the training—"

"That is presumption, Dr. Harris. An untested assumption, a—"

"What you must do," Ruth continued, ignoring him, "is clear out an area at the police station—no, it would be better up here, I think. I will call Mr. Dillon's contacts and get the real experts in here. Captain Parker will handle operations at this end. The press, of course, will be cleared through my office, and—"

"And I should do what? Boil water?"

"Sheriff, you don't have to get defensive. I just feel that a case this big should be handled by the best, and you have to admit that the sheriff's office of Picketsville is hardly in that league. You said yourself, whoever did it are real professionals. I want my own real professionals to find them."

So absorbed was Ruth in her directive, she missed the flash of anger in Ike's eyes, a look that he replaced by one of weary resignation. Ike hitched himself up in his chair and leveled his gaze at Ruth. Finally, he spoke, his voice patient, like a school principal explaining for the fifth or sixth time why there would be no beer at the junior prom.

"Dr. Harris, there are some things you need to understand. First, as I told you before, neither the FBI nor the state police can enter the case, because they have no jurisdiction. The county police can, but only if I ask them, or they feel the investigation is not being handled correctly. That is not yet the case, and if any of these folks were here, they would be doing what we, my deputies and I, are doing now.

"Second, your man, Captain Parker, has been missing since eleven o'clock last night. But if he were here, I would tell him to stay out of the way. If he wanted to be useful, he could do something about the parking problem on campus. He is the last, I repeat, the last person on earth I want mixed up in this investigation.

"Third, you may do with the press and television what you wish, but I am telling you now that details of the case, what we know and what we don't know, will be cleared through me. If you cannot accept that, I will get a court order and have you gagged.

"And last, just for the record, I don't give a damn what you think of me and my deputies. I was elected to this job because folks here believed I could do the job better than your Captain Parker, and I hired the men who work for me. I know what they can and cannot do. I am here to tell you that if anyone is going to find your little collection of pictures, it's me, me and my rural constabulary. So I will give the orders here, not you." Ike was up and pacing, trying to keep his temper under control.

"Now wait a minute, Sheriff." Ruth was aware that she had been told off, and she did not like it.

"No, you wait a minute," he shot back. "You are the single most tiresome person I have met in the past decade. I cannot think of anything that I or any of my people have done today to earn the back of your hand. They know their job and they are pretty good at it. More importantly, they know when they are in over their heads and how to ask for help. Police work is almost all routine and it works best when one group stays with the problem from beginning to end."

She watched as he walked back and forth between two chairs, punctuating his remarks with gentle stabs at the upholstered backs with his right index finger.

"We don't need a lot of jurisdictions and agencies swimming in this pond. All they will do is muddy the waters."

He stopped and dropped into his chair. Ruth stared at him. She was angry and frustrated. She fought off the feeling that, somehow, she was losing. She knew she had asked for the lecture, but she did not like Schwartz giving it to her. Most of her anger, she admitted, was due to the fact that she had underestimated this man and was on the defensive.

"You're not wearing one of those belts," she blurted. "Where's your cop belt?"

"Excuse me? My cop belt?"

"You know, the big bulky one with the big stick and the little boxes and guns and things like that hanging on it…where's yours?"

"Never wear it…too bulky. Anything else?"

She closed her eyes and wondered what possessed her to ask about his belt. She decided to make one last stab at reestablishing her position. Gathering her strength and the last vestiges of outrage, she flared out at him.

"Look, Sheriff, you can give orders, take orders, or go screw yourself. I do not care. I'm just telling you straight out, I think you lack the expertise, the equipment, and the brains to handle this business, and I intend to get some people in here who know what they're doing, and I don't care whether you like it or not."

He did not reply, did not react to the determined set of her chin, the fire in her hazel eyes. He gazed at her, his face expressionless. Thirty seconds passed—a minute. Ruth felt her determination beginning to crumble. She had lost. A minute and a half slid by like molasses on cold pancakes. Finally, he spoke. His voice was quiet, but his words and the force behind them were unmistakable.

"Dr. Harris. If you would just put aside all that radical crap that used to be your credo fifteen, twenty years ago. And if you could be, if not pleasant, at least tolerant of others, irrespective of their background, their profession, or political persuasion, and if, in short, you would shed all that left-liberal bigotry and concentrate on the problem at hand, we would get along fine. If you will not or cannot, I will come down on you like Godzilla.

"I am a very patient man, most of the time. People tell me I am good at what I do. We will soon find out how good, but until I screw up, please stay out of this investigation. I do not want to fight with you or anyone else. On the contrary, I need your help. And I need the cooperation of your staff, faculty, and students. So please, please, make it easy for all of us and back off."

Ruth relaxed and leaned back in her chair. Her hands fell into her lap. She blinked and let out a sigh. Enough, she thought, I have had enough. I am tired. I am hungry, and there is no fight left in me. Maybe he is right—a stiff drink, and a hot bath. She closed her eyes. God, I do not even know why I am giving this man a hard time. He is right. She opened her eyes and studied him, took in his angular frame, dark eyes and hair, and rugged good looks. Not handsome, she mused, but well put together. His face fits the rest of him. And, God help me, he even seems like a decent sort of man.

"Okay, Sheriff," she said. "For now, you win. I will back off. I might even owe you an apology. Will you settle for a truce?"

"On one condition...."

"What's that?"

"Let me buy you dinner."

"What? You're kidding." Ruth was amazed.

"I never kid...well, not often, not now anyway."

Ruth stared at him. She had been caught off guard. The last thing she expected was a dinner invitation. She felt beaten and disappointed in herself. The angry words, in spite of the hard shell she built around herself, battered her spirit. Now this. Here, she decided, was a very unusual man. He had just won, and instead of leaving her to lick her wounds, instead of rubbing her nose in her defeat, he offered her a kindness. The man was one of those rarest of creatures, a good winner. Ruth swallowed.

"Sheriff, you are amazing. I think I had better accept, if only to find out what makes you tick. You're sure about this?"

"Absolutely. Dinner, the works. Why not?"

"When?"

"Tonight?"

"You're kidding, right?"

"I told you, I never...."

"Kid, right, but shouldn't you be, I don't know, on duty or something? What about the reporters, TV hook-ups?"

"There is nothing I can do between now and tomorrow first light. The bunker is sealed off, my cell phone is on. My people are working. I'm available twenty-four seven. And anything I can do to avoid the press is a plus for me. Besides, this may be our last chance. You reported the break-in late, too late to make important deadlines. By tomorrow morning this place will be crawling with press, politicians, and all kinds of people ready to exploit the situation. Some of my law enforcement colleagues are going to find the opportunity to become celebrity cops irresistible."

"How are you planning on avoiding all that now?"

"I know a place."

"A place. Like a place where all those people can't find you—find us. That kind of place?"

"Right."

"Do I get a chance to go home and change?"

"You have half an hour—tops. Where we are going takes time and it's almost seven already."

Chapter 13

One half hour later on the dot, Ike pulled up to the central entrance of the college just as Ruth rounded the corner of the long porch that ran the length of the main building. The building, the subject of hundreds of pictures and thousands of postcards, was famous for its wisteria. Its purple panicles covered the length of the porch, climbed upward to the second story, and back to disappear around the far corner.

Ike had had just enough time to jump into the shower and touch up his shave. Now, smelling of Old Spice, he stepped out of the car and opened the door for Ruth as she emerged from a riot of purple and descended the steps to the gravel drive.

"I could have picked you up at your house, you know," he said.

"That would have been difficult. The driveway to the house comes up to the back, to a garage added as an afterthought. The front door is only accessible by that path you passed on your right as you drove in. Much easier to meet me here." She looked at him and the car. "Well, it's an improvement, Sheriff. I halfway expected to be taken to dinner in a police car."

"That can be arranged, if you'd prefer."

"No, this'll do just fine. The last ride I took in a police car was anything but pleasant and I'm not sure I could rise above that."

Ike installed her in the passenger side, walked around to the driver's side, and slipped in.

"I've been thinking about your belt."

"My belt?"

"I can't imagine why I asked you about it this afternoon, what I was thinking about."

"Probably had something to do with guns."

"You think so? I guess you are right. Aren't you supposed to pack a gun? Is that what you guys say? Pack a gun?"

"Carry. We carry, not pack."

"Sorry. Where is it?"

"What?"

"Oh come on, where are you carrying it?"

"Stop. What is this all about?"

"Guns, I guess."

"Okay. I do not wear my cop belt as you call it, because ninety percent of my time is spent doing things that do not require all that stuff. If I need a gun or handcuffs, they are available. But that is not what this is about, is it? You want to engage me in a debate about guns, the NRA, and all the baddies the folks in the community you come from have identified. Am I right?"

"Don't you worry about hand guns and the rise of deaths attributable to them? I mean even the police recognize the need to get them out of the hands of people, don't they?"

"That's too many questions in one sentence. Sure, I worry about shootings a lot, but I am more concerned about the culture of death we have created in this country. It's the source of most of the awful things we have to live with now."

"The what of death?"

"The culture of death. What's on television? What're the lead stories on the nightly news? Last week I watched the local news and kept score of the items reported. There was a lead-off of a robbery and shooting at a local convenience store. Then there was a report of a drowning in a backyard pool. That was followed by a story on road rage and finally a fire in a local warehouse, which ended with the commentator saying, 'luckily there were no deaths'—as if we should expect death and luck will sometimes prevent the inevitable."

"Well, yeah, but I fail to see—"

"A culture is defined by the way it spends its leisure. Look around you. What's at the movies? What do people do, watch, and admire most in our culture? And have you seen the video games our children play? As soon as a child is big enough to get its thumbs around a Playstation, we begin its education in violence and mayhem. The popular ones are about shooting, blasting, or one way or another demolishing some imagined enemy. We are training a whole generation of killers."

"Oh, come on now, you don't really—"

"People watch HBO and admire, no, award, a show about men who cheat on their wives, lie to their children, deal drugs, some of which end in the schools their children attend. They murder their friends, enemies, strangers, and the ones they don't kill, they destroy. It is a culture of death."

"What's your alternative, Sheriff? Do you want us to go back to *Father Knows Best* and *The Brady Bunch*?"

"Not really. But let me ask you this: how many Columbines and teenage murders were there when those shows defined the culture, instead of what we see now? The answer, by the way, is zero."

"So you don't think there ought to be limits put on guns?"

"I didn't say that. Register them, make it hard to purchase one, close the loopholes in sales at gun shows—all that is fine with me, the tougher the better, but I think if someone wants to own one, he should. When I was growing up, everyone I knew had guns, long rifles, pistols, the works. And in those days there was not a single shooting in this town—not one. Today we have the same number of guns and ten times the shootings. What's changed?"

"But wouldn't your job be easier if the guns were gone?"

"Sure it would. I think anybody who has a gun and never intends to use it should get rid of it. People who do keep guns should keep them locked up, and in the event someone is injured or killed by their gun, they should expect to be charged with contributory negligence."

Ike caught his breath. He had surprised himself with his speech. What he said, he believed, but he had never put it together that way. This woman, he thought, seemed to bring out the best and the worst in him. He did not know whether that was a good thing or a bad thing.

"My, this is a cheerful beginning for our first date, Sheriff. You got any more thoughts on the state of the world you'd like to share?"

"Later, maybe....It's not a date."

"Right...and I'm not done with this gun business."

Harry stared at the two sleeping forms in the half-light. Even though the girl and boy were handcuffed to the bedstead and the phones removed or deactivated, Donati had insisted they be watched round the clock. He assigned the duty to Angelo and Harry. Red, over his protest, was not involved.

"You got a thing, Red, about young helpless girls and you hit too hard. I don't need that on top of the screw-up with the cop, so you stay away." Donati's voice was always velvet smooth, but there was no mistaking the menace behind it. Red stayed away.

Harry looked forward to his watches. It got him away from the other three, the smoke, and the uncomfortable closeness to people who were and would forever be strangers to him.

The girl stirred and opened her eyes. "I was hoping it would be you."

Harry grunted, thought a moment, and responded, "Why's that?"

She stretched and took a few quick breaths. Her eyes focused, and with the resiliency the young and innocent seem to have, she was at once awake and alert.

"Because you let me go to the bathroom alone. The other one won't. He doesn't look, but, I don't know, I just can't get used to sitting on the john with a chaperone."

Harry walked to the bed and unlocked the girl's handcuffs. She rubbed her wrist and sighed. "When will this be over? Harry? Is that your real name? That's what they call you."

"Yes…a couple more days, then it's over. The Dillons come through, we get paid, and we all go our separate ways."

"Except me and Jack, we know too much. You can't let us go, can you?"

She was right. He did not want to think about it, but she could identify all of them. The boy, Jack, presented a lesser threat. Red had rung his bell the night of the robbery and he was still out of it. He might or might not remember, someday, but not anytime soon. Harry wondered why Donati had not eliminated them sooner. But Harry knew his employer never acted without a reason. Donati must have something in mind.

"Everything's going to be all right, I promise. You and your boyfriend will be fine."

"He's not my boyfriend. He's an oversexed jock whom I met for the first time the night you found us, and if I hadn't listened to that honey-mouthed, social-climbing, airhead roommate of mine, I'd be back at the dorm in my own bed right now."

The girl was a complete stranger to him and half his age, but Harry felt a sense of relief that the boy was only a date. Strange.

"Oh, I almost forgot," Harry said, "I went in town today to pick up food and I bought you these. I hope they'll do."

Harry handed her a paper bag and watched while she opened it. She took the items out one at a time and laid them on the bed—a toothbrush, toothpaste, a comb, two sets of underwear, a flannel shirt, and a pair of jeans. Her face lit up.

"Oh, my God, I know this sounds crazy, I mean, here I am, about to be murdered—it's true, I know it, you'll have to, sooner or later—and all I can think about is a shower and clean clothes. Underwear. Do you know how it feels to be naked under your clothes? I mean—to be that way and know that everyone around you knows it? You feel so…defenseless. Thanks, Harry."

"I just thought you could use—"

"I mean it, Harry…can I call you Harry? I mean if you aren't on a first-name basis with the man who buys your underwear, you're in trouble, right?"

Harry grinned. "Go clean up and make it quick. I'm done here in forty-five minutes, and then the other guy takes over."

"Call me Jennifer, and you are a nice man, Harry. I don't know why you're here or how you got into this business, but you're not like the others. You just aren't."

Jennifer rushed into the bathroom, shedding her dress as she went. Harry caught a glimpse of her naked backside as she turned the corner and shut the door.

Chapter 14

Ruth studied Ike out of the corner of her eye. They drove in silence, through town, east to the interstate. He turned north toward Lexington. Ruth settled back in her seat and closed her eyes. They took the exit to Buena Vista and headed up toward the mountains. A mile or two out, Ike turned left and the car bounced up into the mountains.

"Sheriff," Ruth said between potholes, "it's your party, but for the record, where in the name of all that's holy are you taking me? You said dinner and it is almost eight. I could eat a horse."

"Just a little farther," Ike replied, his eyes fixed on the dirt road. The car lurched. Tree branches scraped its windows and doors. Just when Ruth had decided that she was the victim of a diabolical double-cross, that he was taking her out into the woods to get rid of her once and for all, the car careened to the right and pulled to a stop in a clearing. There were seven or eight other cars parked in front of a log building. Soft light streamed from its windows. Ruth could make out tables and diners inside.

"Where on earth…what is this place?" she asked, turning to him.

"Le Chateau—best-kept secret in the state. It's the only restaurant west of Richmond worth dining in," he replied, grinning.

"But there's no sign and the road is a joke. How do they survive?"

"Well, they're usually busy, especially on weekends," Ike said. He got out of the car, walked around to the passenger side and opened the door. "It's all word-of-mouth, no pun intended. Rumor has it an orthopedic surgeon in need of a tax write-off owns it. I'm not sure. My guess it's Mafia owned and operated to launder money. Who knows, it might be just what it appears to be. All I know is, they have a menu you're not going to believe, a wine cellar as good as any I've seen, and a chef who's fantastic."

They stepped through the rough-hewn door into the warmth and the aroma of good cooking. A short, dark *maitre d'* greeted Ike by name and escorted them to a table in the corner. A dozen tables, twos and fours, two stations and a small bar filled the small room. Candles in pewter holders, a bud vase with a single rose, Limoges china, and linen napery set up each table. Artfully placed indirect lighting and candles in pewter sconces lighted the room.

"Well, I'm impressed, Sheriff. You are a man of many parts, it seems," she said, shifting her inspection of the room and its occupants to the man who could debate with some force and knew food.

They ordered drinks and waited in silence until they were brought to the table. Ruth felt herself relax. She decided that in spite of their ideological differences, Schwartz might not be so bad after all. In fact, something about him intrigued her. Life in academia and earlier flings at the fringes of the radical movement had given her the opportunity to meet and know many men. But she found only a handful interesting—none like this one.

"Sheriff, with all due respect, you are a puzzle. I can't picture you as the pride and joy of Picketsville and certainly not as a small-town cop. I'd like to know who you are, and why I keep thinking I know you from somewhere."

"I'd prefer you call me Ike, if that doesn't tread on your sensibilities. Well, believe it or not, I spent the first eighteen years of my life in Picketsville. My daddy, as we say down in these parts, is Abe Schwartz. He was, and in his retirement still is, a political wheeler-dealer. His last office was comptroller. When he was younger, my age, he wanted to be governor. He made a very successful run from minor county posts to the state legislature. He was elected speaker of the house and stood in line for statewide office. But back then, thirty or forty years ago, things were not all that favorable to someone of his, ah, persuasion. And he was told, by those who could make it happen, that 'there wasn't going to be no Jew governor of Virginia as long as they were alive.' Abe, my father, decided then and there that his son Isaac was going to realize that goal for him."

"So you're going to run for governor? Excuse me for saying it, Sheriff—Ike—but being the top cop in Picketsville does not strike me as much of a political base to launch a gubernatorial campaign. Your father, the wheeler-dealer, does not expect you to go upward from there. He must be very put out with you."

"Well, as a matter of fact, he is, but not the way you think. I said he wanted me to run. I went away to college and then went to work for the government and never came home...until three years ago. It's too late now to think about that anymore, even if I wanted it."

"Children do that, don't they," Ruth said. "They rebel against their parents' plans for them. They go off and do their own thing and then end up as carbon copies of the parent they thought they rejected."

"Like you, Dr. Harris? You and your father, the dean?"

"If I am to call you Ike, you must call me Ruth. How do you know about my father?"

"Ruth? Not Sydney?"

"No one's called me Sydney for years. How did you—?"

"You said a while back you thought you knew me. We did meet, a long time ago."

"We did? Where?"

"At your house. A group of us were there one evening and you breezed through. You were in your grunge phase then, black baggy jeans, bare feet, lots and lots of black makeup, fringed jacket, and long, very black hair. As I recall, you had a young man in tow dressed the same, except his hair was spiked up and dyed an amazing shade of red. He looked like a rooster."

"You. So that's it. Now it makes some sense. You were one of Daddy's young men. Mother always called you people 'your father's young men.' She never knew about his connection with the CIA, but I did. She thought he was just the dean of the law school who had these nice young men over for tea and conversation. She didn't know he was screening and recruiting for the Agency. You were one of them. The government job you had, it was with the CIA, am I right? You were one of his recruits."

"Yes. You still want to have dinner with me?"

"What? Oh, well, I'll be. In all those years I never knew any of you—not one. It drove Daddy crazy. He'd keep urging me to go out with solid people, you guys, and stop hanging around with weird types."

"But you never did?"

"Nope, never, until tonight. Well, I'll be." She beamed at him, inspected him with renewed interest. He squirmed under her scrutiny.

"Whatever happened to the one you were with that night?" he asked.

"Bobby? I haven't thought about him in ages. The last I heard, he was in the construction business with his uncle in Providence."

Ruth sipped her drink lost in thought, her eyes out of focus. She returned to the present and fixed Ike with a no-nonsense look.

"No fair, Sheriff. You have me doing all the talking. What about you? What's a college graduate—what college, anyway?"

"Harvard."

"Holy smokes. What is a Harvard graduate, Yale Law School graduate and former spook doing playing sheriff in Picketsville, Virginia? There has got to be something more to you than you are willing to share. You married?"

"Once."

"What happened?"

"She died. An accident."

"Oh," Ruth said, subdued. "I'm sorry."

Their waiter appeared to take their dinner orders. The cuisine was French, the menu English, an unbelievable menu. When the waiter left, she pressed on.

"So what about you?"

"There's nothing to tell. You know all the important parts, born and raised in Picketsville, sent by my father to Harvard, supposed to come home for law school, Virginia or Washington and Lee, but I went to Yale instead. I met your father, and the rest is, as they say, history. I worked for a dozen years for the Agency, in Europe, and when my wife was ki…died, I quit and came home, to get out of it."

"What did you start to say about your wife, Ike, just now?"

"Nothing. It's all past now."

Ruth wondered again what she was doing here. Her college faced an economic crisis, there were police, press, and curiosity seekers trampling all over the college's lawn, and the guy who declared he would sort it out had her in the middle of the boondocks for dinner. The whole thing struck her as a bit from *Alice in Wonderland.*

She studied him. Questions begged to be asked…about his wife—*When my wife was ki*…killed? And why sheriff, of all things? She saw the evasion in his eyes and something else—pain and anger. He covered it well, but no mistaking the look. Ike Schwartz perched on a personal volcano. She decided to let it go and try later, maybe…but not now.

"Wine," she said, changing the subject. "We need wine, Ike."

Ike scrutinized the wine list.

"White or red?"

"White or pink, please."

"White, it is." Ike beckoned the waiter back and pointed to a Macon-Blanc. The waiter beamed. Ike asked for the wine straight away. The waiter disappeared, to return a moment later with the bottle resting on his arm. Ike inspected the label, nodded, and watched the waiter uncork. Ike felt the cork, sniffed it, and nodded again. He sniffed the splash poured into his glass, sipped, chewed, and rolled it around in his mouth.

"Very nice," Ike said.

The waiter poured a glass for Ruth, filled Ike's, and disappeared again.

"Tell me something," Ruth said, her chin in her palm, "Do you know what the hell all that's about, the cork, the sniffing, the wine-tasting ritual? Be honest, now."

Ike grinned. "I haven't the foggiest, Ruth, but waiters always seem disappointed when you don't do it."

"Aha," she crowed, "at last, an honest man. I do not know how many people I have asked that, and they all give me some bogus story about bouquet and texture and the most incredible bullshit, and none of them could tell you there was a fire if their pants were in flames. But you do it because you don't want the waiter to be disappointed. That is terrific. I am beginning to like you, Ike. You've got possibilities."

He smiled. His face relaxed.

The waiter brought their food and hovered over them, checking and rechecking, swooping in to pour sauce on the duck, on the beef, to grind fresh pepper on the salad. Finally, satisfied they could manage the rest of their meal without him, he left them to dine alone.

‹›‹›‹›

They busied themselves with their meal, filling in the silences with small talk, about the town, the college, speculations on the robbery, Parker's whereabouts. He told her about Loyal Parker. Parker, the local redneck bully, was the kind of kid who would throw cats out of speeding cars, make lewd remarks to Callend girls, and if he and his oafish friends could, beat up their dates. He and his pals went to Roanoke to harass gays. As far as Ike was concerned, Parker had not changed much in twenty years. That was one reason he had decided to run for sheriff.

Ruth shifted in her chair as she crossed her legs. Ike heard the whisper of nylon. He thought, not for the first time, about the erotica of ordinary sounds and smells, of sensory stimulation, the sound of nylon against nylon for example, and where that took his thoughts.

"Ike? Problem?"

Just in the nick of time, Ike was jerked back from the images that were beginning to form in his mind.

"No, nothing. My mind just wandered off for a minute. Must be the backlash from a busy day," he lied.

Ruth's eyes scanned the other diners. "You know any of these people?"

"Well, yes I do, as a matter of fact. You see the silver-haired man sitting with the short fat guy in the corner?"

"The two men with the two young women?"

"Yes. Well, the distinguished older man is Senator Rutledge and the man with him is the attorney general."

"So that's Senator Rutledge. He's on some of my boards but I've never met him. He never attends meetings but always sends a nice note. Is it too much of a stretch to hope the woman with him is his daughter?"

"Way too much. They are, or one of them is—not to put too fine a point on it—bait."

"Bait?"

"The attorney general, Bob Croft, wants to be senator. Rutledge has hinted he might step down, but everybody knows in the end he won't. So Croft has brought the good senator to dinner and, I'm guessing now, set him up with one of those bimbos—excuse me, professional women, in the hopes of putting the good senator in a compromising situation, thus advancing the time the said senator declares his retirement."

"And will he?"

"Senator Rutledge did not get to Washington by being stupid. He will see through this and will report it to his friends, and the attorney general's career will end before the next general election."

"Just like that?"

"Just like that."

"Wow. Life must be tough in the fast lane."

"You're having me on. Now look over in the corner. Do you see those three men and the woman together? Well, that's Gloria Barnes, Clint Davis, William Danzinger, and Mordichai Blum. You know who they are?"

"Only by reputation. I think Ms. Barnes attended my inauguration. The others run Fortune five hundred companies and she owns a chain of newspapers or something."

"Newspapers, television stations, cable TV, and major stockholder in more big companies than you can imagine. If Daddy Warbucks had a female rival, she would be it. What do you suppose those four are cooking up tonight?"

"I'm afraid to ask. Do you have an idea?"

"No, but I do know that they all have two things in common: one, they all have bought development rights to vast tracts of land south of Washington, adjoining the Manassas battlefield, and two, they are the honorary chairpersons of the Roanoke College capital campaign. You choose what they're up to tonight."

"It staggers the imagination."

Chapter 15

Time slipped by. They didn't notice the other diners finish and leave for home, or assignations, or whatever came next on their program. Ruth kept Senator Rutledge in view from the corner of her eye, fascinated by the process unfolding at the table. The waiter appeared with the dessert cart.

"Oh my, did you ever....A person could gain five pounds just by looking."

"Well, are you going to slide all the way into decadence and take one of those or are you just going to drool down the front of your blouse?" Ike said.

"In for a penny, in for a pound," she said and pointed at a big éclair on the cart. "That's got to be at least thirty-five hundred calories—one pound. I'll risk a pound."

Ike waved off dessert. The waiter shrugged and rolled the cart away.

"So, how about you? How did the gum-chewing grunge child I saw years ago end up in the Shenandoah Valley?"

"Oh, it's not much of a story. I went to college, tried my best to outdo my parents in upholding the great causes of the day. Then my father had his first heart attack. It sobered me up, I guess. It is one thing to be forever young and believe you are on society's cutting edge, another when you realize that your father might die and you haven't done anything with your life except embarrass him. All the fun went out of hell-raising so I settled down. No more marching, no more provocative articles in the school paper, that sort of thing.

"Graduate school was a logical next step, and before I knew it, I became my dad. Academia is a safe haven for us left-liberals, you know."

"Oh yes. So what did you study?"

"Majored in political science, switched to history in graduate school. It gave me a wider range of things I could study."

"Let me guess—you did research on the history of women in politics."

"Close. I did my doctoral thesis on Margaret Sanger."

"No romance? No great affair of the heart?"

"I got married. Does that count?"

"But you're not married now?"

"No, not any more."

"It's none of my business, but what happened?"

"I'll tell you my story, but only if you promise to tell me yours. Deal?"

Ike hesitated. Could he? He had not spoken of those events in three years. Why now? Why this woman?

"Okay, it's a deal."

"Well, by the time I'd finished my doctorate in history, I had made a name for myself. I signed on as a faculty member, published journal articles, and wrote chapters—earned my academic merit badges. I sat on committees, commissions—all the usual stuff. But I did not feel good about me. Too many men. Don't raise your eyebrows like that, Sheriff. There weren't *that* many.

"Then I met David. He was four years younger than I, a graduate student in the medical school studying reproductive physiology. We used to meet at night in the rat lab, gave the rats lessons in reproductive technique. We got married. I loved him, and it might have worked—only it didn't."

Ike signaled the waiter for more coffee. When he left, Ruth continued.

"I married David because I wanted stability. He gave me self-respect. In return, I supported him while he finished his

Ph.D. He got a junior faculty position at the medical school and everything seemed to be fine. The problem was—I was doing better professionally. As hard as he worked, he couldn't get into a tenure track. I got promoted and started receiving offers from more prestigious schools.

"We told each other nothing changed, that the differences didn't matter, but they did. I resented having to turn down offers. He resented my success. But we could never bring ourselves to talk about it. That was our big mistake.

"Then, one day I got an offer I couldn't refuse, department chair at the University of Chicago. We talked about it, or rather I talked, and David listened. 'Don't worry,' I said, 'there're six or seven medical schools in the area. I'm sure we can find you something.' What a terrible thing to say.

"I moved from New York and commuted home on weekends. It wasn't too bad at first. He began to look for jobs, but all his prospects fell through. He wasn't that good professionally, to tell the truth, and he was in a crowded field. I got more and more involved in my work. I stayed in Chicago one weekend a month, then two. I was flying high and I never noticed. I was meeting new people. I was important. I was appreciated and—"

"Another man?"

"No. Yes. No, it just happened. The pressure got to me and I went crazy for just a moment. It meant a fifth weekend in a row away from home, the sixth in two months. You know the funny thing about it? I intended to tell David, say 'look at what's hap-pened to us.' I reached a point where I was ready to quit even, come home if that would save the marriage. I came to believe what I had only given lip service to before, that I loved him.

"When I got home to put my marriage back on track, he'd gone—left me a note. 'Dear Ruth,' it said, 'I accepted a posi-tion in La Jolla. I wanted to tell you when you came home for the weekend, but you never came. I called, but you were out.' Then he put in the clincher. He said, 'Don't worry, there are six or seven undergraduate schools there, I'm sure we can find you something.' It was dated two weeks earlier. Two weeks.

"I called him and he said, 'How's your friend?' and I said 'I love you, David,' and he said, 'I can't live with that kind of love' and hung up. Since then I made a vow—no more messing up other people's lives. No commitment. Have fun, but do not get involved. Besides, my work takes up most of my time. There's not much left for a social life outside it. Do you know what I mean?"

"I'm not sure. I think I do, maybe. It sounds pretty final—a commitment to not commit. I guess that paradox ought to be explored sometime."

"Maybe, but not now, not by me." Ruth glanced around in surprise. "Ike, do you realize we're the only people here?"

All the tables were stripped of their linen and silver and the candles out. Their waiter chatted with the *maitre d'*, glancing in their direction. Ike looked at his watch.

"Good Lord, it's nearly twelve. This place closes at eleven. We're holding these people up."

"Is it that late? Make it up to them, Ike. Give him a big tip. Did you know you're an easy man to be with? And all this talk about the past makes me very sentimental and sad. But I have a full day tomorrow and we, sorry, you have a tiger by the tail. Home and to bed."

They drove down the mountain in silence.

"Pull over here," she said.

Ike slowed the car and then pulled into an overlook. He killed the ignition and turned off the lights. A nearly full moon bathed the pull-off in silver-blue, its carefully ragged stone walls contrasting sharply with the soft symmetry of the forest. Puzzled, he got out of the car and went around and opened the door for her. She walked across the few feet of gravel to the wall.

"In all the time I've been here, I've never gotten away from my desk long enough to see any of this." The ground fell away at her feet creating a magnificent panorama. She gazed across the tops of trees and down into the Shenandoah Valley. She stood in silence, unsure if she was overwhelmed by the view, the day's events, the wine, or inner turmoil as she realized, to her amazement, that this man had more than just charmed her. He stepped up behind her and for a brief moment she let her head fall back on his shoulder.

She turned to face him. The moonlight filtering through the pines made his features seem dashing and mysterious. Ruth felt her heart turn over. This is crazy, she thought. What am I doing here?

"Ruth?" Ike murmured. She said nothing but turned back to the view, as if she might find some guidance from the twinkling lights scattered across the valley floor. A shadowy movement caused her to jump.

"Something moved down there."

He moved behind her and looked in the direction she pointed.

"A doe and her fawn."

"Oh, I've never seen one, not in the wild. They're beautiful."

They watched as the slender wraith-like forms, washed in moonlight, ears alert, stepped from the brush into a small glen, stiff legged and cautious. They hesitated, nibbled the tough mountain grass, and drifted silently into the trees. Ruth turned to face Ike.

As a child, when left to play alone, she had invented an enchanted place—the Fairy Ring she called it—where she imagined wonderful, magical things happened. Her dolls were no longer plastic and stiff, but moved, talked, and drank tea. Later, when the dolls no longer served as her companions, she dreamed of adventure and romance. Inside the Ring, she believed, anything could happen.

As she gazed into Ike's eyes, the moonlight worked its magic and the world drifted away. He moved closer and time slowed, then stood still. She felt the Fairy Ring coalesce, circle, and enclose them. She waited. Ike put his hand on her cheek. It was not a caress, just a touch. Ruth felt her eyes begin to tear.

"Oh," she said, eyes wide, lips parted. "Oh."

Ike drew in his breath and exhaled. "Time to go."

They returned to the car and rode in silence. As they neared Pickettsville, she turned to him.

"Ike, what happened just now?"

She searched his face in the dim light, looking for some hint, some clue, perhaps just reassurance.

"It's not you, Ruth. God knows…."

The pause seemed to last forever. She realized ghosts stood in the space between them. They defeated the Fairy Ring's magic.

Chapter 16

Ike ignored the stares when he walked into the office. In his three-year tenure as sheriff, he'd never been late. But today he wandered in, waved vaguely to his staff, and closed the door of his office behind him without a word. He had some serious thinking to do and did not wish to deal with the idle chitchat that usually marked the beginning of his day. He'd managed to cool the relationship between himself and the formidable Ruth Harris to something approaching normal—at least he hoped he had. Something good happened the night before, he knew that, but he didn't feel brave enough this early in the morning to explore what it might be. He put his feet up on the desk and closed his eyes. He needed to think.

When he caught himself dozing off, he dropped his feet to the floor with a crash loud enough to earn a worried look from Essie.

She peered around the doorjamb.

"Ike, are you all right?"

"Fine, Essie. Long night."

"Well, I'm sorry, but it looks like its going to be a long day, too." She handed him a fistful of pink phone slips. He shuffled through them and called after her, "None of these press guys gets a return call. If they insist, say we can't talk while the investigation is still in progress. There will be a press conference soon."

"How soon?"

"Never. Then call my father and have him deal with this stack." He scowled at the messages from the governor's office, local congressmen, the chief of the county police and an assortment of current and wannabe politicians. "This is right up his street. He'll have a ball. Put the rest in a pile for later."

Essie smiled and nodded.

Calls, he had to make some calls, but not to that bunch. He heaved a sigh and decided to call Charlie Garland. He punched in the number at the Agency. Funny, Charlie's number was the only one he could remember. All those years dialing Operations and myriad departments and offices and the only number he could remember was Charlie's.

The phone rang twice before Charlie's nasal baritone came on the line. "Garland."

"Charlie, a voice from the past. It's Ike. I need some help. Have you heard about the robbery down here?"

"Oh, a little something, Ike, little of this, a little of that, you know, office scuttlebutt."

"Charlie, whoever did it were pros, real pros, our kind of operators—well not mine anymore, but your kind. Someone who knew his business deactivated the alarm and surveillance system. There can't be more than a half dozen or dozen people in the world that could have done it. Can you get me a line on who might have been available?"

"Oh gee, Ike, I don't know. You know we don't fool around with local stuff, not since 9/11. Holy Hannah, if we even so much as ask about stuff like that, the FBI and every local police agency in the country's likely to climb all over the boss. I'd like to help, but I don't have a thing for you, pal."

"Charlie, just poke around, will you?"

"Ike, I can't, but say, I do have something for you. Do you remember a guy named Elwood Farnham?"

"Elwood who?"

"Farnham, Elwood Farnham."

"No, never heard of him."

"That's funny, he remembers you. I saw him six or seven days ago at O'Rourke's in Georgetown. He says he went to school or something with you. He'd like you to call him."

"Charlie, I don't know any Elwood….He wants me to call him?"

"Right. You should call him, fill in the gaps for you, maybe."

"Thanks, Charlie, I'll do that, and if you hear anything, you'll let me know?"

"Sure thing, Ike, but don't expect much from here."

Ike hung up and stared at the phone. Now what the hell was Charlie playing at? It had been how long? Five, six years since he had pulled that one. It was a wonder either of them remembered. There was nothing to do now but wait.

Ike dialed the college and asked for Ruth.

"President's office." Ike recognized the inflated tones of Agnes Ewalt.

"Is President Harris in, Ms. Ewalt?"

"Whom shall I say is calling?"

"Isaac Schwartz, Sheriff Schwartz."

"President Harris is in a meeting right now, Mr. Schwartz, and she can't be disturbed."

"Thank you, Ms. Ewalt. Would you tell her I called?"

Ike hung up and wondered at the mentality of this executive assistant, that's what they called themselves now, not secretaries. Who would ask for a name when she knew she was not going to put the call through anyway?

Ike left the office telling Essie he was going home and then out to Lee Henry's to get his hair cut. Essie sat, mouth agape, a new fistful of pink call slips in her hand, and watched as he left the office whistling.

<><><>

Shaved and freshly dressed, Ike drove down on one of those rural roads that zoning boards and planners like to ignore. All sorts of businesses get located in and around their owner's residences. Body shops, truck, and auto repair garages operate from large buildings at the rear of the properties. He pulled into the

parking area in front of Lee Henry's house. A sign on the front
steps read: *Lee Henry, Hairstylist.* Lee set up shop in a room just
off her kitchen in what would have been a mudroom or family
room, between the living room-dining area and the garage. The
house was a fairly new split-level south of Picketsville. Lee "did
hair" and told stories. For her male customers, the stories ran
to raunchy. For that matter, so did the ones she told her female
customers, but holding to an old tradition, she never told an
off-color story in mixed company, at least not very often. Ike
hoped she was not busy. He had no appointment, but he also
knew from experience that Lee would fit him in somehow. Lee
greeted him with a smile like summer at the beach.

"Ike Schwartz, you old Jewish Paul Newman, where have
you been for the last God knows how long?"

"Busy, Lee. Busy stamping out crime and corruption, appre-
hending villains and bringing malefactors to the bar of justice."

"That means you've been handing out a lot of parking tickets,
right?"

"Something like that. And we had a robbery—I guess you
heard about that."

"Heard? Honey, there ain't nobody in the county that ain't.
Robbery and, bless the Lord, that son-of-a-bitch Parker missing.
You think he did it?"

"I doubt it. He is not smart enough, and the people who
did it are very good. He might have been party to it somehow,
you know, looked the other way, but that wouldn't jibe with
his disappearance. I don't know what happened. He's probably
sleeping it off somewhere."

"Shoot. I was hoping to see that bastard behind bars."

"Parker's not one of your favorite people?"

"Not mine, not anybody around here who knows him. You
were away when he was sheriff, but you saw enough when you
got back to know, Ike, no disrespect intended, but we would have
voted for an old yellow dog for sheriff if we had got the chance.
Best thing that ever happened to the town, when you ran. You
were the only one around who could and get away with it."

"He hurt you, Lee?"

"Not me—my baby sister, Ike. Locked her up one night when he caught her and her boyfriend smoking a little grass. He and them goons he had for deputies. They had her searched, you know what I mean? Strip search, they call it. There she was, a sixteen-year-old girl scared out of her mind and four grubby grown men watching her undress, feeling her panties, saying things, you know. Then they said they had to make sure she didn't have anything hidden inside her."

"I get the picture."

"Four grown men groping her, and her just a kid, a terrible, rotten thing to do to anybody, and all the time them remarking. That little thing like to went crazy. Almost twenty-five before she'd even look at a man again, much less go out with one."

"Did anybody do anything?"

"Do? What could we do? Parker owned the town. You cross him and your life was miserable, you know?"

"Yes, I guess I do."

"Well, anyway," she brightened, "them days're all gone. You're the sheriff now and I'll tell you, Ike, if you've a mind to, you can strip search me anytime you want. I'm best in the morning, though, when I ain't been on my feet all day. Gravity's not kind to you when you cruise past forty. Sit down, honey, and let me see if I can make something out of that mess on your head."

Ike sat and allowed Lee to tuck the sheet under his chin and around his neck. Lee clucked and tut-tutted as she combed, measured, and began to clip.

"Ike, I got one for you. What's the difference between true love and herpes?"

"I can't imagine. Tell me, what is the difference between true love and herpes?"

"Herpes is forever! Ain't that a hoot? Georgie Tice told me that one—herpes is forever," Lee chortled. "Had a big night last night, did you?"

"Big night? No, not really, not if you mean what I think you mean, then definitely not."

"I say you were out with a lady last night and it got pretty up close and personal."

"Why would you say that?"

"Oh, a woman can tell. There's the look—and other stuff."

"The look? What look?"

"Oh, you have a little glint in your eye."

"Lee, I didn't sleep last night at all."

"There, you see, I was right. Lover, you need to learn to pace yourself. Love a little, nap a little, that is, if you're going to pull an all-nighter."

"Enough already. Nothing like that happened. It was just dinner. What other stuff?"

"Well, the big tip-off is this twelve-inch-long brunette hair on your collar. It's not yours and it sure ain't mine. Got to be someone else—another woman. I hope she was nice to you." She dissolved into another paroxysm of laughter.

"Lee, when you're done wetting your pants at my expense, I have a favor to ask, as one detective to another."

"Shoot, Ike, I'm all ears."

"Your ex-husband and your friend Roy are both truckers, spend a lot of time on the interstate, right?"

"Pretty much. They'd rather pull north-south and be close to home than go east-west so, yeah, they try to pick up loads running up and down I-81."

"Lee, whoever pulled the robbery loaded the stuff into trailers. My guess is that they are not too far away. Ask your friends if they have seen anything, anybody that is…I don't know…different, suspicious. That could give us a line on where the pictures are… anything at all. I don't even know what I'm looking for. I could be fooled by a bogus trucker, but a trucker couldn't."

"I'll ask around. There, you're done, lover. If you're going to see that lady again, this ought to get her panting in a hurry."

Ike paid and left the shop. Lee called out after him.

"And if the lady don't take good care of you, you tell her me and the rest of the horny old bats in the county are going to scratch her eyes out."

Ike was halfway back to town when the radio's low static coalesced into Essie's voice.

"Ike, you got your radio on? I called out at Lee's and she said you just left. Ike?"

"Essie, for God's sake, just call. I'll answer if I'm on. You do not have to work your way through your day for me. What is it?"

"Sorry, I just can't quite get used to all this formal stuff on the radio and all. I was telling Momma last night—"

"Essie, stop right this minute. Just give me the message."

"Oh, right. Ike?"

"Yes, Essie, it's me. I'm here and you're going to tell me something, aren't you?"

"They found Parker."

Ike pulled into the parking lot beyond the bunker near the point where the overgrown lane ended in the trees. Whaite Billingsly waited for him with the coroner. The three walked down the lane, stepped over the log that blocked it, and went into the trees for about ten yards. Whaite motioned to Ike's left, toward a small depression six or seven yards away. It was the early stage of one of the sinkholes that characterize the area's topography.

Ike walked to the edge and looked down at the broken body of Loyal Parker. In death, he looked only pathetic. The eyes that once froze people with their malevolence and terrified the helpless were blank, covered with the curdled milk scum of death. The coroner explained to Ike it appeared Parker had been dead at least thirty-six hours. The cause of death, he guessed, a professional guess, was a tremendous blow on the back of the head that shattered the base of the occipital bone and a fair portion of the right mastoid.

"I think he was hit once, very hard, with a crowbar or tire iron, something like that, Ike. I'll know for sure after I've posted him."

"You'll get a report to me soon, Doc?"

"Soon's I'm done. Okay to take him out?"

"Whaite, you got everything you need here?"

"Been over it with a fine tooth. There's nothing new here. Footprints same as over at the building, only better. No sign of the weapon, and we've gone over the whole area. Funny thing, though, they didn't take his gun. You'd think that'd be too tempting to pass up."

"These guys are professionals, Whaite, they don't want, or need, a very traceable piece like that. Okay, Doc, you can take him out. You got anything else, Whaite?"

"Well, I don't know for sure, Ike, but I got a bad feeling about something. You know that loop on the surveillance tape showed a car down here two nights ago. 'Course it wasn't here yesterday, and we guessed Parker shooed it away after the TV was tampered with, but before the robbery. Now with Parker dead, I reckon it means he was killed about the same time." Whaite scratched his head and frowned.

Ike respected Whaite's intuitive, if not particularly articulate, method of sorting out possibilities, probabilities, and arriving at inevitabilities. He waited.

"Well, look here, Ike. I found these over there, about forty feet from where the car was parked." Whaite held out a pair of woman's underpants, the elastic band broken.

"And old Parker, he's over there away from the car, and over here, here by this tree trunk, you can see where he was standing for a while. Ike, you know his reputation—he got his jollies, you know, watching. He couldn't do anything himself. Well, he used to come here a lot, see. He shifted that surveillance camera so he could see anybody who came back here. He'd sneak down, watch a while, maybe, you know, get it off with himself, and then jump the kids, scare the hell out of them and send them away.

"So anyway, you can see where he was lying, and you can see where he fell here by the tree."

"And?" Ike felt the knot begin to form in his stomach. He knew what Whaite would say next and wished it were not so.

"Well, Ike, I don't know. But it seems to me like old Parker caught it here and was toted over there and chucked down the sink hole before he went to the car. His zipper's still down, but the car is gone and we got these britches past where the car was at. They got to be the ones from the car on account of it rained here Wednesday night and these are dry. I reckon the thieves got the car and whoever was in it."

"So we're looking at hostages," mused Ike.

"Or more bodies."

"Whaite, let's stick with more bodies. We'll keep this local as long as we can." At least, Ike thought, until after he talked to Charlie.

"I want you to go back to the security office up on the campus. Fill those clowns in on what's happened and tell them they work for me now. If they give you any trouble, tell them I have deputized them. Then see if you can get a license plate number off the videotape, registration, description, anything, and track it down. Have Essie call the college and find out if anybody is missing, and send those pants to the lab in Roanoke. I don't expect we'll find anything interesting, but you never know, some DNA maybe."

"You going to stick around here, Ike?"

"No, I've got another stop or two to make. You can get me on the radio or the cell phone."

Chapter 17

Ike glanced at his watch. It was still early, too soon to call Georgetown. He thought about calling Ruth, stared at his cell phone for a full minute, and decided to wait. He would drop in on her later. Things were getting complicated, and he needed some information and an outside opinion. He hesitated and then, his mind made up, drove back to town, turned north at the stoplight, and made his way past the golf course to the Meadows, the town's only upscale residential section. He searched mailboxes until he found the one he was looking for: *Tice*. He turned in the driveway, parked, and went to the front door and pressed the doorbell.

"Well, if it ain't Mr. Ike. Land sakes. Seems like a hundred years since we seen your face 'round here."

Amy Cartland filled the doorway, large, black, and beaming. She had been an institution when Ike was growing up. No one knew how old she was, only that no one in town could remember a time when she was not around.

"Afternoon, Mrs. Cartland," Ike said, smiling. "Is Mrs. Tice in?"

"Yes, sir, Mr. Ike, she is. She expecting you?"

"No, she's not. I just thought I'd drop by, to chat."

"Well, she sure going to be surprised when she see you, that's a fact. She's out back, by the pool. You know where that's at, Mr. Ike?"

"Oh, yeah." Ike turned and walked around the house.

Marge Tice was lying face down, her still youthful body gleaming with suntan oil and barely covered by the pale blue bikini, its top untied at the back. Ike cleared his throat as he approached so as not to startle her. She cocked one eye open, squinted, and smiled when she recognized him.

"Hold it right there, Ike," she said, "while I try to get myself more or less decent." She gathered the two skimpy strings that served as straps for her bra, and in the classic maneuver that only women seem to have mastered, reached behind her back with both hands, and tied the straps together. Satisfied that they would hold, she rolled onto her back and sat up.

Marge Tice was one of those women who never seem to age. It is not that they stay perpetually young, propped up with surgery or silicone, but they just hold their looks. They are beautiful at every age, with a beauty appropriate for that age. Ike remembered when she was just Margie Davis, the most popular girl at Rockbridge High, the all-American girl with her short blonde hair, pleated skirts, always-white tennis shoes, and what must have been the largest collection of cashmere sweaters in the county. Margie, vice president of the senior class, head cheerleader, and, for one brief moment, the most important person in Ike's existence. That was over twenty years ago.

"Well, to what do I owe this honor? I've paid all my parking tickets, bought all the chances I can afford on the sheriff's office annual raffle, and I don't think anyone saw me coming out of the Carousel Motel last month, so what is it, Ike?"

"The Carousel Motel," exclaimed Ike. "I didn't figure you for the Carousel, Marge. Anyone I know?"

Marge grinned. "Don't I wish? I guess you're here about the robbery, although I can't imagine why you want to talk to me."

"Well, I could say it was just routine. That's what they used to say on the TV, isn't it, 'just routine, Ma'am.' But the fact is, there are some things that don't make sense to me, and I thought you might be able to help."

"Sure, such as what?"

"The timing, Marge. There is something screwy about the timing of the thing. If you were going to rip off the art, why do it now? Why not later, say, next month, after the college closed, or on the Fourth of July?"

"I don't know, Ike. Stealing isn't in my line of work. But if they had tried later, even a week later, they would have come up empty-handed."

"What do you mean, empty-handed?"

"You didn't know, Ike? The whole collection was being moved to New York next week. I thought that you would have been notified right away. With so much valuable stuff going through town, you should have known. Didn't Ruth Harris' office call you?"

"Well, to tell you the truth, Ms. Harris and I weren't exactly communicating all that well then, and Parker would not have done it unless ordered to," Ike said with chagrin. "But even so, we should have known. He's dead, you know?"

"Who's dead? Parker?"

"Conked on the head with the proverbial blunt instrument."

"No loss there. Sorry, that was a terrible thing to say. But I have to tell you, Ike—"

"No need. You have to take a number and get in line to dance on that man's grave. But back to the art collection, when was the move decided?"

"Gee, a week ago last Monday. You were there—I saw you when we all came out of the meeting."

"I remember." Ike thought a moment. Something someone said, then something he saw, but what?

"So that happened a little over a week ago. I know the names of most of the people at the meeting, but I don't know anything about them. What can you tell me?"

"Not all that much. We meet once a year to rubber-stamp the decisions made regarding the collection, usually about things like air-conditioning, burglar alarms—things like that."

Marge squeezed a generous dab of lotion into her hand from the tube at her side and began to massage it into her skin—shoulders, chest, stomach, and legs. The effect, Ike thought, was very erotic. He wondered if women were aware of the effect it had on men when they did that. He guessed they were.

"Marge, tell me more about the alarms. You approved them?"

"Oh, sure. Dillon senior is a gadget nut. He was always adding something new to the system. Then about two years ago, he had the whole thing redone, with a fancy central panel, laser beams, Star-Wars stuff. He had enough security put into that building to protect Fort Knox."

"Well, not quite enough, it appears."

"No, I guess not. They got through, didn't they?"

"They did, indeed. Of course, if they had the plans and specifications, it would have been easier. When you all approved this new system, did you get a copy of the details? How it worked?"

"No, not really. We got a written description of the plan. You know, a list of all the elements, but we were spared the details."

"Still, even that would help. The people on the committee, who are they? What should I know about them?"

"I can't tell you much, Ike. They put me on the committee because they needed someone local, and I think they were looking for a woman. I was a 'twofer.' The other members are from all over. There's Callend's ex-president, Dan Clough. You remember him. Mr. Dillon, Charlie Two, grandson of *the* Mr. Dillon and son of the current Dillon patriarch, M. Armand, Sergei Bialzac, Ruth Harris, of course. Ben Stewart, the gallery owner from New York, Senator Rutledge, who never comes to the meetings, and me. You know most of them, I guess, except for Stewart and Dillon. Dillon is the shadow of his father from what I gather, and Stewart is a little swish if you know what I mean. I can't see how any of them would gain from being involved. In fact, they all stood to lose."

"How about insurance? Is Dillon in trouble, do you know?"

"I couldn't say, Ike. From what I've seen of their annual statements, they may be healthier financially than General Motors."

"Who else knew about the planned move?"

"Oh, Lord, I don't know, Ike. Anyone might have known. It is not the sort of thing that stays a secret very long. Small towns and small colleges are famous for their grapevines. I expect that just about everybody in town knew by the end of the week."

"Everybody but me, it seems." Ike let his mind wander over what Marge had told him. Something nagged at him, something she said that reminded him of something someone else had said, but who? When? He wrestled with the thought but it slipped away. He shook his head like an annoyed bear.

"What is it, Ike?"

"I'm trying to remember something, but I lost it. Something important."

They sat in silence for a moment. Ike became conscious of Marge and her near nakedness. Her body, tanned and slim, could be the body of a twenty-year-old. He shuffled his feet.

"Well, I'd better be off, Marge. I've taken up enough of your time."

Another period of silence followed while Ike tried to figure why he had not, in fact, gotten up to go. Then, with a sigh, he stood.

"Ike?" Marge's voice was softer, almost girlish, "Can I say something to you that I've been meaning to say for, God help me, twenty years?"

"It couldn't have been twenty years," Ike answered in a half-hearted attempt at gallantry.

"It was, Ike, longer actually. I'm sorry for what happened that night."

"Marge, it's not necessary. It was a long time ago. We were very young."

"I've got to. I have been sitting on this for a long time and it bothers me, even now. No." She waved away his protest. "I told you I'd come to you that night, and I didn't."

Twenty-five years ago, the senior prom and Margie Davis, the most beautiful girl in the room, the only one who could wear a strapless gown and make you notice, with George Tice as her escort, as usual. Margie and Ike in the parking lot in his candy-apple red Mustang convertible, its top up, hers down, two adolescents fumbling their way to adulthood. Margie saying, "Not now, not here, I've got to get back. Georgie is looking for me." And then, "Tonight, in the pool house, here," and she pressed a key into his hand, "Meet me after...." And she tugged the top of her dress into place, straightened the rest of her clothes, her hair, and darted away.

Ike waited for her in the little house by her father's swimming pool for four hours, surrounded by damp towels and the smell of chlorine. When the sun rose, he went home, humiliated. He had barely talked to her since.

⟨⟩⟨⟩⟨⟩

"It's not important, Marge, not anymore."

"Oh, but it is. I almost came, Ike. I got home, went upstairs, and waited in the dark until everyone was asleep. I even went so far as to change into the right clothes, or what I thought would be the right clothes. I wore a sundress that was held up with elastic so all I had to do was let you pull it over my head and, bingo. Oh Lordy, I wanted you—the way kids want...whew. You never recapture that first one. It seems like you'll die if you don't get it."

"What happened?" he said, remembering his own ache.

"I got cold feet. It took a long time for my parents to go to bed. They were arguing about something, me, I think. The longer it took, the more I thought about what I was about to do, and the more hopeless it seemed. I couldn't marry you. My life was all planned for me, college, and then George. I just couldn't say, 'No, I won't do that. I'm going to marry Ike Schwartz someday.' Don't you see, Ike? That's the way we were brought up. Kids in the city discovered the sexual revolution early, but out here...you only went 'all the way' with the guy you were going to marry, and I couldn't marry a...Daddy would never permit me to marry a—"

"Jew?"

"Yes. I'm sorry. I was seventeen, for God's sake. I didn't know anything. For what it is worth, that's the only time in my life I ever committed an anti-Semitic act."

Ike gave her a crooked grin. Here were two near middle-aged people reliving an aborted love affair over two decades old and so much a product of full moons and new hormones as to be laughable, but neither laughed.

"I cried all that night, and most of the next month. Then we went away for the summer and I forgot, almost. When I got back, you were off to Harvard, and I never saw you again until three years ago. But I still remember. I hurt you, and now I want to say it. Ike, I'm sorry."

"So am I, Marge, so am I. You did the right thing, you know. Maybe not for the right reasons, but you were right, it would have never worked."

"That's the awful part, Ike. You know what my father told me on my wedding night? He said that Georgie was a nice boy and he hoped I'd be happy, but he'd always hoped I would hook up with you. Sweet Jesus, all those years, I thought I was acting out what he wanted, following his plan, because Daddy always knew what was best, and I blew it. He liked you and I never knew. I wasn't living out his plan at all. He didn't have one. I was living out my own. I didn't even know my father well enough to know what he wanted or didn't want, what he liked or didn't like. And I found that out on my wedding night."

"Even so, Marge, it wouldn't have worked. I was not going to live out my father's plans for me, and I was not going to come home or have anything to do with it. I would have hurt you sooner or later. But I will tell you one thing, I have thought about that night often, and what might have been."

"Me too. Still do, as a matter of fact. You won't tell George, will you?"

Ike grinned. "How is George, anyway?"

"Oh, he's just fine. He does what all his bank buddies do, play golf and go to important meetings."

"And the Carousel Motel?"

"Just rumors, Ike, just rumors."

Chapter 18

Ike sat in his office and stared through the glass panel at the room that served as police headquarters. Six o'clock. Essie gone for the day. The press corps, reluctant to cover a story that seemed to be going nowhere, had decamped to Roanoke where a gruesome murder story took front and center. Ike had no illusions—they'd be back, but for the moment he had some peace.

Billy had the three to eleven shift and sat in front of the radio transmitter reading *Playboy*. Saturday night. Things would get busy in five or six hours when paychecks were converted into beer or shooters, when kids in pickup trucks began to miss turns in the road, when college students with more money than sense began to tear through town on their way to God only knew where. But now things were quiet.

Ike picked up the phone and dialed information.

"What state, please?"

"The District of Columbia."

"What listing?"

"I want the number of a bar in Georgetown, O'Rourke's."

"Thank you, just a moment."

Ike waited, picked up the pencil, jotted down the number, and hung up. Six-o-five. Charlie had said between six and seven. Ike decided to wait until six-thirty, twenty-five minutes away—time to have a quick beer, read the paper, work a cross-word puzzle, or call Ruth. Instead, he sat and stared at the glass partition thinking.

For three years, he'd enjoyed the luxury of quiet anonymity, and a career as sheriff away from all of it. Now, the whole world beamed in on him. Television crews from the national networks set up at the college. Stringers from all the major dailies were ensconced in Picketsville's only hotel. The curious, the morbid, and people seeking a peripheral role in history arrived hourly to this little backwash of a town, filling its motels, boosting its economy, and annoying its inhabitants. The town's only prior claim to notoriety was a very messy lynching of an African-American man accused, but never tried or convicted, of raping the lieutenant governor's daughter. That was seventy years ago. The lynching had been given wide publicity. The discovery two days later that the girl had not been raped, indeed medical evidence proclaimed her virginity intact, had been buried with the shipping news, and the whole incident had not created half the coverage the robbery had.

On the whole, he preferred the attention the town received now, but wished it had happened before, or later, or somewhere else to someone else. He had picked this hiding place so well. Who would have known he'd be found so quickly? Well, he couldn't do anything about it now. Maybe, when it ended, the last picture taken, everyone would go away and leave him alone. Of course, if the case weren't solved…my God, he thought, they might never let me go.

Work it out. What? How? Who—it had to be someone inside. The Board decided to move the collection eleven days before the robbery—a coincidence? Not likely. The best time to pull this kind of job would be July or August, the Fourth of July, when nobody was around, students gone for the summer, police distracted by traffic jams, fireworks, accidents, entire families off to the beach, backyard barbeques, people asleep, not watching. Why do it now? All wrong, students coming and going—parked in the lane, a Thursday night, the slowest night for police. Too many things could go wrong, so why now?

Because someone knew and they had to move the time up. What else?

The locksmithing job rated as a work of art. Only a group with access to tradecraft could have planned and executed a job like this one. The Agency, the Bureau, the Mafia, or maybe one or two of the other private groups he'd run into from time to time, groups operated by large corporations with financial interests and assets more widespread and substantial than the government itself.

They knew the collection was going to New York and it would be difficult if not impossible to steal it there. They knew, so someone told them. The board members and the people at the Dillon Foundation knew before the robbery. But they would be the last to engineer this, or would they? Why? Check the financial status of Dillon and the whole Dillon enterprise. Who else? Marge Tice? Ex-president Clough, the guy from New York? Maybe. Better check his background. And there was Ruth. Would she? Was some of that old radical, anti-authority dynamic still at play? What a mess. And where are the paintings now? If he could just recover them, it wouldn't matter who stole them. Let the FBI track them down. If the paintings were back, he'd be left alone.

Six twenty-five. Ike dialed the number for O'Rourke's. On the twelfth ring, a voice with a false shanty Irish brogue answered. Ike asked to speak to Elwood Farnham. Forty seconds later, he heard Charlie's voice recite another number and say, "Gimme a minute," then, click, the line went dead.

Ike hung up, waited sixty seconds, and dialed the new number. Charlie answered on the first ring.

"You're very prompt, Ike. I'm glad you remembered."

"Charlie, the whole business was schoolboy simple: you give me a name, a place, and a number. Six or seven days means today between six and seven—six or seven weeks means next week, same day same time and so on. Even if I had forgotten, I could have figured it out. And if I could, anyone could. Aren't you worried someone will?"

"With my job, who'd want to?"

"You've got a point. Maybe a newspaper guy would like to catch you before a press conference or something. Why are we doing this, anyway?"

"Ike, trust me. I needed to keep this conversation off the phone log and away from any possible monitor. You remember the drill—all phones in the Agency are monitored from time to time, and I need to talk to you. It's important and I couldn't get to you before. But now you need me and I need you. We can deal. I have information and a name for you, but you will have to tell me things first. And speak up, I'm on a phone outside O'Rourke's and you remember what Georgetown's like on Saturday night."

"Charlie, I will never understand you. It must be the copper absorbed into your system from your penny loafers that makes people like you go mad. What do you want me to tell you?"

"I need to know about Zurich, one step at a time, exactly as it happened."

Ike paused and considered. It made no sense. Why would Charlie want to know or care what happened in Zurich?

"That's the deal, Ike. I help you with your robbery, you give me the story. Don't ask why, please. That comes later, if ever. Just talk to me."

Could he? He'd managed to suppress the images and pain for years. Why open it up now? Ike drew a breath and began, slowly at first and then more rapidly. He concentrated on the details, the technology, the precise sequence of events. As the words flowed he carefully pushed back the images, the sweaty little man, the blood and Eloise…. Someday, he thought, I will tell the whole story, but not now. Now it's just facts. He forced himself to remember sounds, who said what, and when. Charlie listened, interrupting only twice; once to ask him to repeat the part about Peter Hotchkiss' phone call, and then to ask if he were sure about the number of shots.

"Two. You're sure it was two?"

"I'm sure. An SKS or an old Kalishnikov, maybe an AK47. Charlie, no mistake. Two."

When he finished, Charlie only said, "Thanks, that's a help."

Help for what, Ike wondered. By now enough time had passed for it to cease being a public relations problem.

"Okay, Charlie, your turn. What have you got for me?"

"Two shots and a clean hit, a perfect hit. That's interesting; Hotchkiss calls and then—one, two."

"Charlie, we have a deal. Tell me what you know about this robbery."

"Oh, right. Sorry. I was just wondering. I will need to talk to you again, Ike. When you're all done with your robbery, promise me something…you'll meet me in Washington, and go through some of this again. I'll send you an address and we'll meet."

"Sure, after the robbery is taken care of and if you don't start talking to me about it, that could be sometime after I start drawing Social Security."

"Right, but remember, you promised." He paused. "The problem you put to me was: who was available to do some professional, very professional, locksmithing. There are, or to be accurate, were, three possibilities. In order of likelihood, George Smythe from Great Britain, Achmed Harreem from Syria, and a new one, a guy named Grafton, Harold Grafton. He's local. Smythe was my first choice because he could enter the country and mix in almost unnoticed. Harreem, on the other hand, would stick out like a sore thumb. We are a little sensitive about Middle Eastern passengers on our airlines. But Smythe is out, he got picked up for, of all things, too many traffic violations, and an English magistrate decided to make an example of scofflaws. So Smythe, a movie starlet, and a member of parliament were all spending fifteen days in the slammer when the job was pulled.

"That leaves Harreem or Grafton. Grafton used to be one of ours, or, more exactly, the Bureau's, a good one from what I hear. Things went sour for him a couple of years back, when his wife got that slow-to-kill cancer. Grafton ran out of money to pay medical bills, started to booze pretty bad. Then his work started to slip a little and he got into some kind of fight with his bosses. Anyway, four months ago he got sacked at the Bureau, and his kids were snatched by the wife's parents and trucked off to Chicago, North Side somewhere. Two weeks ago his wife died and he disappeared, told his landlady he was going camping in the mountains. He paid his back rent in cash and took off. I think he could be your man."

"Any description, Charlie? I got a make on a guy, maybe five ten, graying curly hair, blue eyes, and class ring with a green stone, right ring finger. He may go one seventy-five—no, closer to one sixty-five with one of those faces that looks like was living on coffee and cigarettes, but not bad-looking."

"Sounds like our man, but I hope not. I hear he's good even when he's drunk, and the Agency could use someone like him. You know Crotty bought it in Istanbul?"

"No, I didn't. Tough."

"Yeah, well, we've been trying to get this Grafton guy to replace Crotty, but we can't find him. The Adirondacks is a big place. We're waiting for him to come out, unless, of course, he's mixed up in this."

"Yeah, sure, the Agency worries about that stuff. You guys would hire Jack the Ripper if you needed him and wouldn't care a rat's rear end what he'd done before or did after you're done with him."

"Now, Ike, you're not serious. We sometimes contract with specialists but—"

"Like the Mafioso when we wanted to snuff Castro?"

"Now, you know nothing ever came of that. It was just an idea, a little conversation, which leads me to part two. They're involved in this somehow."

"Who? The Mafia or Castro?"

"I can't be sure but it sounds like the guys doing this job are contract professionals, and that means the Mafia directly or indirectly. I can't tell you for sure, but whoever is behind the job didn't do it themselves. They bought talent from New Jersey."

"Thanks, Charlie. Anything else?"

"Well, if you can get us Grafton...."

"You want him that bad?"

"The boss wants him. Since Crotty died, we are pinched. Something must be cooking, something big—the director pulled out all the stops to find him."

The new director was a man of unremitting honesty and surprising modesty, who possessed no political skills whatsoever. Given these characteristics, it was problematical how long he'd stay in office. Whatever negative feelings Ike had for the Agency, he liked and admired its director.

"Charlie, I don't think I can do much, but I'll try. Is that good enough?"

"It'll have to be. I'll send you some stuff to give him and tell him if he's available. Thanks, and if anything else turns up, I'll be in touch. By the way, how do I do that?"

"Pick up the phone and call."

"You're kidding."

"No, down here we just talk to each other—no codes or instructions to call out-of-the-way bars or use funny, made-up names. Just pick up the phone and say, 'Ike, this is Charlie, I've got some information for you.'"

"I can't do it, Ike. It would ruin the image I've been working on for almost twenty years. Tell you what, I'll call and say I'm Elwood Farnum, which will mean it's urgent. If you can't talk, or you just get a message, you call O'Rourke's. If I say, 'It's me, Charlie,' then there's no rush and you call me at the office. Okay?"

"Charlie, you are nuts. By the way, I need a picture. Can you send me a picture of Grafton?"

"Sure, I'll e-mail it to you. You do get e-mail out there?"

"Sheriff," Ike rattled off, "at Picketsville dot gov. By the way, who is Elwood Farnum anyway?"

"Can't say, read it on a Christmas card my sister got last year. Liked the name. Has a nice nasal quality to it—Farnum, lovely. Be talking to you." The phone went dead.

Ike wrote Essie instructions to make copies of the picture, but to remove any indication of its source or the person's name, and give them to the team. Then, with time on his hands, Ike sat and took inventory: contract professionals, murder, possible kidnapping, possible Mafia, a rogue FBI man, and not a clue why the job was done. Who would steal five hundred million dollars in traceable, unsellable artwork? And for what? I am missing something, something important, but what? The phone's ringing broke his train of thought.

"Ike, it's Ruth, I think you'd better come out here now."

Chapter 19

Ike scanned the letter twice, an indistinguishable product of computer-generated word processing. The message, exclusive of its political rhetoric, was simple and straightforward: fifty million dollars in diamonds, none to exceed two carats in weight, were to be paid to the New Jihad as ransom for the stolen art work. A representative of the Dillon family, M. Armand Dillon himself, preferably, was to buy time on a specified local television station, agree to the terms and apologize for the role his company played in the oppression of the poor of the world. A second sheet of paper—this one was fuschia—bore a message from the New Jihad—a hate-filled anti-American, anti-Semitic tirade that ended in calling for the downfall of the "Great Satan of the West and its Jewish lackeys."

The letter went on to say that they, the New Jihad, would contact the Dillons to give instructions for the delivery of the diamonds and when they were away would inform them of the exact location of the paintings.

"Ruth, tell me again how you got this letter."

"I don't know. It appeared in my inbox sometime this evening. It was not there earlier because I would have noticed. I stayed in the office late because meetings I had all day kept me from clearing my desk and I wanted to get that done so I could at least have Sunday off. I hoped you and I might do something together. Sorry, maybe I am presuming. It's just that last night…anyway,

I stepped out of the office for a minute to use the restroom and when I got back, there it was."

"You noticed it right away?"

"No. I had another letter I wanted to finish first and when I did, I put it in my outbox. That is when I noticed this envelope. It surprised me because I cleaned everything out, and except for the letter I just completed, I thought I was done for the night. I started to return your call and picked it up.

"I opened it, wondering how I could have missed it. It is addressed only to me so I thought it might be a note from Agnes or one of the other office staff. But it isn't, is it? And when you answered, I told you to come. Not the message I had in mind for you, I'm afraid."

"No. Are we the only two who have handled this?"

"Yes, except, I suppose, for the writer, assuming, of course, whoever put it in my box was the same person who wrote it."

"We'll want to check it for fingerprints. We won't find any, except yours and mine, I'm sure, but you never know."

Ike looked at the letter a third time. It took up more than three quarters of the page. The wording seemed strange, awkward. Some of the sentences ran on. Phrases were repeated and peculiar constructions were used. The message was clear enough but could have been stated in half the words.

"Odd bit of writing, don't you think?"

Ruth inspected the letter again. "It looks like it was written by someone not very familiar with English, or maybe someone under the influence."

"I wonder. Too bad we don't use typewriters anymore. Typewriters, especially the old Selectrics, were traceable, if you knew how. The ribbons did not reverse, so you could read everything written on them. The Agency used to burn their ribbons inside the building and would never use them outside. But we live in the age of computers and word processors, and they are sterile and anonymous. Even the paper is indistinguishable. You don't use watermarked paper, do you?"

"I don't know, Ike. I have to delegate things or go mad. Paper, pencils, furniture all goes to someone who has the patience to deal with it."

Ike tilted Ruth's desk lamp up and inspected the paper. "We're in luck. This paper has a Callend College watermark on it."

"You're kidding."

"No, see for yourself."

"I didn't even know we had the stuff." She grabbed a piece of paper from her desk drawer and held it up to the light as well. It had the mark. "So that means that the letter was written here."

"Maybe. Or by someone who works here, or at least someone who has access to the buildings."

"That doesn't help you at all, does it?"

"Oh yes, but how much I can't tell just yet. It depends on where this paper is used, everywhere, or just some places? And if only in the confines of the college, then maybe we can trace the computer it was written on. They tell me that there are ways of doing that. I'm not a computer person so I don't know."

"I could ask Sam."

"Sam?"

"We got a big grant from the Dillon foundation right after I got here, an inauguration present from M. Armand himself, to be used to install a sophisticated information management system. Dillon makes those things—computers, chips, electronic things—and he wanted us to showcase the future or something like that. I would have settled for having the roads and parking lots repaved."

"Yes, but who's Sam?"

"Oh, well, the grant meant installing an elaborate computer system, software, hardware, cables—I don't know—all the stuff that goes with it. And that, in turn, meant hiring an information management systems coordinator—Sam Ryder, our techno-geek. We can ask Sam about the computer stuff and the paper, too. If I can figure out how this new phone works in house…let me see…." Ruth consulted a card taped to the glass top of her desk. "Pound and the number…no, call the home number first then.…"

Ike left her to her problem solving and paced around the room. The office was almost Spartan in its appointments—a few knick knacks and a handful of books. He glanced at the titles. Ruth, he noticed, had authored two of them. She failed to reach Sam at home and dialed an office number.

"Sam? Good, Ruth Harris, yes, fine thank you, could you come to my office? What? You are in the middle of a what? Oh, I see. Well yes, I think you might want to do that. Ten minutes? Good."

She hung up with a puzzled look. "Sam said, 'I will put the program on paws.' Paws? Like little furry feet? Does that make any sense to you?"

"Pause, not paws, to stop temporarily, pause."

"Oh. You have no idea what thirty-six hours without any real sleep does to my brain, Sheriff."

‹›‹›‹›

Harry Grafton's hands started shaking. He stared at the bottle of sour mash bourbon on the dresser and licked his lips. He needed a drink. One couldn't hurt—just something to steady his hands. He tasted the bile in his throat. His eyes felt like they were filled with sand. His collar was damp even in the air-conditioning. He looked at a sleeping Red Burnham and wished with all his heart he had the courage to shoot him.

Red left the bottle out in plain view to torment him, he knew that. One drink, that's all. He heard Red laugh. Harry looked up and saw he was awake, waiting.

"What's the matter, Grafton, bottle singing a love song to you? Go ahead, have a drink. Have two. Take the whole bottle." Red laughed again and sat up. "Go ahead and drink up some courage, Rummy."

Harry left the room—walked out into the warm May night and wished he were dead.

‹›‹›‹›

"Tell me about Parker. All your man said was he was hit on the head. It must have been a very hard hit."

"Or a lucky one."

"Well, I'm sorry. Robbery is one thing, murder another. Terrible. Nobody deserves that."

"Lots of folks in town would disagree with you about that. If anybody deserved it, they'd tell you Parker was at or near the top of their list."

"Your list, too?"

"Mine, too."

"Ike, nobody deserves to die. You're not a capital punishment supporter."

"No, I'm not, as a matter of fact. But deserve and warrant are different concepts. I don't think the death penalty is warranted. But some people agree that if anyone deserved to die—"

"I don't see the difference but I'm happy to discover that you and I do agree on something."

"Yes, that's a nice change, isn't it? But I'm not sure we agree."

"No arguments tonight, please," she said. "Cruel and inhumane is enough—leave it."

"Except cruel and inhumane punishment is a sliding scale, formulated when beheadings and torture and public hangings were in style. Joseph Guillotin invented his gadget as a humane way to behead people, a great leap forward in the humanitarian approach to death. The electric chair was thought to be a similar advancement over hanging, the gas chamber an improvement over it and so on to lethal injection. Now you will say all capital punishment is cruel and inhumane. It is a moveable target and, for me, not substantial enough to affix a moral code. So I prefer the sanctity of life."

"If I weren't so tired, I could start a major debate here."

"You could, but I'll bet you dinner and a movie that you'd get a draw at best."

Ruth sat up, challenge in her eyes and about to reply, but she was interrupted by a knock at the door.

Chapter 20

Donati took the telephone from Angelo. "Yeah."

"This is Artscape. What are you doing? I told you to be careful with the pictures. They're ruined."

"You wanted the collection taken. We took it. You didn't say anything about being neat. Besides, do you have any idea how long it would have taken us to do the job your way?"

"But it will take years to restore the pictures."

"What's with you? Your people are threatening to burn the damned things. What difference does it make if the paint is scratched?"

There was a pause at the other end. "My people say they don't want to pay the full price for the goods. They're damaged."

"Tell them if they don't pay, they go down—starting with you. Do you think I am stupid? Do you think I don't know who you are, where you live? I know who you talk to, who you sleep with, and I know how to get to you. Would you like me to tell you your address? How about the name of your lover—lets see, he's—"

"All right, all right. I take your point. What happened to Parker?"

"Wrong place at the wrong time."

"Is there anything else I should know?"

"You might get a line on two students. Find out if they're worth any money. You could sweeten the pot by throwing them into the mix. You know, return the hostages, an extra five mil."

"Hostages? What hostages?"

"Minor complication. The Parker guy went to spy on some kids in the bushes. Had to drop him and take the kids. We can kill them, or sell them back with the paintings."

"That's crazy. They know who you are. They can identify you."

"They won't."

"Why?"

"For the same reason you won't. They will want to stay alive. They will want to be sure their families and friends do not have accidents or hurt themselves. You know drive-by shootings are a real problem nowadays. They, and you, don't want something like that to happen, do you? No, they won't say anything. Besides, I have an airtight alibi. Feds won't believe it, but they won't be able to break it either."

"You are a monster."

"I'm a monster? The people you represent kill women and children in suicide bombings. They drop skyscrapers full of people, and you call me a monster? Did you think this operation could be done without somebody getting hurt? People die. I have people working with me I will eliminate as soon as I get my payoff. I can't risk having them run around loose. One talks too much, the other's a drunk. Push me and you get added to the list. Do we understand each other?"

"Yes."

"Good. You got a pencil? Write down these names."

"Oh, Sam, come in. This is Sheriff Schwartz. He has some questions he wants to ask you about our computers. Sheriff, this is Samantha Ryder, our resident computer expert."

Sam turned out to be a woman with mouse brown hair that clung to her shoulders, thin and unremarkable in every way except that when Ike stood to shake her hand he found himself looking at her nose. She stood at least three inches taller, in sandals. She could not weigh more than one hundred and forty-five pounds. Except for a chest that would turn a Hollywood starlet green with envy, she looked like she could be sucked up through a soda straw. She shook Ike's hand. She had a grip.

"Sam, we need help. Dr. Harris received a letter relating to the robbery. In a minute I want you to read it and tell me if it is possible to trace it in any way, assuming someone wrote on one of the machines here. I've been told that something like that is possible, but I don't know for sure. The letter is on the desk."

Sam leaned over the desk and examined the letter. She picked it up by its edges and held it up to the light, as Ike had done earlier.

"It's our paper and that means it was probably printed here. I can't be sure about where though."

"Because of the watermark? Do all of the departments or printers use this paper?"

"Yes, at the moment. The vendor who sold us our printers included a couple of hundred reams of that paper as part of the deal. I guess he hoped we'd be impressed and maybe buy more. Either way it helped with the sale. The margin we work with in purchases of this sort is pretty thin, so anything extra helps. Of course, it's possible that whoever wrote this took paper home, printed the letter, and brought it back, but I doubt it."

"Why?"

"Well, nobody except me and the staff in IS knows about the watermark, and it's not noticeable unless you go out of your way to look for it. As far as most people know, it's just plain twenty-pound bond."

"So, if the letter were typed and printed here, could you tell us who wrote it?"

"Not who wrote it, but where it was written, at which work station. We installed a very sophisticated network. All work stations are connected to a main print server in the basement. There are other servers, of course, for backup, data bases and so on."

She looked at the puzzlement in Ike's eyes and continued, "A print server is a machine that spools—lines up print jobs and sends them to the printer. We have thirty-five printers in the LAN…sorry, that's the local area net, LAN. So we have one for each department or office like this one. Oh, and there are three printers in the library for student use. The job comes to the server and it sends it back to the appropriate printer."

"Why not just send the job straight to the printer? My computer just sends the stuff straight over to my printer. It seems a lot of trouble to send it to a server and back."

"Well, in your case, part of your hard drive is your server. Check out your printer utility sometime. It has all the features a server has and...sorry again...I tend to go on. Anyway, no matter how we set all this up, the job would have to go to a print server of some sort. It could be another computer in the department or a separate box, but unless you have a printer for each computer, like yours, you need a separate server. We chose a high-capacity server to assure that the printing got done no matter what situations came up. For example, if a departmental printer went down, or even ran out of paper, the server would route the job to an alternative printer, usually the nearest one, and then tell you where you could pick it up. Folks get ticked when their jobs get backed up."

"Every printer in the college is connected to the server?"

"Yes, sir, every one."

"Okay, but I don't see how this helps us."

"Well, as I said, we have very sophisticated servers. One keeps a log of all the documents processed. The log can tell us where the job came from, file name, and so on. We can look at the log and see what jobs have been done and when."

"You can do all that?"

"We can. Look, this is a one-page document, so that eliminates all of the files that are larger. Next, look at the number of words in the document. The log keeps track of them too. That will narrow it down even more, and so on until we have the document and the source. Of course, if the person who wrote this knows the system, it might take some time."

"And if they know a lot about it they could beat it?"

"Well, yes and no. It's iffy either way."

"What do you mean, iffy? You either can or you can't."

"It's not that straightforward, Sheriff. First there is the matter of a search warrant and then—"

"A what? I'm not tossing a room here. I just want some information from you. Ruth, tell her to give me the information."

"Dr. Harris, there is a whole new corpus of law covering electronic data. Information of this sort is viewed the same as paper files and property. If I give the sheriff the information and it leads to an arrest, and if there was no search warrant issued to obtain it, it would be inadmissible in court."

"Sam, I appreciate the point. How do you know all this anyway?" Ike asked.

"I had a double major in college. The second was criminal justice. I hoped to be in law enforcement, computer forensics. Got turned down by the FBI—bad eyes."

"She's right, Ike, we can't let you have the information without a warrant."

"I don't believe this. It's Saturday night. It'll be Monday before I can find a judge and get that warrant. Here's a chance to cut through a lot of details and you are going to scruple over this?"

"Have to, Ike. Matter of principle. How long is that whatever…how long before the data will be available, Sam?"

"It depends. The library files are backed up and the system rebuilt every night—they tend to get corrupted. But these files will be logged in for ninety days. All the data will be there on Monday."

"I can't wait until Monday," Ike shouted. "Sam, you want police work? You got it. I am hereby deputizing you into the Sheriff's department. Under county law, you don't get a choice in the matter if it is clear that we are in a state of emergency, smoking gun and so on. Determination of that state is left to the prerogative of the instituting officer—that's me—subject to appeal and review, and so forth. Now, as my deputy, you will go and find me the source of this letter."

"You can't do that," Ruth protested.

"Can, and just did."

"Do I get a badge?" Sam asked.

"What? A badge. Well yeah, but—"

"Does it mean I can carry, too?"

"Carry. You want to carry? You own a gun, Sam?"

"Yes, sir, a Glock 17."

"Well, I don't think you're going to need one, but yes, as a deputy, you can carry."

"Sam," Ruth interjected, "You can't be serious. What about search warrants? What about the—"

"Well, you're right, Dr. Harris, but as his deputy, I have to do this. Sheriff, there's something else you should know—something that will make this easier."

"What? There's more? Look Sam, in case you hadn't noticed, I am a computer ignoramus. I just want to know if you can get me what I need....What should I know?"

"I, um...don't know how to say this, but I can get your guy—absolutely."

"Now you can, five minutes ago you said iffy. What happened?"

"Well, as your deputy, I am required to inform you of some things that I...um, the truth is, I installed a root kit last week and with the right password I can tell you the activity level of every computer in the net."

"A root kit? It sounds like something a plumber would use."

"In a way I guess it is." Sam looked at the floor.

"There is something about root kits I should know?"

"They are hacker tools, Sheriff, not routine additions to systems—illegal maybe—depending on policy and federal restrictions....I'm sorry, Dr. Harris, but I have this interest in forensics and I told myself that as your IS guy, I should have the capacity to find out things, if the need ever—"

"Well, it has. You haven't been using the college's facilities to hack...." Ruth's eyes began to signal early storm warnings.

"Oh, no, ma'am, I just, you know...to keep my hand in, I sometimes...see, anyone can hack, if they know how. I thought we ought to be prepared if one of our people took it up, that's all."

"It's all right," Ike cut in. "Given the history of college hackers and…very sensible." He did not know what he was talking about but the last thing he needed was an angry Ruth Harris.

Sam looked relieved. "How about I secure the data and begin processing it in anticipation of a warrant?" she said. "Then, when it comes, I will have everything you need. It's going to take that long anyway."

"You can't get it now?"

"No, sorry, but I can start now. Whoever sent this letter knew what we were up to. I haven't counted the words but I'm guessing it's two hundred and forty-seven."

"Why two hundred and forty-seven?"

"Well, we printed out a big mailing this weekend, a letter to all of the students scheduled to enroll in the fall, about the collection not being on campus. That letter ran two hundred and forty-seven words. To speed up the printing, we sent it to all the departmental printers over the weekend. Whoever wrote this letter knew a little something about our setup and I think ran this letter through with the others."

"That explains the wording. The writer tried to force the word count. So, we can't trace it after all."

"No, I didn't say that. There are more features on the log that he might not know about. The first is character count. The log tells us source, pages, words, and characters. It's unlikely he got the same number of characters as the form letter, but even if he did—there's spaces."

"Spaces?"

"Yes. The log keeps track of spaces, like between words. The probability that he got that right, too, is astronomical."

"Not that it would mean anything to me, but what is the third feature?"

"Keyboard logger."

Ike began to feel the same way he did when he tried to read Hawking's *A Brief History of Time*. "And it does what?"

"It logs the keystrokes into the main log. If I can narrow down the choices, I can have it type the letter over again—if you want me to. It all depends on how much the writer knew about our system and how to beat it, but I'm sure whoever it was didn't know everything. We'll find your writer."

"Ruth...you satisfied?"

"No, but I'm too tired to argue. How about you bribe me into silence by taking me out for a cheap dinner and then take me home."

"Happy to. Deputy Ryder, you may proceed."

"One last thing. Dr. Harris?"

"Sam?"

"About the picture IDs. When do you want me to start putting that online? I thought you would want to start next term. If we do, we will have to have the locks and card swipe units installed and that, with the wiring and all, could take all summer."

"What picture IDs are you talking about? What locks?"

"It was all in the committee report you approved. We are to issue picture IDs to the students and the swipe stripe on the back will activate the new locks on all the building doors so that we can keep track...." Sam's voice trailed off.

"Report? You mean the Information Services Committee report had that as a proposal?" Ruth's face was thunderous.

"Yes ma'am, toward the back."

"Thank you, Sam. I'll let you know about the IDs."

Sam left, closing the door behind her.

"Don't look so smug, Schwartz, I had no idea, and by damn I will not allow it."

"Right."

"Oh God, what can happen next? I have to tell you, I have been in contact with Mr. Dillon Senior, or more accurately, he has been in contact with me."

"And?"

"He's mobilizing. Called his friends in Washington, the FBI, everybody. They will be all over the place by tomorrow or the next day. I know what you said before. I'm sorry."

"It's all right. I was about to call the Bureau anyway. He saved me the trouble. We may have a kidnapping to go with the robbery. That makes it an automatic call to them."

"Kidnapping? Is that why your people called to ask if anyone was missing? You think one of our women is missing?"

"It's possible. We think the car parked in the lane, the one you can see in the television picture, got there before the robbery and the people in it were taken. That or...." He let the words hang in the air.

"Or they are dead like Captain Parker. What next?"

"Well, we wait for Dillon to respond to the letter. We keep digging around hoping to find a lead. We go on about our business."

They sat across from each other. Ike's earlier happy state of mind had been replaced hour by hour by a sense of gloom. He felt tired and depressed.

"Well, at least now we know what the robbery was all about in the first place," he said as much to himself as to her. "I mean, up until now, the whole thing made no sense. Paintings worth millions, a king's ransom, but not sellable. I guess that is progress. And who knows, maybe Deputy Sam will turn up something. Didn't you say something about dinner?"

"Hamburgers and beer, my place. Now."

Chapter 21

The call came just as Tom headed to bed. He'd stayed up to watch the late news and catch part of *Saturday Night Live*. His wife had been asleep for an hour. He scowled. Only business would prompt a call this late. A glance at the caller ID confirmed it. He took the call and cursed his luck that he'd pulled duty officer. Seven and a half hours later and someone else would be on the spot. He went upstairs, put on his jacket, kissed his wife, and told her he would be back soon. She searched his face for the signs that would tell her if he was in danger and seeing none fell back to sleep with a mumbled, "G'night, babe."

Tom unlocked the drawer in the highboy, retrieved his badge and gun, pocketed the first, holstered the second, and let himself out the door into a chilly May night. He shivered a little, climbed into his car, and headed downtown.

In all his years with the Federal Bureau of Investigation, Tom Phillips had visited the director's office only once, when the late Mr. Hoover, too old by then for the job, had received him and five other elementary school students, finalists in a national essay contest. Different days, different ways.

He drove downtown, parked in his spot, and rode the elevator to the lobby. The guard at the desk, a man who had been at that post as long as Tom could remember, checked his ID as if he were a stranger and logged him in. Tom took the second bank of elevators to the director's office, knocked and let himself in. The director waved him into an overstuffed chair. He waited while the director finished talking to someone on the phone.

This was the new FBI and the man across from him no J. Edgar Hoover. Just as well, he thought, although, as bad as the press and the liberal establishment wanted to paint him, Hoover had his moments and no other man could have built the Bureau the way he did. Just stayed too long at the dance.

"Phillips, what do you know about the robbery in Picketsville, Virginia?"

"Only what I read in the papers and what came in on the dailies. We haven't been called in yet, have we?"

"We have now, and that could be a problem."

"Sir?"

"It's big, Phillips."

The director had a habit of enlarging operations. "It's big" was one of his favorite expressions. Next, Tom guessed he would say, "I can't stress this enough."

"I can't stress this enough. I got a call from the White House. Some big shot friend of the President is on the warpath, got the President's attention. I said we'd go when the locals call or the jurisdiction changes, but going into Senator Rutledge's territory uninvited and unannounced could create problems. He could kill us in the committee hearings if I did."

"Well, sir?" Tom peeked at his watch. One o'clock in the morning and he still did not know why he had been called and what he was supposed to do. "I guess we could put a group on standby."

The director leaned back in the black leather chair and gazed at the ceiling. Tom stared at the ceiling too.

"No. I called you in here to put operatives in the field. But we have to be mighty careful on this one."

"Because of the President?"

"No, not for him, for us."

"Sir?"

"We are in this mess up to our eyeballs, Phillips. One of our guys did the job."

"Sir?"

"Call me Chet."

"Yes, sir. You said one of ours?"

"Did you know an agent named Grafton?"

"Yes, sir, slightly. We never worked a case together. He was in the covert section. I always worked the field." The director returned his gaze to eye level. Tom noticed for the first time that he suffered from a mild case of amblyopia. His left eye was fractionally off center.

"Yes, yes, I know. Look, he was a screw-up and a drunk and we dumped him. He gave us some sad song and dance about a sick wife and whatnot, but with the budget cuts and all, we cleaned house. No big deal. But this Grafton guy turns up working with whoever pulled that heist in Virginia."

"Sir, are we sure it was him? I mean, it's a pretty big jump from out-of-work FBI agent to crook."

"Is it? You've got some learning to do, son."

"Yes, sir, but I don't see the problem. If we fired him, the publicity will be bad, but shouldn't come back on us too much."

"You're kidding, right? They told me you were on the ball." The director's eye apparently bothered him enough that now he squinted at Tom, an expression that made him look like a full-figured Popeye. "I told you, this is big. How do you think it is going to look when the press finds out that someone with Grafton's assets and knowledge of Bureau operations ended up with some Mafia types in the biggest robbery in the century? We are in deep shit here, Phillips."

"Yes, sir."

"Deep. And it gets deeper."

How much worse could it get? And did it qualify as all that bad? He guessed it must or he wouldn't be here in the middle of the night.

"You put a team together to help with the investigation and at the same time extract Grafton before anyone gets near him. Do you understand what I mean?"

"Yes, sir, I believe I do. But if we are to work with the locals, that may be tough. You said it was worse than just Grafton. Something else?"

"I want the team in the open. They will have two jobs. They are to do everything they can to slow the investigation down. Then find and cancel Grafton."

"Cancel?"

"You know what I mean, Phillips. Grafton gets whisked out of there before anybody can say hot damn—that's best case. Worst case, he comes out smelling like dead fish, whatever. Clear?"

Tom stared at the man across the desk. Had he heard him right? Tom felt his shirt getting damp. He did not like the direction this conversation was headed. The director disappeared into the relative shadows beyond the pool of light from his desk lamp.

"Look, we have a double whammy here. Grafton is only problem number one. You're right, bad publicity we can ride out, but there's the other."

"And that is?"

"The locals are Agency. The sheriff down there is CIA."

"What? How can that be? They're not domestic. They can't be."

"They can and they are. My guess is that they pulled the robbery—one of their games to draw attention from something else. They're hip deep in the Middle East and are still trying to save their cookies from all the aid and comfort they gave Bin Laden in the old days. Remember the arms deal to the Arabs a couple of years ago? This is part of that or I am the Little Mermaid. And I told the President so."

Tom did not reply. The director was off on a rhetorical odyssey and Tom must wait until he finished. Meanwhile, he studied his boss, the man who held his future in his hands. After Hoover, a variety of men had held the job. Some of them were good, some were not so good, and one or two were disasters. "Call me Chet's" appointment had come as a surprise. After Ruby Ridge and Waco, the embarrassment of misreading the intelligence in the Phoenix memo and hundreds of Al Qaida operatives and sympathizers in the country before September eleven, the post looked like a political graveyard. The President brought this man in because he thought a nonpolitical type might be able to bring a fresh look to the Agency.

Fresh indeed. His years as the CEO of a couple of Fortune 500 corporations meant he intended to run the Agency like a business. He created lines of accountability, reorganized departments, subunits, all the way to the library, and dozens, no hundreds of employees, some with decades of service, were let go, the biggest housecleaning in the Agency's history. Tom had to admit the place did run better, and for those, like him, who had survived the storm, it was a good thing. For the likes of Harry Grafton, it was awful. Most of the personnel had been offered early retirement. Tom had nearly jumped at that. He had the years, and the bonus out would have cleared his debts and allowed him the chance to move to the Outer Banks at last. The offer was still on the table and looking better all the time. The director wound down.

"Phillips, I want him out of the way. Do you understand me?"

"Yes, sir, but—"

"No buts, Phillips. Look. I want you to get him one way or the other. Nobody touches him and we bring him in. However, if the CIA….Do you have any idea what those guys would do to us in the Oval Office if they get him first?"

So much for closer working ties between the nation's intelligence communities. "Sir, I don't think—"

"Even the spinmeisters downstairs couldn't get us right. No, if it looks like the CIA will get him…." The words hung in the air like day-old fish.

"What?"

"Friendly fire, Phillips. It happens all the time. Collateral damage, that sort of thing. You know the drill."

A lack of previous law enforcement experience may have left some gaps in his grasp of the finer points of the Bureau, but this new guy was either on a steep learning curve or corporate America operated as ruthlessly as the rest of the system. Tom swallowed hard. There were times, he knew, when an agent had to be brought in. If he compromised an operation, or jeopardized the lives of others, certainly, but eliminate someone to avoid a public relations fiasco? Tom didn't think so.

"About the CIA, sir," he said, hoping to redirect the conversation. Tom knew, orders or no orders, he would not set in motion any operation that could end in the death of an agent, ex or otherwise. Early retirement started to look better and better.

"Don't ask me how or why, but the sheriff down there is one of theirs. They must have been setting this up for years. Look, the guys in intelligence link this robbery to the mess in New York three months ago."

"Terrorists? Grafton is working with terrorists?"

"Yes and no. Our information sources say this job was contracted out to the New Jersey Mafia. He might or might not know who is behind it. Either way it doesn't matter. He has to go. Put your best people on it. Okay, that's all."

◇◇◇

Sooner or later, the scuttlebutt went, the director's chickens were going to come home to roost. Business acumen and efficiency notwithstanding, this man had become a loose cannon, and Tom was sure he heard chickens flapping nearby. He thought about his options. For the moment, he had no choice but to put together a team and send it to Picketsville. As soon as he finished, he would fill out retirement forms and send them through. There would be no problem in the first instance because he intended to assemble the most inept team possible. That would guarantee no one would be caught, much less killed.

Chickens at twelve o'clock, he thought.

Back at his desk, Tom opened a drawer and removed the pint of rye hidden under some folders. Strictly against Agency rules but often a necessity. He emptied some cold coffee out of a Styrofoam cup and poured himself a double, logged in on the computer, and began to search for agents with little or no possible competence. He knew they were there, assigned to library or document work, their field evaluations so weak they were never considered for that work again.

He found them. Next, pick a leader. He studied his roster. "Eeny, Meeny, Miney, Moe, who's the dumbest one to go?" His finger stopped on Dennis Kenny. Perfect. Kenny was a likable thirty-something who did not fit anyone's idea of an agent. He was on the bubble and he knew it. He would jump at the chance to shine. Perfect. He clicked on the phone number and picked up while it rang. Six rings and a sleepy Dennis Kenny answered.

"Sorry to wake you, Agent Kenny," Tom said in his most official voice. "Director's orders. You will assemble a small team of men and take charge of our operations in Picketsville."

"Who is this?"

"Phillips, Central Operations, Director's Office. Hang up and call me back. But go wash your face and wake up first. Are you always this slow?"

"Yes, sir, I mean no, sir. I mean…I'll call you right away." The line went dead. Tom waited. Two minutes later Kenny called.

"You awake now?"

"Yes, sir."

"Right. I'm going to read you a list of names and phone numbers and I will fax you the pertinent files on the men and the case. You will contact them and then get down to Picketsville pronto."

"Yes, sir."

"And Agent Kenny? This is big. The President has a special interest in this one, so don't screw it up." Tom could almost hear him swallow. He hoped Kenny had good bladder control when he discovered his assignment included the removal of someone who could take him barehanded and drunk.

"Oh well, all in a day's work," Tom said to the now silent phone. "The chickens have landed." He thought it would make a great title for his memoirs if he ever wrote them.

He sent an e-mail to the director's office outlining the operation, logged off, turned out the lights and left.

"Buck, Buck, Buckah," he clucked to the puzzled guard at the lobby desk.

⟨⟩⟨⟩⟨⟩

"I can't keep this up, Ike. Between the press, TV, board members, alumnae calls, and trying to run the college, I am dying. Too many nights out past midnight with you.…You are killing me, do you know that?"

Ike winced.

"Sorry. That was a stupid thing to say."

They sat in silence contemplating the empty plates in front of them. They'd eaten and talked through their burgers and salad, had a couple of beers and let the day wind down. Ike sighed.

"No harm done. I'm the one with the problem, with the history, not you."

They moved to the veranda and watched moonlight paint the lawns and buildings its silver blue, wisteria black against gray foliage. Nothing stirred.

"We had a deal, Ike."

He looked at her. Why this woman? Why now? Telling Charlie had been painful. Did he really want to go through that again? He toyed with the idea of brushing her off. When he'd returned to Picketsville he'd invented his go-away story—guaranteed to satisfy those who couldn't resist asking. His narrative to Charlie had been technical, accurate, but now he felt he needed to tell the whole of it—the real story. Why not this woman?

They sat side by side and, as the moon inscribed its course across the night sky, they slowly disappeared into deepening shadows.

"You're right, we had a deal."

Chapter 22

Charlie Garland had said it would be the last great crab feast of the season. Ike allowed himself to be talked into going, not because he wanted to crack crabs, which he did, or because he felt any particular need to be in the company of other people, which he did not. But, because he was bored and restless, and anything sounded better than spending an evening alone in his apartment, he drove to Montgomery County, found Charlie's townhouse, put on his company smile, and determined to be pleasant.

Charlie offered and he accepted the obligatory gin and tonic and a deck chair on the tiny backyard. When Conrad Anton arrived with her on his arm, Ike's world changed forever. She was tall, slim, and very blonde. She had inherited a set of wonderful green eyes and Ike thought her the most beautiful woman he'd ever seen.

The evening blurred—a kaleidoscope of bright, disconnected images of Eloise McNamara and Ike surrounded by faceless people. Ike showed her how to use the little wooden mallet to crack the claws to get at the meat. They both laughed at her first attempt when, with more enthusiasm than skill, she'd smashed the claw, meat, shell, and all to a pulp. He explained the fine points of getting out the back fin, eliminating the dead man's hands and all the intricacies of eating steamed crabs. She told him she did not mind crabmeat but eating one seemed a bit like eating a big bug. They laughed and drank beer and piled the shells in the center of the table, oblivious to everyone else.

Sometime after midnight, Ike took her home. He did not remember leaving or how he managed to disengage her from Conrad, or even how they got to her place. He did remember climbing two flights of stairs, pausing at her door, and then kissing her, at first tentatively and then, when she responded, kissing her again and again.

‹›‹›‹›

Three days later, they got married in North Carolina. Four days later, with some string-pulling to get passports, they were on a hastily arranged honeymoon in Europe. The first leg was London, then Paris, Zurich, and Rome. Ike had accrued leave and Peter Hotchkiss approved the two weeks.

"You've earned it, Ike, and besides, after twelve years, you should be riding a desk like me. Marrying Eloise means we can get you to come out of the field. You are too valuable to the Agency to be in the field. Have a ball. We'll talk when you get back."

And so it had been arranged.

By the time they got to Zurich, they both wore the satisfied expressions of those who have loved much and are convinced against all common sense that they are the only ones who ever have. They discovered Europe together like any other pair of tourists. They wrote lists of restaurants and bars and shops they liked. They took pictures, bought postcards, and saved menus.

It was Eloise's first trip to Europe. In a way, it was Ike's as well. Before, perhaps two dozen times, he had been on the continent, but always on business, meeting strangers at night, in airports, train stations, cafés, staying in one- and two-star hotels, false identities, and never knowing what was going on. Was he the pawn or the queen in this particular game of chess?

Now, Ike saw Europe for the first time. He had his own passport, his own money, his own time, and Eloise. No two people had ever been in love like that—never, or so he thought, with the forgivable arrogance of a newlywed.

Hotchkiss called him in Zurich.

"Ike, I hate to do this to you, but we need a favor from you, a little job to do, nothing complicated."

"Peter, it's my honeymoon. Get someone else. I am not on duty. I'm not here."

"Ike, I know, believe me I know. I would not do this to you except we're a little pressed for time and you're right on the spot. It would take me a couple of days to set this up without you, and our man is getting scared. He needs to make contact today or he says it's off."

"What kind of contact? What do you want?"

"Piece of cake—a single drop. You meet, he passes you an envelope, and you process it in the usual fashion…take about a half an hour."

"What's the drop? What's he giving me?"

"Ike, I can't tell you, you know that."

"You will this time, or it's no deal. I'm a married man now, remember? And besides, I'm off duty. If you want me to work, you will tell me, at least enough to let me decide whether it's dangerous or not. Peter, I don't have any cover, no backup— nothing."

"Okay, Ike, it's easy. The man is passing bank data, financial stuff. The bad guys are laundering money through Swiss banks and this will tell us how and give us some numbers. We need the information so when we want to we can cross-wire the process. It's not big stuff, just some documents we can get from our man the easy way. It would take us months to dig it out the hard way, and you know how the Swiss are about bank account confidentiality. But this guy is spooked. He doesn't do this stuff as a rule, a first timer, and it is now or never with him."

"That's it, Peter, you're sure?"

"That's all of it, the whole package."

"Okay, where's the drop and how do I make contact?"

"He'll find you. There's a café just off the Bahnhof Strasse, not far from your hotel, Der Sturm. Get there about four-thirty in the afternoon when it's crowded. He will approach you and ask if you mind sharing your table. You say no. He drinks his chocolate or whatever he is drinking, pays, and leaves. The envelope will be on the table with your map and guidebook or whatever."

"Do we talk or just stare at each other?"

"Whatever feels right. You are an American tourist; that should be obvious. You want to ask about the country or whatever, feel free."

"Okay, how does he identify me?"

"He doesn't exactly. He will be looking for an ugly Jewish face, that's you, by the way, and a beautiful blonde. Just to be sure, he'll ask you if it's all right to sit down and will expect an answer in German from Eloise. Got it?"

"Eloise? Eloise is not part of the deal, Peter, for God's sake. Why bring Eloise into this?"

"Ike, it's easy. Besides, it is the best make I could put together on short notice. No kidding, you wait and see, it's a walk in the park. Your bride is going to be excited, and there is no danger. The stuff we are getting isn't important enough to stir up the Swiss or anyone else. Trust me."

And he had.

Hotchkiss had been right. Eloise acted as excited as a kid at Disney World.

"What should I wear, Ike? I have a black dress, but no hat. Should I buy a hat? A big one with a brim maybe, and a veil. Do I wear sunglasses? I could wear a wig—"

"El, honey, stop. The last thing you want to do is look conspicuous. This business is conducted by the banal for the benefit of the mediocre. I want you to dress like, talk like, and behave just like you. Unless you watch very closely, which you should not, I repeat, should not, you will find you have spent an uninteresting half hour in a café with me, and for a time, a stranger. Got it? No cloaks, no daggers, no wrist radios, and no sunglasses, unless," he added absently, "the sun's out."

They went off on their mission, Eloise bubbling over with excitement, Ike with the same gut-tenseness he had whenever he worked. His mind turned over details, as he watched faces, scouting for exits, lines of fire, hiding places. Lord, he thought, it's just a drop, stuff we give new green kids from Fort Belvoir, even recruit private citizens from time to time—just a two-bit drop. Eloise prattled on, raving over items in shop windows, architecture, native costumes and then, under her breath, "How am I doing, Chief?"

"Lord, El, back off, I am not Maxwell Smart and you are not Ninety-nine."

"Sorry, Chief."

Holy cow, Ike thought, if I had to work with Eloise full time, I'd be dead in a New York minute—that or fired for not making contact, not even getting out of bed on time.

"Ike." Eloise tugged at his sleeve. "Isn't this where we're supposed to...whatever?"

He had nearly walked past the café. Oh, he was in great shape—top form. Off on the spying business with his new bride, who acted like someone out of a Sandra Bullock movie. Terrific.

They found a table and ordered drinks.

The request was made in French; Eloise responded in halting German and then there were three.

He was short and rumpled. He could have been anybody and nobody. Five minutes after he left, Ike would be hard put to remember anything about him.

His nervousness disturbed Ike. A very frightened man, Ike thought, too frightened—and the accent, not Swiss, not German. My God, the guy's Russian. Alarm bells went off in Ike's head. Something's wrong. On a cool afternoon this man sweated like a Georgia patrolman, sweat that reeked with fear.

The man said something. Ike turned his attention elsewhere, not listening. To hell with him. Need to get out, get Eloise out. All wrong. Ike pushed his chair back. It careened into the people behind him. Everything seemed to slow down. His arms weighed hundreds of pounds. People moved like participants in a water ballet. The pot of chocolate in front of him exploded, sending a geyser of brown liquid arcing upward. He heard the sharp slat-crack of the rifle. His eyes found Eloise's face. She looked puzzled, puzzled and disappointed, the look a mother has when her one-year-old smacks its chubby fist in a bowl of pureed carrots.

He was screaming at her, trying to push the table over, push her to the ground. Eloise's face slowly changed expression. Her mouth formed an O, her eyes widened—shocked. Ike saw the fabric of her dress twitch. Then, the hole formed—brown, black, and ragged, and a red stain bloomed across her breast. His body crashed against hers. Too late. He sprawled on the flagstone terrace cradling her, and watched, helpless, as the life drained out of her. Too late. Another shot. The little man, the little frightened man, rocked back and then crumpled down next to them. The back of his head was a mass of jelly.

Ike heard screaming, voices, people running away, the hee-haw of police, ambulances.

"Help me," he heard a voice plead. His voice. It was wrong, all wrong.

Captain Durant sat opposite Ike, polite and very correct—legs crossed, creases in his pinstriped trousers crisp, precise. A lean, ascetic man, his thinning hair brilliantined to his skull, horn-rimmed spectacles in his left hand and a handkerchief, with which he polished them, in his right. Only the large yellow-dotted bowtie seemed out of character.

"M. Schwartz, that is your name, I suppose—ah, ah." He held up a hand and handkerchief to cut off Ike's response. "It doesn't matter. What matters is that we, the Swiss government, you see, wish for you to leave the country at once. We are aware of the special place our country plays in the world of politics and finance. Years of neutrality, our banking laws, *et cetera, et cetera*, make this country suitable for, invite even, activities of the sort you and your colleagues pursue."

"I don't know what you're talking about." Ike's voice sounded calm, cold. He heard his own words, but as if they were spoken by someone else, in another room. A dozen years of this and it became automatic. You turned off your mind and let your heart go to ice.

"My name is Schwartz, Isaac Schwartz. I work for the International Development Bank and I came here on my honeymoon as a tourist, nothing more." Eloise was dead and the sun no longer occupied the sky.

"As you say, M. Schwartz; nevertheless, I have been sent to escort you to the airport and make sure you are on the first flight out. As I was saying, we understand the reasons for our country being, shall we say, the arena for your activities. And as long as you, the British, the Russians, Poles, Chinese…behave and remain discreet, we look the other way, but we cannot allow violence. We do not have a police force large enough to take care of that sort of activity. You will tell your superiors that this will never happen again, you understand?"

Ike said nothing. Why answer? When he saw his superiors. Oh yes, he would tell them. Indeed he would.

"Your *baggages* are packed and await at the airport. I have made all the arrangements."

"My wife." The word sounded strange. He had not been married long enough to have a wife. A wife is someone who makes a whole out of the parts of your life. In time, we would have been a unit, but ten days—not enough time to be anything, to fall in love, to know happiness bordering on ecstasy, and lose it, but not time enough to have a wife. "I want to see her."

The light provided by the single, bare bulb in the overhanging lamp cast a long shadow over the plain wooden table. Only an ashtray filled with the leavings of previous interviewees broke its scarred surface. The smoke from those interviews and years of others like them permeated the air, the walls, the thin curtains, filing cabinet, papers—all the detritus found in rooms like it in every police station from Seattle to Singapore.

Durant polished his glasses again, concentrated on them, and, still scrutinizing them, addressed Ike.

"You will forgive me, M. Schwartz, but that will not be possible."

"Why, not possible?"

"Your wife…the arrangements are all made by your embassy, her effects, passport, *toute*—all removed and taken by your people. M. Schwartz, your wife did not survive the, ah, excitement."

"I know that, Durant. I want to see her."

"My instructions are to return your belongings and put you on a plane. I am not authorized to do anything else."

"Well, you listen to me and listen carefully, because I'm not going to repeat myself. And when I am done, you will do as I say or I will get on that phone and raise such an almighty stink, you will wish you'd stayed in the cheese and yodeling business instead of becoming a Swiss bureaucrat cop.

"My story is true, every bit of it. I am a tourist. My passport is authentic. We were on our honeymoon, and someone killed my wife in your country. And you, instead of getting out and finding the bastard who did it, are harassing me." Ike held his hand up. "Wait, I'm not through."

Durant had opened his mouth to protest. His glasses, at last polished to his satisfaction, perched on his nose, caught the light, and flickered like an Aldis lamp sending a message to a ship at sea.

"Durant, it doesn't matter to me whether you believe me or not. What you need to understand is the media will believe me. They will report another case of Swiss police paranoia and incompetence. They will want to know how such a thing could have happened. Do you follow me? Do I make the call?"

The blinking stopped. Durant gazed at Ike for perhaps thirty seconds.

"Your wife is in the mortuary, two blocks away. The coffin is being prepared for air shipment to the States. I cannot be sure if she is, that is, if the body is.…I do not know what has been done, M. Schwartz, but if you insist, we will go there on our way to the airport. You will have five minutes. That is all."

Ike nodded his agreement.

"These are your belongings, all except your passport which I will give you when you board your plane."

Ike watched as the policeman emptied the contents of the manila envelope onto the table. Nothing much—wallet, keys, loose change, the guidebook he'd bought when he left the hotel, the one they needed to put on the table for the man—and the envelope.

Ike's face did not betray the shock he felt. The exchange had been made and he'd missed it.

"Thank you, Captain. I believe that is everything. Shall we go?"

It was a six-minute walk to the funeral home. Durant spoke to the proprietor, glancing twice in Ike's direction.

"This is Herr Grundig. He will take you to the viewing area. He asked me to tell you that under the circumstances, he cannot be responsible for…appearances."

"I understand, Captain. Thank you."

"Five minutes only."

Ike followed Grundig into the back of the building and into a small tiled room filled with the scent of formaldehyde and phenol. Grundig pulled the chain on an overhead light. Ike winced at the glare. Eloise's casket, simple gunmetal gray, lay across two trestles. Grundig opened one end and stepped back, eyes downcast.

Pale. She was so pale. They'd wrapped her in some sort of sheet. At least she looked at peace, he thought. He leaned forward as if in prayer, a one-man *Shiva,* dropped his right shoulder and slipped the envelope out of his pocket. Screened from the door and, the very uncomfortable M. Grundig, he slit open the envelope, withdrew and unfolded the single piece of old-fashioned onionskin paper and glanced at the writing, names, and addresses. The typing was bad, amateurish, but there was no mistaking the content, thirty—thirty-four names.

Ike replaced the paper in the envelope and dropped it into the casket. He turned so that from where he was standing, Grundig could see him. He slipped off his wedding band and placed it on Eloise's cold finger, next to hers. At the same time, he nudged the envelope deep into the folds of the sheet.

"I'm ready. You can close here."

"*Ja wohl.*" Grundig glanced into the casket and, satisfied that all was in order, closed the lid.

"Seal it, please," Ike said in a tone that brooked no argument. Grundig hesitated, uncertain what he should or could do.

"Captain?" Ike was sure that Durant was close by, watching him. He was not wrong. Durant's voice came from the hall just beyond the pair of swinging doors with their matched square windows.

"Yes, M. Schwartz."

"Captain, I want to witness the sealing of the casket. You may too, if you wish."

"Certainly. Herr Grundig, seal the casket. M. Schwartz is quite right."

They watched as Grundig closed the lid, tightened the recessed setscrews, and slipped four short loops of cable through the hasps. After the loops were closed and set, they were sealed shut with lead slugs, the slugs marked, and the marks recorded.

"You are satisfied?"

Ike looked at the seals, gave each a perfunctory tug, and said, "Okay, Durant, to the airport."

Chapter 23

Four hours later, Ike booked into the Chelsea Hotel in London's East End, not the most glamorous stopping place, but the safest for what he had to do. He unlocked and opened his luggage, placing each piece on the bed. Eloise's things made him wince and he decided that he would leave them in the room when he left. He put his wallet, passport, and papers on the dresser, picked up his key, and left the room.

He sat in a little park across the street feeding the pigeons and wondering who they would send. Kamarov sat down on the bench forty-five minutes later and threw some crumbs.

"Ike, I am sorry about your lady. I do not understand how it happened. The man, the shooter, was a new one, and I suppose very excited on his first assignment. He was careless. For whatever it's worth, he has been disciplined."

"I know, Alexei. It's not your fault."

"We want the envelope, Ike."

"You know I haven't got it. You've searched my room and luggage."

"Yes. Thank you for making that easy for us."

"It's new luggage, wedding present. I didn't want your fumble-fingered friends busting it all up. I haven't got it, Alexei. I didn't get it."

"Our man didn't have it, Ike, which means you have it or the Swiss police have it. Our people say they don't have it. That leaves you."

"You can search me too. I haven't been out of your sight since it happened. I haven't got it. He never passed it. He was being followed, and told me where to meet him later to make the pass, when you nailed him. If you waited, you could have gotten the stuff then. Now, we'll never know."

Kamarov studied Ike, one tired old pro sizing up the other. Someone had watched Schwartz since the shooting. There were only two opportunities to get rid of the envelope: at the mortuary, and on the airplane. They had removed the cushions in the latter, and the contact in Switzerland had assured him that only a ring was placed in the casket. Schwartz was good, but not that good.

"Very well, Ike, you haven't got it. You understand it makes no difference now whether you do or don't. If we do not have it, then adjustments will be made to assure that whoever does cannot use it. You understand?"

"Certainly."

"Ike, I am very sorry about what happened. You know none of us likes that approach. None of us would do that to colleague." The Russian paused and looked at Ike, his brown eyes searching. Finally, he asked in a puzzled voice, "Why, why on a meet as important as this one, did you bring that beautiful young woman?"

"Orders, Alexei, orders, and misunderstandings, the usual crap."

"Ah, my friend, I am sorry. You didn't know, yes? What was being passed?"

"No."

They sat in silence a few moments.

"This may be the last we shall see of each other," Kamarov said. "You have been an admirable opponent and occasional ally. Do not be too bitter, old friend. We chose to play this game and accept the risks that go with it. It is a crazy game, and those of us who play it are not Olympians earning laurels. We are more like your professional football players. We play for the money or the thing it does for our ego. We respect one another only for the skill we display, not for whom we display it. In this, as in the football, only the spectators care which uniform we wear or what the scoreboard says at the end of the day. Good-bye, Ike. Be very careful."

‹›‹›‹›

Ike landed at Dulles two hours before dawn. No one met him. He drove a rental the seventeen miles to Langley, parked in a spot reserved for visitors and passed through the security checks. If anyone wanted to know where he was, now they knew. Once signed in at the Agency, you were tracked as closely and as thoroughly as modern technology allowed.

Hotchkiss waited for him.

"You look as bad as I feel, Ike."

"Bullshit, Peter, you don't feel bad, you don't feel anything. For you, it's just another job."

"Look, I am sorry about Eloise. We all are. There was no way we could have known."

"Shut up, Peter. I am an old-timer, remember? Ike Schwartz, dumb but dependable, not quick enough for a slot in Operations, but good—very good in the field. After twelve years, Peter, even the dumb ones learn something."

"Ike, you're upset. Take it easy. You've had a shock."

"I told you to shut up. I do not want to have to tell you again. I am going to talk and you are going to listen. When I ask you a question, you will nod yes or shake your head no. I am not fooling, Peter. I am very angry—angry enough now to take your head off at the shoulders and punt it out the window. You have been behind that desk for a long time, Peter, translating musings from King Henry into forays on Archbishops. You've lost a step and you're soft, so shut up and listen."

Hotchkiss stared at Ike for a full minute without speaking. Ike knew he was on shaky ground. Oh, he could take Peter if he wanted to. He always could, but he also knew that he had been expected. There might be four or five gorillas listening to him right now who could be all over him in thirty seconds if

Hotchkiss wanted. Hotchkiss sighed and slouched back in his swivel chair.

"Okay, Ike, you talk. By the way, you're safe. There's no one here but me. That's the truth. We've been together a long time."

"Thank you for that, anyway. The only question I have to live with now is why? In fact I have a long list of whys. Why me? Why Eloise? Why the rush? You are very good, Peter. They pulled you out of the field because you are very good at operations. You have a success rate that is the envy of the section. You never—I repeat—never leave loose ends if you can avoid them. So there I was caught up in the most screwed-up operation I have ever seen, and I ask myself, why?"

"I told you, we were short on time and we didn't believe it would get, um, complicated."

"I said no talking. So I ask myself why? Then it hits me. You knew, Peter—you knew. You said some trivial bank records, but that is not what was passed. You told me a minor official, a Swiss banker, an amateur, but I met with some guy from the Russian Embassy and, I'm guessing, a pretty high up somebody."

"There were no financial records in that envelope. Just names, thirty-four names and addresses. Am I right?"

Hotchkiss started to speak, then stopped and nodded.

"Very good. 'Let me see,' I said to myself in the funeral parlor. 'What names would be worth killing for?' And you know what I concluded? None of them were. So why is everyone dead?"

"Ike, they were agents. My God, we had a chance to get the names of every one of their agents operating in the Switzerland/ Northern Italy zone. We had to take the—"

"They are dead, I said to myself, because they are supposed to be. Simple. When you refuse to accept complexity as a necessary condition of existence, things can be made very simple. The reason, for example, that you are so good at what you do is that everyone expects complicated plots and counter plots, disguises, and ruses. But you design simple, straightforward plans, and then let those caught up in it miss the boat because they can't believe it's so simple. Sometime, you have to lie to get what you want, and that helps create the illusion of great complexity.

"Well, knowing that about old Peter, I think, 'What the hell is going on?' You do not care about those agents. Hell, half the people on the list we already knew about, and none of them were important. And now, they are dead, too, aren't they? As we sit here talking, thirty-four unexplained accidents, homicides, and disappearances are cluttering up the police blotters all over Switzerland, southern France, and Italy. They didn't get their list back. They do not know if we have it or not, so they can't take a chance. Thirty-four agents are erased in a week or two, and later, thirty-four more will take their places.

"And who wins? Nobody. We lose the names of the seventeen agents we did know, and it will take us a year or two to discover the new ones, so we don't. They're out of business for a month or more, so they don't. And you knew that. You knew it all the time. You weren't after the names at all."

"Ike, I swear to you…yes, I lied about the documents, but we needed to get those names and set up the meet."

"Oh, I believe that. Yes, indeed, but not for the reasons you want me to believe. The names were meaningless. You wanted the meet with that sweaty little man. He was the important piece. The only thing needed? He meets me and passes that envelope. He could have given me a recipe for chicken soup and you have what you wanted. I need a yes or no, Peter."

Peter nodded.

"Good, so what are we looking at here? First, there is a need to do something about the Russian intelligence in Switzerland for a while, say, one or two weeks. You have got their number two or three guy wired somehow, and he is ready to give you some names. Now, all you need is the time and place and the reason. Somebody upstairs says, 'Peter, there's a big one going down on such and such a day in Switzerland and we do not want the Russians to know, so deactivate them.' And you say, 'The whole area?' And then you get lucky. Big, dumb Schwartz rolls into your office asking you to fix up a passport for him and his bride, and what do you know, they're going to Switzerland. Your number one agent is going to be on the spot. So you say, 'You bet, Ike, no problem,' and off we go.

"Well, it's simple after that. You con me into a meet with whoever-it-was, and you leak it to one of your double agents so they know, and bingo, their whole intelligence apparatus in the area is blown. They have to replace agents. They have to find out who else is involved, and while they're doing that, we sneak some stuff through the country, right?"

"Ike, it was important, big, one of the biggest. We had to. The Middle East, Arabs, oil, and the terrorist groups we have been after—"

"I don't want to know, Peter. I do not want to know the product, but counting the shooter and Eloise, over three dozen people died for whatever it was. That is a high price to pay. I do not want to hear Eloise died so that some economically strapped arms manufacturer from Chicopee, Massachusetts, could unload his surplus inventory of rocket launchers on some two-bit Arab terrorist, our terrorist this time, without interference from the Russians."

"How did you find out, Ike?"' Ike heard the fear in Hotchkiss' voice.

"Peter, do you think I'm stupid? I worked Europe a dozen years. There isn't anything or anyone out there I don't know or I can't find out. Three phone calls and a confirmation from Kamarov—it's done. When will you desk types learn? When will you learn to say 'help me' and 'thank you'?"

Ike had not slept for close to forty-eight hours. He gazed through bloodshot eyes at the man who had trained with him, a man he liked, respected and had worked with for years. He felt empty.

"Ike?" Hotchkiss' voice was tentative, probing, and wary. "They know?"

"They know. It's not going to work. The shipment is going to go badly, the plan will be exposed, and the Agency is either going to have to eat another public exposé, or it will have to throw the arms company to the dogs and hope they don't blow the whistle. That could get, what was your word? Complicated."

Hotchkiss leaned back and closed his eyes. Back to his scheming, Ike thought, looking for a way out, his mind ticking off possibilities, maneuvers, and strategies. He was startled when Hotchkiss spoke.

"Ike, I am sorry about Eloise. That was not in the script, believe me. I thought they would confirm the meet and pick our man off before. It is not their style to blast away in public. I don't understand."

"Kamarov said the guy was new and nervous, and by now is no longer with us."

"I hate this. Dear God, forgive me, I hate this. I believed I used you as a minor player. You are right. The fact you were there would ring their bells and then the meeting time and place would be all that was needed. He wasn't even supposed to show up."

"But he did, Peter, and now, it's over."

Two men sat in silence for a while.

"Ike, you knew when you signed on how the game was played, the risks involved."

"Peter, you're the third person in forty-eight hours to call what we do a game. It is what is wrong with this business. It is all a game, and we play it like summer campers playing Capture the Flag, all rah-rah and removed from reality. But it is very real, Peter, and lots of people feel what we do personally, and usually tragically. If those rocket launchers get through, a lot of Israelis—men, women, and children—are going to die. Why? For oil? For twenty cents off the barrel price of crude so we can keep our gas-guzzling SUVs rolling down our superhighways? And the Israelis will retaliate with their rockets and Mirage jets and a lot of Arabs are going to die.

"Don't you ever wonder, Peter, what the hell this is all about, all this death and destruction in the name of hegemony? It only makes sense if it is a game, not if it is real. So we play games, and sleep at night." Ike paused, the weariness washing over him with the first real stirrings of the grief that would embrace him for the next year.

"I'm finished. You've got me this time. Schwartz is hanging up his cleats, turning in his marker, folding up his board, turning up his cards—*kaput.* I am done, finished. No more games."

"Ike, don't. We need you. Take some time to get over what happened. Take as much time as you need, then—"

"Peter, I'm done. I will never get over losing Eloise and what my country, in its misguided way, did to her and to me. I am telling you, and you can tell the division chief, who can tell the director, who can tell the President, Schwartz is through."

‹›‹›‹›

Ike exhaled.

"And that's it. Sorry. I had no right to burden you with it."

"It's not a burden, Ike. No, I'm glad you told me and I'm honored that you felt safe enough to tell me."

"Yes, well, that's something, I guess." He stood and stepped out of the shadows and leaned against the porch rail.

"That's something, all right. I don't know if I should cry, or be angry or…and here's something else for you to think about, I think you are the most irritating, engaging, infuriating, attractive man I have ever met." And that said, Ruth stepped up and kissed him.

"Wow," she said, eyes glazed.

"Wow, indeed," he replied and kissed her again. Ruth shivered. The Fairy Ring twinkled at her feet, circled, closed, and began to weave its magic.

"You know where this could lead, Sheriff?"

"I hope so."

‹›‹›‹›

*Moonlight becomes you.…*His father would sing the tune, usually on a Sunday morning, and when he did, his mother would blush. He would grin and go on…*It goes with your hair.…*" His mother would scowl and mutter, "Abe.…" There could be no mistaking the warning in her voice.

After thirty years, at last Ike understood the joke. He rolled over on his elbow and admired the smooth naked body beside him. Moonlight streamed into the room through the open blinds, washing her body silver-blue. She turned toward him and pulled at the sheet.

"Not yet."

She pushed the sheet away and smiled.

"Help yourself. It's not much, but it's all mine."

"I'm a very lucky man."

He reached for her again. This time there would be no hurry.

Chapter 24

Agnes Ewalt, called in on a Sunday for service beyond the call of duty, sat at her desk sorting paper clips. She greeted Ike with a vague smile and called Ruth on the intercom. Assured that Ike was both expected and welcome, she ushered him into the inner office, offered him coffee, which he accepted, and left. Ruth sat at her desk half-heartedly examining a foundation report. Ike slumped down in the crewel-covered wing chair and studied her. The morning sunlight filtered though the half-open blinds and formed a dappled pattern on the oriental carpet that reminded Ike of leaves in the woods in New England.

Agnes reentered carrying two cups of coffee, muttered something, and left. Ike sipped his coffee. Ruth stopped shuffling the papers in front of her and sat back.

"Dillon and the rest of the U.S. Cavalry will be here in about an hour, Ike," she said.

"Right."

"He's quite a guy, Dillon. He can be very intimidating sometimes, but he is very quick, and if you remember to lay back and let him go for awhile, you can get to him when he's ready. He hates for people to second-guess him or try to impress him. And whatever else you do, do not try to one-up him."

"I'll remember." M. Armand Dillon was not Ike's major concern. He could be a lion or a pussycat for all he cared. There were things that were going to happen no matter what Dillon or anyone else said or did. Ike's only concern was getting the right things to happen in the right order. He inspected Ruth.

"You look tired, Ms. President," he said, noticing for the first time the lines around her eyes and the sag in her shoulders.

"I am, Ike," Ruth murmured. "Except for the late-night interludes with the local police, it's been a mean couple of days."

"Job not too much for you?"

Ruth's eyes flashed. "A job is a job, and no, it's not too much for me."

"Whoa," Ike said, taken aback, "I didn't mean anything."

"Why does every man think if a woman is tired, or sad, or out of sorts, it's because she is working, has a career, or PMS?"

"I wasn't even thinking about that."

"I know, but that's the way it came out. Do you know what it is like, even now, being a woman in a man's world? You have to do everything twice as well as a man in the same job. And you cannot get tired or, Heaven forbid, angry. Men get angry and they're called hard-nosed. Women get angry and they're labeled bitchy. Men lean on you and they're tough. Women lean on you and they're castrating. I am so tired of all that crap. Sheesh."

"I'm sorry. I didn't mean to sound…that way. It's the kind of remark I might have made to anyone."

"I suppose that's so. But you've got to understand, that's not what I hear, what a woman hears."

Ruth paused, lost in thought. "Look," she continued, "you are as sensitive to the issue as any man. You've worked in situations where your colleagues, maybe even your bosses, were women and you managed. But even with that, you still have to make an effort to keep from calling the students here girls, and I'd bet I could find in your own area the kind of discrimination that drives people like me, women, crazy."

"Oh, come on, Ruth. I am sympathetic. No, that's not it, is it? You got me. Let me try again. I don't discriminate, harass, or treat women in the world of work any differently than I treat men." Ike's words were sincere, he thought, but even as he spoke them, he realized they came only with great effort.

"Ike, I know you don't or wouldn't…the sexual harassment thing. The job discrimination that you're thinking about is not the point. I can deal with overt sexism. It's the little things that hurt. It's our friends that are killing us, Ike. Look, how many women work for you?"

Ike paused and thought. He felt the noose tightening and already knew where he would be in less than five minutes. He decided to take his medicine like a man and smiled at himself for the figure of speech. "Two," he said, "not counting Sam."

"Two, and no, you can't count Sam—she works for me. And the two, your two, what do they do?"

"Ah…well, there's Rita the secretary and Essie the dispatcher."

"No deputies, Ike? No women on the force? And don't tell me about Sam."

"No."

"Why not?"

"Well, um, no one's ever applied."

"You ever advertise for one?"

"No, can't do that, Ruth. Believe it or not, town statutes prevent me from citing race or sex in any ads. Besides, we haven't had but one opening in the two years since I set up the group I've got."

"Ike, I don't want to push you anymore. You are a kind and gentle man, and you are the sort who will always do the right thing. But I want you to know that I think it is criminal that this town, whose main industry is a women's college, does not have even one woman on its police force. The social imperative for that should be transparent and the advantages to you, if you did, should be overwhelmingly obvious."

"*Touché*, Ruth," Ike said with a wry smile. "One point for the lady."

Ruth waved her hand in the general direction of the window, dismissing the topic and the argument. She sent a similar smile back to him. They drank their coffee in silence.

The chimes in the bell tower struck the third quarter. The intercom buzzed again.

"President Harris," Agnes Ewalt said at her officious best, "there's a Miss Billups to see you. She says it's important."

"Send her in, Agnes," Ruth said, and shrugged her shoulders at Ike.

The pretty woman who slipped through the heavy mahogany door could not have been more than nineteen or twenty. She had the sort of soft, curly brown hair that you see on bottles of shampoo and, Ike thought, a very sexy overbite.

"President Harris?" she said breathlessly. It came out "Prizadin Hairs." "I'm real sorry to bust in on you like this, it being Sunday and all, but I just got to tell you."

"What is it, Miss Billups....I'm sorry, your first name is?"

"Betsy Mae," she gasped, surprised, and then added, "It's about my roommate, Jennifer. They said up at the dorm you all were asking about people who might be missing and so I thought I'd better tell you right away—"

"Slow down, Betsy Mae, and start from the beginning. Your roommate is missing?"

"Well, yes, I reckon she is. I don't know for sure, but I think so on account of Jack Trask's missing, too."

"From the beginning, Betsy Mae, and go slow. This is Sheriff Schwartz, and if anything needs to be done, he will attend to it, won't you, Sheriff?" Ruth, the very model of a college president, sat cool, calm, in control, and the authority in the room. The girl seemed reassured, and glancing in Ike's direction began her story.

"Well, Thursday night Jennifer, Jennifer Ames—that's my roommate—had a date with Jack Trask. I shouldn't have made her do it...I wouldn't have, except that my boyfriend really wanted to get a bid to St. Elmo's and he thought it might help. So anyway, Jen went out with Jack and she didn't come back."

"Jack Trask, the lacrosse player?" Ike was now interested.

Betsy Mae was wide-eyed. "Yes, you know him?"

"Only by reputation." Seeing the puzzled look in Ruth's eyes, Ike explained. "Jack Trask is an All-American midfielder, lacrosse player, for the University of Virginia. He is their one, and only hope of winning a national title."

Ruth seemed only slightly less puzzled.

"BMOC," Ike added. Ruth nodded in comprehension.

"Okay, Betsy Mae," he said, "your roommate did you a favor and went out with Trask. That was Thursday?"

She nodded. "And she wasn't in her bed Friday morning."

"Why didn't you mention it then?"

Betsy Mae blushed and looked guilty. "Well," she said, "I didn't want to get Jen into trouble, and you know I thought maybe she and Jack—well, you know how it is sometimes. And then I signed out Friday for the weekend to go to Charlottesville, and I thought I'd see her there Saturday and I'd, you know, kid her about it."

"Why did you think you'd see her in Charlottesville?" Ruth asked, the puzzlement back on her face, still struggling with the girl's narrative.

"Well, because of the game, of course."

"What game? Betsy Mae, please try to be a little more to the point. I'm losing you," Ruth pleaded.

"The lacrosse game between UVA and Hopkins. It was the most important game of the season. That's when I knew that something was wrong." Betsy Mae was trying to be clear, but it seemed beyond her capabilities.

Ike cut in, hoping to save Ruth from having to sort through the girl's tangled narrative.

"What happened at the game, Betsy?" he asked, knowing what was coming.

"They lost because he didn't play."

"Jack Trask didn't play?"

"Wasn't even there. The biggest game of the season and Jack is a no-show. Nobody knew where he was. Well naturally, I thought he and Jen...well, I don't know what I thought. I was so upset, I asked Bobby to bring me back last night, and when

I heard you all were looking for missing people, I thought I'd better come right down."

"Thank you, Betsy Mae." Ruth said, "You were right to come down."

"Is everything going to be all right?" she asked.

"Everything will be fine," Ike replied. He hoped he sounded more confident than he was.

"Is there anything I can do?" Betsy Mae asked, reluctant to leave without some assurance.

"Can you remember what she was wearing Thursday? Anything that we could use for a description?"

"Well, I reckon I could do that. I'll write it all down on a piece of paper. Anything else?" she asked.

"Nothing now," Ike said. "You go to church much, Betsy?"

She nodded.

"Well, fine," Ike said with a smile. "You just hustle off to church and maybe say a prayer or two for Jennifer and Jack, and all of us, if you can work that in. Everything will be fine."

"I shouldn't have made her do it," she cried and hit her right fist into the palm of her left hand. "I just shouldn't."

"Thank you, Betsy Mae," Ruth said, dismissing her. "Let us know if anything else occurs to you, or if you hear from Jennifer."

"Yes, ma'am." She retreated from the office.

Ike picked up the phone, frowned, and looked at Ruth.

"Hit nine, and then that red button," she said.

He did and got a dial tone, and punched in his office number.

"Essie, put Whaite on."

"Whaite, did you get anything on the car from the tapes?"

"Not enough, Ike. We got the make and year, it has New Jersey plates, and we know the last two digits, but that's all. New Jersey State police are trying to make a match for us, but it's Sunday and they don't expect much to pop out today."

"Never mind that—call the University of Virginia campus police and get all you can on Jack Trask."

"The lacrosse player?"

"The same. See if they have the car registered—parking sticker application, whatever. Get parents' names, then get back to New Jersey and see if you come up with anything. Call me as soon as you can."

"Will do." Whaite hung up.

Ike replaced the phone on the hook and scratched his head. There it was again, that little bell that went off in the back of his head, something someone said, but he just could not put it together.

"Ike?"

"It comes and goes...a nagging little thought, but I can't get it out to look at it. I think it's important but it just won't come." He sat down again and stared at his empty coffee cup.

"Do you suppose I could have another one of these?" he asked.

"Sure....Agnes," Ruth grumbled into the intercom, "could you bring us two more coffees, please? And is there any sign of Mr. Dillon yet?" Ruth listened and sighed. "Damn," she said, "I hate waiting."

‹›‹›‹›

It was time to move again. Angelo and Grafton slipped out of the Dixie Motel. The two hostages were bundled into the back seat of the car and they drove off.

Sunday morning and shades were drawn, the parking lot quiet. They headed out of Lexington south toward the Picketsville exit. They would be at the Lee-Jackson for the next two nights.

"Son of a..." Angelo exploded as the heavy Cadillac limousine roared by them, its smoked windows hiding its occupants. Another, smaller car with government tags followed, and then a state police car followed it in hot pursuit. "Those guys drive like lunatics." He steadied the wheel and followed, maintaining the posted speed limit.

Harry watched the retreating cars, wondering if they had something to do with him. The limousine could belong to anyone, and the state police car needed no explanation. The other car, however, could be a problem. He knew a Bureau car when he saw one, and he was pretty sure he recognized the driver. He did not remember the name, but he worked out of the Richmond office. Did they know? He closed his eyes and fought the panic that began to rise from deep inside. No good, he thought, no damned good.

Chapter 25

"They're here, Dr. Harris," Agnes gushed over the intercom.

"Send them in, Agnes."

The door burst open before she finished, and M. Armand Dillon, flanked by Colonel Scarlett and a short, rumpled, sandy-haired man with FBI written all over him, marched into the office. Dillon struggled with a bulky package wrapped in newspaper.

"M. Armand Dillon," he announced to the room, and turning to Ike, said, "You must be Sheriff Schwartz. Excuse me for saying so, no disrespect intended, but that is as unlikely a combination of words as I've heard in a long time, right up there with Whoopi Goldberg. This is Dennis Kenny, Richmond FBI, and Colonel Scarlett, state police."

"We've met," said Ike.

"Fine, that takes care of the formalities. Now, Dr. Harris, if you'll just let us boys use your conference room, we'll get to work."

Dillon breezed out the door and headed toward the adjoining conference room. Ike, Ruth, and the others followed. She pushed the door open and ushered them in.

Dillon dismissed her with a wave of his hand and seated himself at the head of the table.

"Coffee, a pot, if possible, and a telephone," he said to Ruth's back. She froze in mid-step, her shoulders braced like a marine recruit, and she seemed to grow two inches in height. Ike held his breath. He blushed at the memory of the recent lecture he'd received about women. No more than a second passed, but it seemed an eternity while he waited for the explosion he felt sure was coming. Dillon money or no Dillon money, Ruth would not let this one pass.

"Dr. Harris?" Dillon said. "Problem?"

She spun on her heel and looked at the men standing around the table. Her gaze stopped at Ike. He read the anger in her eyes. She opened her mouth to say something. He stood and, taking her by the arm, guided her to a chair.

"Mr. Dillon, we need President Harris' input."

"We do?" Dillon caught Ike's eye, noted the lightning flashing in hers, swallowed, and agreed.

"Quite right. Dr. Harris, sorry, please join us."

She sat in a corner, face flushed and tapping her foot, anger seething like lava just below the surface. Ike pleaded with his eyes. She stared at him, tight-lipped, then nodded and settled back in her chair. Ike prayed Dillon would can the good-ole-boy routine. He would have enjoyed seeing these two have at each other, but not now.

The others seated themselves on either side of the table. Ike sat across from Scarlett but pulled back from the table, excluding himself from their group. He felt Dillon's eyes on him. Sizing me up, he thought. Ike turned toward Dillon and returned the stare. M. Armand Dillon peered at Ike through rimless spectacles, the kind with their lenses squared off on the corners. His face was pink and what was left of his hair had retreated to form a red-gray fringe above his ears and neck. He was short and round but Ike guessed very hard and fit. He looked anywhere between fifty and seventy years old. Ike knew from his file that Dillon was over seventy-five. His expression, though genial, Ike thought was very deceptive. Dillon would be easy to underestimate.

Dillon reached into the upper vest pocket of his gray pin-striped suit and pulled out a box of wooden matches, and a pack of cigarettes, Lucky Strikes, unfiltered.

"My God," Ruth said, "I didn't know they still made those things."

"They do, Madam President, and I smoke 'em. Been smoking 'em for over fifty years. They taste wonderful. When I was young, that was sometime just after the Flood, you understand, I spent some of my misguided youth enrolled in the university up the highway from here. One of the upperclassmen took it on himself to teach us freshmen how to drink. 'If you can't taste it,' he said, 'don't drink it. You've got to know what and how much you're getting.' Good advice, by the way. Same holds for cigarettes. I want to taste what I'm getting."

He struck a kitchen match and lit his cigarette, exhaled a plume of smoke, and spit a tobacco shred from his lip. Ruth rolled her eyes, got up and opened a window.

Agnes entered and placed a tray with five cups, a pot of coffee, creamer, sugar, and spoons on the table. She left and returned with another tray with half a dozen limp Danish, left and returned a third time with a telephone, which she plugged into the wall-jack.

"Thank you, Miss…?" Dillon said, and gave her one of his snaggle-toothed smiles.

"Ewalt. Agnes Ewalt," Agnes twittered and left.

"Okay, Kenny, what have you got?" he shot at the FBI man.

Kenny began a long and technical report, which Dillon interrupted after a minute.

"Never mind that crap," he said. "Just tell me the big stuff. Who are these people and what do they want?"

"They call themselves the New Jihad and they want fifty million dollars," Kenny replied.

"I know all that, man," Dillon barked, "but who, what, where, can you give me some specifics?"

Kenny flushed. Ike could not tell if it was from anger or embarrassment.

"Well, sir, as nearly as we can make it out, they are a terrorist group, a splinter of what is left of Al Qaida, the same bunch that tried to break into the library in New York. They are holding your pictures for ransom. You are to go on local television tomorrow night and read a prepared statement denouncing yourself and your militaristic industrialist friends, apologize for a variety of so-called crimes, and agree to pay fifty million dollars in reparations to them." Kenny recited his piece like a well-rehearsed schoolboy.

"Good Lord, son, I know all that, too. What I want to know is, are these the same ones who stole my paintings? Any crackpot whose been watching the news could have written a ransom note. Do you think these are the people?" Dillon demanded.

"Yes, sir," Kenny said, "I do."

"You agree, Scarlett?"

"Could be," the colonel replied. Scarlett had a genius for not having a firm opinion on anything.

"How about you, Sheriff?"

Ike let his gaze shift out the window. The sun beat on the wisteria outside and made the light filtered through it a pale blue. He thought of moonlight and caught himself drifting into the previous night.

"Sheriff? You with us?"

"I don't think the robbery was pulled off by the New Jihad, no. sir," Ike replied. Kenny's head snapped around to stare at him. He had to be careful. He wanted to maintain his jurisdictional control, and he wanted to know why Kenny, who should know better by now, wanted to sell the theory that the terrorists were also the thieves.

"Why not?" Dillon asked. His voice quieted and the bark seemed at bay.

"This was a professional job, Mr. Dillon, a very professional job. Whoever planned it had some high-powered talent, not the sort you find in terrorist groups. More like the folks who work for Mr. Kenny here. And don't forget, the New Jihad is the same crowd that botched the New York Library job."

"You got a problem with that, Kenny?" Dillon asked, eyebrows arched, forming parentheses on his forehead.

"Well." Kenny hesitated, frowned and shot Ike a look. "We believe, sir, with all due respect to the sheriff here, that information from the Bureau is a little better than what can be generated out here in the boondocks."

"Sheriff?" Dillon looked back at Ike, eyebrows up.

"I'll stick with my analysis and," he added, looking at Kenny, "my sources." *So Kenny knows about Harold Grafton,* Ike thought, *and the Bureau wants to cover its collective rear end. I would hate to be in Grafton's shoes if they get to him before I do.*

"Next question is for you, Kenny, since you are so sure of things—are they serious? Will they burn the pictures?"

"No, sir, we are pretty sure they won't. They are a small group and an act like that would lead us straight to them."

"Positive about that, are you?"

"Yes, sir."

"Then explain this." Dillon peeled the newspaper from the package he'd carried into the room. He laid the charred remains of a painting on the conference table.

"It's a small Chardin, not a very good one, either. Its provenance is a little shaky and I never liked it, but there is no question it has been torched. You agree?"

Kenny swallowed. "I, uh, we didn't know about that…."

"You don't know a lot about too many things, son. Your boss knew about it. Didn't he tell you?"

"I guess he must have." Kenny slouched down in his chair and looked like he wanted to disappear.

"Either way, what do I do? Kenny? Scarlett? Sheriff? Dr. Harris, you have a thought or two for us?" Ruth shook her head and looked at Ike.

"The Bureau thinks you should pay the ransom." Kenny burst in. "We will set up surveillance at the drop, or whatever, and when they come to get it we will apprehend them."

"Can you do that?"

"Yes, sir, we can."

"Colonel Scarlett?"

Scarlett agreed. Dillon asked a series of logistical questions. The phone rang. Dillon snatched the receiver off the hook.

"Hello?" he rasped. "He's right here." He handed the phone to Ike. "It's for you."

"We got a make on the car, Ike." Whaite said. "You were right. It's Trask's and registered in his father's name in Saddle River. I put an APB out on it."

"Thanks. Get the boys working on it, will you? It's important. I want that car."

"Sheriff?" Dillon asked as Ike replaced the phone in the cradle.

"There was a car parked near the bunker during the robbery. We think they got it and the people in it."

"Hostages? Kidnapping?" Kenny, confidence restored, sat up and licked his lips. "That makes it ours, Sheriff."

"Maybe. No one has been reported missing. We have not received a ransom note. We have no evidence that they are in custody anywhere or left the state, just supposition so far. For their sake," he added, "I hope you're right. That means they are alive. Much as I hate losing control of this investigation to you, I'd rather do that than keep it so I could work a triple homicide."

Dillon was becoming impatient. "I do not give a diddle-dam about who does what here," he snapped. "I want to know what I'm supposed to do next. You, Kenny, want to set a trap baited with my fifty million, that right?"

"Yes, sir," Kenny said.

"And the state police will cooperate and back the Bureau up. Is that right, Colonel?"

"As best as we can," Scarlett said.

Dillon swiveled around in his chair and stared out the window. The room fell silent. A beetle flew through the open window and zigzagged the length of the room. It made a sharp right turn at the wall and circled, gained altitude, bounced twice against the ceiling, and nosed over into a power dive. It landed with a soft plop in Kenny's coffee cup.

"Kamikaze," said Scarlett. "Must be a Japanese beetle."

It was the first time Ike had ever heard Jack Scarlett say anything remotely funny. Scarlett took the opportunity to remove a large wad of chewing tobacco from his jaw and put it in the coffee cup with the beetle.

Kenny fidgeted like a hunting dog waiting to be turned loose. He wanted the operation, and his urgency overflowed into his speech, his posture. Dillon turned and inspected him, the way an entomologist inspects a bug, interested, curious, but all the while withholding judgment until he has time to think, classify, identify, and then stick a pin in it. He glanced at Ike and then turned back to Kenny.

"Mr. Kenny, you act like a young lad who has to go to the bathroom. Either learn to hold it, or raise your hand. I need a little more time here and a cooler head than yours."

Kenny's always flushed face turned a shade redder.

"Why don't you and the Colonel slip down to the cafeteria and get yourself a cup of coffee or something, about a half hour's worth of something. The sheriff and I will chat a bit and then I'll tell you what I'm going to do. Dr. Harris, I reckon you might want to stay, too, but if you have other—"

"I'll stay. I've watched the sheriff work over people. I want to see how he manages you."

"Pardon?"

"Thank you, Mr. Dillon, but on second thought, I'll get back to my desk. Ike, try to behave yourself."

"What was that all about, Sheriff?"

Chapter 26

Angelo was sprawled across the small couch, asleep, when Harry entered the room. Harry shook his arm and started as Angelo recoiled. The gun seemed to appear in his hand as if by magic. It was leveled at Harry's stomach.

"Easy. It's me, Grafton."

Angelo relaxed, then looked anxious.

"I was asleep. You going to tell the *Patrone*?"

"Hell no, why would I do that? You are babysitting. They're handcuffed, what could happen?"

"He would be very angry with me, Grafton. Please, you will not tell."

"I won't tell, Angelo, if, of course, you don't tell him when you catch me asleep either?" Harry attempted a smile. He got a blank stare in return.

"We understand each other, and also something else—you don't worry about afterward. I take care of that, right?"

And with that cryptic remark hanging over him, Angelo let himself out the door. Harry scratched his head. Afterward? What afterward?

He looked at the two kids. The boy slept curled in the fetal position. The girl was awake and staring at him.

"Hi," he said. "How are you doing?"

"I'm okay. Thanks again for the clothes. They fit pretty well. I'm not that big on top or that small on the bottom, but they'll do fine. A little loose here, a little tight there."

They sat in silence. After a minute or two, Harry spoke.

"Where are you from, Jennifer?"

"Are you sure you want to know, Harry? Are you sure you want to get that close to someone you may have to shoot later?"

"No one's going to shoot anyone, Jennifer, I promise. In two or three days, this will all be over and done with."

"I can identify you. I know your name, what you look like, everything—the others, too. You can't let me go."

"It will work out, you'll see. You will just have to forget for a while and then it will be over. See, the other one, Donati, is untouchable, you know. He will have an ironclad alibi for the whole time. They all will. And so while you're trying to convince the police you're right, Donati will stalk you, or your family. He can do that. And he will tell you he can, and so you will forget. Jennifer, you will forget me, him, Angelo, Red, all of us. You must."

"Is that how it works, Harry? Is he—are you so sure of him that you can risk letting me go? Really?"

"That's how it works, really." Harry wished he believed it himself and hoped she would. She looked dubious.

"I don't know."

"Jennifer, listen to me. The boss of this operation is a contractor with the Mafia. He can do what he says he can do. Look, if it were otherwise, wouldn't he have killed you both before now?"

"Yes, I guess so. You believe it's going to be all right?"

"No doubt about it."

She relaxed.

"Where am I from? All over. My folks are divorced. Daddy lives in Philadelphia with his trophy wife. He makes lots of money by investing other people's and collecting fees. Summers in Rehoboth Beach, side trips to New York, Europe, that sort of thing.

"Momma tried working for a living, but found she could get more money by marrying it. She's on her fourth now. Counting Daddy's settlement and her inheritance from the late number three, she's worth about six million dollars."

"Poor little rich girl."

"Don't patronize me, Harry. You asked. That is what they are. What I am is something else."

"I'm sorry. What are you?"

"I'm…me. I am my own person. When I graduate, I have a job in Chicago with the Art Institute and I got it all by myself. My parents do not even know about it yet. I am going to Chicago and have a career. I want to write, be a curator, and someday maybe collect fine art. Like the paintings you guys stole."

Her determined look and confidence, the strength of her voice, convinced Harry that if she got the chance, if he could get her out of this mess somehow, she would do all those things, and more, much more.

"I believe you, Jennifer. You're the kind that can make things happen."

"And what about you, Harry? You can't make things happen? You're one of life's losers, reduced to crime to meet your needs? I don't believe it."

"Well, you may be the only one who doesn't."

"Harry, if what you said is true—they will let me go, if I shut up—I won't hurt you, you need to know that."

Harry nodded. He supposed it was true enough. Hoped so.

"So tell me. How'd you get caught up in this, Harry?"

He thought a moment and decided it did not make much difference one way or another if she knew. But he wanted her to know for his own reasons. He wanted this girl's friendship, goodwill, whatever. He wanted one person in the world to think well of him. He had had precious little of that in the past.

"I am here because I had no other choice. It is true what I told you about Donati's long arm. He can get me through my children. I had a choice. The good way, the way I chose, he offered me enough money to be able to get my kids back, lawyers, that sort of thing. The bad way, he hurts them.

"I was out of work with no prospects. I owed a lot of money. Things were closing in on me and I took this path because it promised release, one way or the other. If the plan works, I'll have enough money to buy my way out of my troubles. If it fails, I'm dead. I haven't the courage to kill myself so I'll let someone else do it for me."

"Are you always so hard on yourself? I don't believe for a minute you mean that. I think in the back of your mind, you are already working out how you are going to get out."

Harry grinned at that. She had it right, but getting her out, too, had so far stymied him.

"You said you have children. Where's their mother?"

"She died two weeks ago." It seems like two years, two decades, he thought. "It took a long time for her to do it, but she died."

"And you loved her very much?"

"Yes. No. I don't know. It wasn't much of a marriage in the end—too many disappointments. She was impossible to please. I didn't have the kind of job she could feel proud of, not in business like her friends' husbands, like her father. And even though I made good money—people like me are expensive—there was never enough. The house, well, too small, or mildewed, or in the wrong neighborhood, or…something. She wanted Jaguars, not Chevrolets; country clubs, and I couldn't please her. I tried, but it just never worked. And she began to resent her lot in life; to feel cheated, I guess. She quit college to marry me—her great sacrifice—her hopes for a career in the United Nations or the Foreign Service went out the window when the babies came. The role of housewife and mother didn't suit her. Anyway, the anger and resentment built, and ate away at the marriage."

"Why didn't you just get divorced, be done with it?"

"We, I, come from a group that doesn't believe in that. We believe marriage, good or bad, easy or hard, rewarding or awful, is forever. It's like an Army chow line—you eat what they put on your tray or you go hungry. It never occurred to me to change lines."

"So you endured it and began to hate her back?"

"Hate her? Maybe I did. But in my own way, I was devoted to her. I tried to reason with her, help her see what her anger did to me, but I failed—a catch twenty-two. When you are reduced to believing you are a failure, when your self-esteem goes, it's not possible to convince someone of anything. You are beaten before you start. And so the hatred becomes two-sided. You're right. I did grow to resent her as she resented me."

"So what did you do? I know that sounds silly, but you were employed, making money. Others must have seen your worth. Wasn't that enough?"

"No. That helps you do your job and I guess counterbalances some of the crushing weight of what is going on at home, but no, not enough. I didn't do anything. My circle of friends got smaller each year as she edited out the ones she didn't like, who failed to meet her standards. I didn't know anyone well enough to confide in. Even if I did, I wouldn't, because by then she'd pretty well convinced me that the problems were mine. I thought about having an affair or leaving—all kinds of things."

"But you didn't…have an affair, I mean."

"No. There were offers, you know, I could have. But that would have made things worse. I was not very good at lying and if she found out.…Well, there is no joy going into an affair when you know the outcome. Some days I wished she would die, you know. I prayed for that sometimes, that she'd die, without pain, of course, heart attack, plane crash, and then I'd feel guilty as hell, and wish I were dead. I thought about suicide, how I would do it—what I would write in the note. Planning or wishing for your own death is a guilt-free preoccupation. And then she developed breast cancer, a late diagnosis, and she began to die for real."

"And you felt guilty, felt like you were responsible, like you'd wished it on her?"

"Something like that. My drinking went over the top. I lost my job. Then her parents snatched my girls one morning when I was so hung over I couldn't get up to stop them. I don't think I've ever seen a look of contempt like the one on her father's face when they broke into the apartment, took Karen and Julie, and all I could do was throw up. On my knees in the can, throwing up my guts, too weak, too helpless to stop them from taking my children. I guess that was the bottom. That was a month ago. My wife died two weeks later, and Donati offered me a chance to put my life together. Money to pay medical bills, lawyers, rent—serious money."

"What you did in the robbery, the alarm business, you did that before?"

"Yes, only legally. But when you drink, you become unreliable. Well, they couldn't risk it, and then I had a disagreement with the new administration about whether I would carry a gun and broaden my, um, area of responsibility. Anyway, I was let go."

They sat in silence. Harry felt tired, but at the same time better. Just talking about it helped ease the hurt, see himself better. He wished he had met a Jennifer two years, five years before. He looked at her. She sat cross-legged, lost in thought. She looked like someone who was about to buy a house, weighing the advantages and disadvantages of location, taxes, school districts, transportation, and mortgage payments. Then, without warning, she began to shake. Harry got up and went to her, uncertain what he should do.

"Hey," he said, "you okay?"

Her eyes filled with tears and she fought back the sobs that wracked her.

"I'm scared, Harry. I don't want to die."

"No one's going to die."

"We are. We all are."

Harry reached for her without thinking, cradled her in his arms. Her free arm circled his neck and she buried her face in the angle of his neck and shoulder and gave way to the tears. Harry stroked her hair and back. He murmured reassurances he really did not feel, and without realizing it, kissed her hair and forehead. After a few minutes, her sobbing slowed, stopped, and ended in hiccups.

"I can't face it, you know?"

"It's going to be okay, kid."

"Harry, if I get out of this alive—no, let me finish—I want to...."

She dissolved into tears again, this time not so body wracking. Through them, she murmured, "I'll never see you again, will I?"

"We'll see each other, sure," Harry said and hoped it was so.

"But how will I find you?"

"You won't. I'll find you. Art Institute, Chicago. Remember?"

Chapter 27

Ike and Dillon watched Ruth and the two men leave.

"She's quite a woman, don't you think?" Dillon said.

"Yes, sir, she is that."

"Kenny able to play in this league? God, he looks like a teenager. Am I getting old or is everyone else getting younger?"

Ike smiled. He was beginning to think the same thing. "He'll be okay. I'm a little surprised they didn't send someone with a little more experience. You'd think with the press and everything, the Bureau would send an agent with a little more pizzazz."

"It's the new guy. I told the President he should hire a lawman, but he's got a bug in his ear about MBAs from the Ivy League. Anyway the Bureau is in turmoil and that's why we got the schoolboy, I guess."

Ike wasn't so sure.

"Now, Sheriff." Dillon's voice turned serious, the curmudgeon gone. "I think maybe you're the one I need to talk to. I do not believe for a minute that you are what you pretend to be. I have dealt with small-town cops in practically every state in the nation and half the countries in the world. I do not know what you are, and I do not want to know, but you sure as hell aren't a cop. So, you heard all this talk about ransom and operations and so on. What do you think I should do?"

Ike stared at Dillon. He knew a little about him. Who didn't? He appeared on the cover of *Time*, hobnobbed with Presidents and royalty. But beyond those surface things, Ike did not know very much. Money had a way of distorting people. He guessed this man, a second-generation industrial baron, could be as tough as he needed to be. Dillon could handle just about anything he or anyone else might dish out to him.

"Mr. Dillon, I will not tell you what to do. You are far too smart to need that from me, and I am not dumb enough to try. I will tell you what I think, what I believe, and if I can, I will try to project odds. You will do the deciding."

Dillon lit another cigarette.

"Okay, Sheriff. You do that. What do you think?"

"Well, first, there is the ransom—to pay or not to pay. Whether you pay will depend on how much you value one of two things: the money and the paintings. If you value the money, you won't pay, unless you think there's a chance of recovering the diamonds or at least most of them. If, however, you value the paintings, you will pay, but only if you're sure they will be returned to you. If they are already destroyed or will be irrespective of payment, you will not pay."

"The government and the state police think I should pay."

"Yes, I gather they do. Unless you agree to do it, they don't have much to work with. Remember, this was a professional operation using very sophisticated talent. You know the security system in the bunker. I'm guessing they sailed through that in less than an hour. They will be hard to find, maybe impossible, they're that good."

Dillon nibbled at the corner of a pastry, made a face, and dropped it into the trash basket behind him.

"You talk like you know them."

"I guess I do, in a way. I worked with people like them...ah, in the past. They are good, Mr. Dillon, very good. If you pay the ransom, Scarlett and Kenny hope they can set up an intercept and catch one or two and through them, get the rest. If you don't pay, they have nothing to do."

"If the bad guys are as good as you say, that might be tough, too?"

"Bad odds, Mr. Dillon. The days of leaving a suitcase full of money somewhere in a hollow tree are over. These people are prepared to get away clean. Fifty million dollars buys a lot of equipment. They will ask for the exchange in a wide-open place they can watch, like a state park or a beach. The diamonds will be deposited in the open and left. They will wait until they're sure no one can get to them, then come in fast with a helicopter, pick them up, fly nap of the earth to a second point, change to another transport and keep doing that until they're clean and clear. They will have alternative contacts on every exchange and all the FBI or state police in Virginia will not be able to cover all the possibilities. I think it's safe to say that if you pay the ransom you can kiss fifty million dollars goodbye."

"You don't have much faith in your colleagues, do you? What's your name, anyway?"

"Ike."

"Ike, short for Isaac? Father's name Abraham? You'd call a son Jacob, no doubt."

"Not a chance. Bill—he is going to be named Bill. Do you have any idea what it's like to be Jewish in this part of the country, with a name like Ike?"

"Ike the kike?"

"You got it."

"How'd you like to be named Millhouse like the geek in *The Simpsons*, or Nixon? Millhouse Armand Dillon. I grew up believing that a natural part of living involved a fistfight on the playground every day. You can't even come up with a decent nickname with Millhouse. At least you had Ike. I solved it by using my initials, M.A.D. Called myself Mad Dog. I got good enough at fighting by then to make it stick, and I was known as Mad Dog, Mad, or just plain Crazy until I made my first million. Count your blessings, Ike. Jacob is a nice name; a kid could do all right in this world as a Jake. Now, about the FBI, the state police—you don't think they can cut it?"

"Don't get me wrong, Mr. Dillon. They're good enough, better than that, but it's just that the deck is stacked against them."

"So you think the money's gone?"

"Yes."

"And if I value it over the paintings, then I shouldn't pay the ransom."

"No."

"I'll tell you, Ike, I don't care about the money one way or another, so tell me about the paintings. Do you think these professional thieves of yours will keep their end of the bargain if I pay?"

"Well, that's complicated. I believe we have two parties involved here: the people who stole the paintings and the people who contracted the first group to do it for them. I told you the first are pros, but I do not know about the second. Terrorists are impossible to predict. They lash out at anything or anybody. They're suicide bombers. They'll kill their grandmothers to make a point."

Dillon pulled out another cigarette and the box of matches. He stared at them for a moment, and then replaced both.

"Then you're saying I may or may not get my pictures back if I pay?"

"Yes, but not exactly. Let's take some hypothetical cases. One, you pay, the group holding the pictures gets your money. When they're away, they tell you where to pick up the stuff, or they notify their employers. If the latter, then you are dependent on their sense of fair play to tell you. Since they do not have such a sense, you have a fifty-fifty chance of getting your paintings back.

"Two, you don't pay, the first group pulls out. They have been paid part of their fee up front. My guess is that they will pack up and go."

"They won't burn the paintings?"

"They're thieves, Mr. Dillon, not vandals. What would be the point? No, they won't touch the paintings, but they may tell their employers where they are and you can bet they will burn them. And call the papers and television stations to watch them do it."

"The terrorists don't have them now?"

"I don't think so. Those truckloads of paintings are the only asset in the game. The thieves need them to get their payday. If you refuse to pay, the pictures are converted from an asset to a liability."

Dillon stared at the ceiling, turning Ike's words over.

"The hard part of an operation this big is keeping track of all the players. Where are the paintings now, Ike? Who has them?"

"I suspect they're close by, in a truck stop somewhere on I-81, a warehouse in Roanoke or Harrisonburg, maybe in an abandoned barn."

"If I don't pay and the terrorists don't destroy them, I'll get them back?"

"Oh sure, sooner or later, they'll turn up…next week, next year…eventually."

"Are you sure about all this?"

"I think so, but as I said, this is only my take, my best guess."

"Ike, you're not the bearer of the most cheerful news I've ever heard. Let me see if I've been following you—if I pay, there's at best a fifty-fifty chance I'll get the pictures, and no chance of recovering the money. If I don't pay, there's only a twenty-eighty chance I'll get the pictures, but I keep the money. In both cases, we aren't going to catch any of these people at all."

"I didn't say that, Mr. Dillon. I said paying or not paying will not catch them. If we get them, it will be because we did our homework and got lucky, but it will also be independent of the payment of the ransom."

"Finding the pictures is also an independent event?"

"Yes, sir."

Dillon stood and stretched. He walked to the window lost in thought. His back was to Ike. The chimes struck the hour, and when the last peal had finished resonating in the courtyard, he spoke as though addressing someone outside.

"Funny thing about art. My father bought fifty, sixty percent of that stuff in Paris in the Thirties. He was a very young man with a little money with no talent for painting. But he knew people who had it, and when they couldn't pay back the small loans he made them, they gave him a picture or two. He came home to the family business with a carload of impressionists. I have an undeserved reputation as a collector of classics. I am offered stuff all the time, Klees, Pollacks, Turners, at bargain rates. I doubt there is more than ten million tied up in the whole lot. It's appraised at half a billion now. It would take me a decade to sell them if I wanted to. But either way, the price is a paper one, it's not real."

Dillon was silent for a few moments, then, turning to Ike, said, "If you had fifty million dollars lying around loose, would you buy my collection, all of it? Any of it?"

"Nope."

"Neither would I. What would you do with fifty million dollars, Ike?"

"Mr. Dillon, there are a lot of underfed, underclothed, and undereducated children in this world. If I had that kind of money, I'd spend it on them, the kids who'll someday paint new pictures, dream new dreams. I'd spend it on the future."

"Thank you, Ike. I knew you weren't a cop. Now, let's get those two hotshots back in here. I've made a decision."

Chapter 28

Ike heard the squeal of brakes that announced the arrival of Billy Sutherlin.

"For crying out loud," Ike grumbled, "how many times do I have to tell him? He drives like a Baghdad taxi hack. Billy," Ike yelled as he entered, "I've told you a hundred times not to drive like that."

"How do, Ike. Hi, beautiful. Got something for you-all."

Billy was the youngest of Ike's deputies and the most unpredictable. He was bright, resourceful, and had a boyish charm that enabled him to find out things that were forever concealed from others on the force. He folded his blond, lanky frame into an old oak swivel chair and beamed, waiting for Ike to ask.

"Okay, Billy," Ike sighed, "what have you got?"

"Well, first of all, Rosalie down at the Shop 'n Save says she might have seen one of your guys on Saturday, the gray-haired one, buying clothes. I showed her the picture like you said."

"Clothes? What kind of clothes?" Ike asked.

"Well now, that's the funny part, Ike. Rosalie said he was buying women's clothes, underwear, and stuff like that. Oh, and a pair of jeans. Said he didn't seem too sure about sizes. She got the idea he was guessing—buying for someone he didn't know too well."

"Women's clothes. You're sure of that?" Ike asked.

"Don't know too many guys around here go in for brassieres and panties."

"That's good news, I think," Ike said.

"You think that means the hostages are still alive?" Essie broke in. "At least one of them?"

"Yes, I hope so."

"It might mean that whoever got them cares about them some, too," she added.

There was that, too. An astute observation, not one he or Billy would make. The woman's touch, he thought, and remembered Ruth's lecture about hiring a woman.

"What else?" Ike turned back to Billy.

"What?"

"You started this by saying, 'first of all.' When you do that, it means there's a 'second' to follow."

"Oh, yeah." Billy scratched his head and thought a moment. "I'm not sure this is as much help, but you can never tell. The county boys been checking the motels hereabouts and they didn't get anything positive. But one of them heard from the girl at Burger King that the big guy might have been in for food—carry out. Enough for a dozen folks, she said. Figured you'd want to know he was close."

"Maybe. He could be anybody, in fact, so could the guy at the Shop 'n Save. We are supposing the two I saw at the diner are involved and that these two are the same ones. It's kind of thin."

"Yeah, I expect so, but she did say when he paid, he emptied his pockets to get some change, and she noticed the keys. He had motel keys. You know, they got those plastic tags?"

"Which motel?" Ike was alert.

"Motels, Ike—different ones, she thought, because the shape and color of the plastic parts were different. She only saw the one good enough to tell. It was the Azalea, up near Lexington."

"Okay, Billy, get up there and check it out, and see what you can make on the other keys. Have her describe them, then check all of the motels around to see if you can find a match."

"Right, I'm on it." Billy launched himself into motion toward the door, clapping his Stetson on his head.

"Slowly," Ike shouted at his retreating back, and then winced as the door's slamming drowned out his words, winced again when he heard the roar of the car's engine, and shook his head at the squeal of tires.

He eased himself behind his desk and stared at the files and mail that had accumulated in the past three days, four if you count Sunday. He faced another Monday and thought how different this one felt compared to two weeks ago. That day he had met the formidable Dr. Ruth Harris. Now they were lovers. He guessed that would be what people would say about them. "I want you to meet 'my friend.' She's on vacation with her 'friend.'" What a culture. There were no boundaries. People moved in and out of relationships as easily as they changed socks. Commitment, if it ever came, ranked last on the list of things people wanted. He wondered how he felt about that. He guessed he did not like it very much, but he also guessed it would be the only arrangement Ruth would consider now, maybe ever. He decided he would think about that later. Right now, he wanted to savor the moment. He had spent most of the previous night at Ruth's again, and the memory made him smile.

Essie poked her head in the door. "Hate to break in on whatever thoughts are giving you that unnaturally nice expression this morning, but the phone is for you."

"Got it, thanks."

"You have the warrant?" Sam, the computer whiz.

"I do. You ready to tell me something?"

"Phone safe?"

"Sam, this is Picketsville, not Washington."

"Right. Just checking. You ready? The letter was typed on a computer in the history of art department."

"You're sure?"

"I tell you this, the guy's sharp, knows the system backward and forward."

"But you got him? It is a him?"

"Absolutely. But it took a while. The sneaky bastard—see, what he did was to wait until the student letter print job ended.

Then he called up the file, deleted the text, pasted in his text and printed it out, went to the printer, collected his copy. He closed the file without saving the changes—that meant the original text got put back and ta-dah—he's done and out clean—no trace. I didn't tumble to that until I saw we had one too many copies. Not something you'd notice right away. See, the log did note the file for the letter had been called up and where. No big deal but, under the circumstances…anyway, I traced the workstation and then…well, you don't want to know."

"Tell me anyway."

"I inspected his hard drive and found the deleted document, downloaded it and printed it out. Oh, and I froze the file on his hard drive if we have to go back for it again."

"You hacked your way into his machine."

"Some might say that."

"But you got the guy and you're sure?"

"Yep."

"Who, Sam? Who is he?"

"Oh, right, it was typed on Sergei Bialzac's machine."

"That doesn't mean he wrote it, of course. Anyone with a key to his office could have done it."

"Well, that's not true either."

"Why 'not true'?"

"How complete is your warrant? Does it cover just the computer stuff, or is it broader?"

"Sam, I don't believe this. It covers everything I could think of this morning—papers, files, personnel records, you name it. I can get the cafeteria cook's recipes if I want them."

"Trust me, I eat there, you don't want them. Okay, here's the second piece. Bialzac got permission to have his office single-keyed."

"What does that mean?"

"It means he has the only key. No one else could have gotten in and used his machine."

"They could break in."

"Possible. The lock was easy to pick."

"Sam, you're a wonder. How can I thank you?"

"Offer me a job."

"Excuse me?"

"Offer me a job. Picketsville may be small potatoes now, but with the industrial park coming in the next year or two, you're going to need me."

Now how did she find out about the park? Nobody in town, not even the mayor knew about that. Then he remembered her skill with computers. She was right, he could use her.

"Get back to you on that," he said and hung up.

"Essie," he shouted through the glass door, "who's close?"

"Billy, but he's looking into those key thingies."

"Oh right. Then call Whaite and tell him to pick up Sergei Bialzac, B-I-A-L-Z-A-C. I don't know where he lives, maybe in the Meadows. Look it up."

Then he remembered.

"And get me Millie Thompkins at the college."

Five minutes passed and his phone buzzed.

"Millie, a couple of weeks ago you were struggling with that new phone system, remember?"

"Not were, Ike, am. The dang thing is crazy. Why we have to have all this new stuff when the old stuff worked just fine is beyond me. I must be getting old."

"Millie, you are ageless. Try to remember—on that day you placed a call for someone to New Jersey. Do you happen to remember who?"

"Well, let me see. I write those numbers down on a pad right here. If I haven't torn off the sheet, I could tell you. Well, shoot, I did."

Ike's heart sank. It did not represent a crucial piece, but it could confirm.

"Wait, you're in luck, it got pushed down in the bottom of the drawer. Let's see. I put one in for Dr. Harris to Rutgers University, and one for Mr. Stewart to his partner in Haddonfield, that's New Jersey, but it's Philadelphia, you know. He was mighty pleased when he put that one through. And one for Dr. Bialzac."

"Millie, this is important. Do you have the number Bialzac called?"

"I do, Ike. You want it?"

"Please."

‹›‹›‹›

The television studio buzzed with activity. Armand Dillon sent his son, Charles, on an errand. He'd loved his son as a small child and watched helplessly as his mother, Dillon's first wife, turned him into an indecisive milquetoast. Now Charles the Second existed in an alcoholic haze. If Dillon had not seen the stuff his grandson seemed to be made of, he would have taken the corporation public, cashed out and gone fishing. But Charlie Three had the makings. All he needed was a reason to quit archeology and come to work for his grandfather. Dillon had a plan. In the meantime, he hired top managers, paid them a lot of money to run his company, and fired them at regular intervals, before they found a way to either steal or wreck it.

A group of men arrived with a heavy suitcase.

"That the stuff?" he asked.

"Yes, sir, thirty thousand dollars' worth of cubic zirconiums. You planning to do Home Shopping Network here?"

"No, son. Just going to play some hardball." He turned to Ike. "Think they'll do?"

"On television, sure. As the real thing, they won't fool anyone."

"Well, I haven't got time to round up fifty million dollars' worth of diamonds in the time they gave me. They think I have more pull than I do. The people at Harry Winston's couldn't put their hands on a pile that big in the time they gave me. I would have to go straight to De Beers and even then I'm not sure they could do it. Well, they're just going to have to put up with them for now," Dillon said and smiled wolfishly.

Ike pulled out his cell phone and called the office. "Anything, Essie?"

"Nothing, Ike. Whaite said Bialzac wasn't at his house and the neighbors don't know anything."

"Well, tell him to keep trying. Anything from Billy?"

"Nothing helpful. There's a ton of motels on this strip of the I-81."

"Okay, my phone's on if you need me."

‹ › ‹ › ‹ ›

The motel room was fetid with the accumulated airborne haze of too many men closed up in a small room for too long. Only Donati appeared calm, cool, and presentable. Red added a cigarette butt to the already substantial pile in the ashtray, belched, and fumbled for another. Angelo stared off into space, a permanent resident of that secret world he alone knew. Grafton fidgeted. He was tired, unkempt, needed a shower, and craved a drink, several drinks. Donati glanced at his watch and nodded to Angelo. Angelo picked up the remote, and the television lit up. He adjusted the channel and sat back, lost again.

The four of them sat and watched as the local station identified itself and announced with a crawl across the bottom of the picture and a voice-over that the regularly scheduled program would be delayed for a special announcement. The picture flickered, went blank, and came up again.

"This air time has been purchased by the Dillon Foundation. Speaking to you now, Mr. M. Armand Dillon."

Dillon sat at a table on what appeared to be a hastily assembled set. Behind him were bookshelves filled with matched bound volumes, statuary, and the sort of odds and ends people expect to see in the library or study of an important person. He faced the camera, a pile of bulky envelopes stacked to his right. The lights glinted off his rimless spectacles. He spoke without notes or cue cards.

"Good evening, ladies and gentlemen. My name is Armand Dillon. As most of you know by now, a substantial portion of an art collection bearing my name has been stolen from the storage facility located on the campus of Callend College in Virginia. The thieves are very professional, it appears."

"You got that right, old man," Red muttered.

"And since they are now watching this broadcast, I will say to them that their work was indeed very, very competent. They only made three mistakes."

He paused, his expression never changing, amiable but serious.

"The first was killing a security guard. Larceny is one thing, murder another. The stakes go up when a felony includes a capital crime. The second—taking hostages. That adds kidnapping to murder and makes it a federal offense. Not smart on their part.

"These thieves are part of a group calling itself the New Jihad. As nearly as we, the police, the FBI, and contacts I have in the Homeland Security department can determine, it is one of a dozen groups supported, I should say sponsored, by elements located in the Middle East, and dedicated to promoting terrorism. We are all aware of the terrible events of September eleventh and their aftermath. Well, these are some of the same people."

"No way," Red exclaimed. "Donati, are we working for ragheads?"

"Shut up and listen."

"The art collection is being held for ransom. Our thieves are smart enough to know that none of the items can ever be sold outright, but they believe that the intrinsic value of the collection is so great that I would be willing to pay a king's ransom for their return.

"I mentioned earlier they made three mistakes, but only spoke of two. The third mistake? Misreading me. I can be very generous or I can be as mean as a snake, it all depends on how I am approached. In any event, anyone with a grain of sense knows that you cannot push a snake, and those who know me will tell you it is a serious mistake to push me.

"Now, where does that leave us? First, there is the matter of this broadcast. The thieves' flair for the dramatic, a common conceit of terrorists, led them to insist I go on local television, at this day and time, and announce my willingness to accede to their demands. For reasons which will become clear later, I purchased time on five national networks, and there is a live pickup on CNN and its affiliates, so that anyone watching television anywhere in the United States is hearing this message."

"What is he up to?" Red muttered.

"Also, there is the matter of the ransom. The thieves demand I turn over to them, at the time and place of their choosing, fifty million dollars in diamonds. The specified sizes and cuts must be untraceable. As I said before, they are professionals.

"I wonder how many of you out there have ever seen fifty million dollars in diamonds, or in any other form, for that matter. Well, here next to me are fifty envelopes. Each contains one million dollars in diamonds. Imagine. One business-sized envelope can hold a million dollars. It can be tucked into your pocket and taken anywhere. It will not be detected at airports or customs. Remarkable."

Dillon, while he spoke, opened in turn ten of the envelopes and poured their contents on the table in front of him. The pile of diamonds grew. It sparkled and shimmered and burned holes in the picture.

"Ten million dollars, and these other envelopes contain the rest." He gestured and two uniformed men moved beside him. They proceeded to open all but five of the remaining envelopes. The pile of diamonds grew, spilled over, and scattered on the floor.

"My friends, these diamonds spell pain, violence, and death for a lot of people if they're put in the wrong hands. Put in the right hands, they could bring hope, joy, and a chance for a new life to thousands of others.

"What should I do? What would you do? Give in to their demands, or give hope to those less fortunate than we? As you can imagine, I wrestled with that for a long time. I consulted my friends and family and I have now come to a decision.

"Even though I may be responsible for the greatest cultural desecration since Caesar's legions burned the library at Alexandria two thousand years ago, I will not, I repeat, I will not put this money into the hands of irresponsible international criminals. No painting is worth even one human life.

"I will, instead, put forty-five million dollars into a trust fund which will be used to foster the development of the next generation of artists—the Dillon Scholarships in the Fine Arts. Dillon gestured toward the shimmering pile in front of him. He paused, then picked up the five unopened envelopes and continued, "The last five million will be used in another way. Our thieves, as I have said, are professionals. They have so far eluded the best efforts by the police. I have no doubt they will someday be caught, but to make that day sooner rather than later, I am offering this five million dollars to the person who brings our thieves to justice.

"I am speaking to them, now. You are in trouble. Every police officer, private detective, bounty hunter, and amateur sleuth in the world will be looking for you. I know people who would sell their own children into white slavery for one-hundredth of that amount. What chance do you have now? The terrorists are now the terrorized. And as for the paintings, return them or burn them...I will not pay."

Chapter 29

His neighbors said Sergei Bialzac often disappeared for long periods of time. Never missed work, it seemed, but lodged somewhere else. What they did not know, what nobody knew was that Sergei maintained two homes. He shared the second with his lover Samir, a Syrian national. Sergei did not know it, but Samir also held a colonel's commission in Al Qaida.

They sat in stunned silence. The television flickered as the regular programs returned.

"What does it mean, Sammy? He isn't paying?"

"That is what he said."

"What will we do now?"

"You have failed. It is over." Samir rose, picked up his jacket, and moved toward the door.

"Me? I failed?"

"Yes, you. It was your idea, this ransom. You dealt with the Italian, who must now die, and you set the time and date. It is your failure."

"But I thought—"

"You did not think. You are finished."

"Where are you going?" he asked.

"Where? To get the paintings, of course. I have buyers on the black market in my part of the world, willing to pay a fortune for them. He thinks he will not support us? He will see how wrong he is."

"But aren't you going to burn them?"

"Burn them? Don't be ridiculous. There is a C-130 Hercules with Egyptian Air Force markings sitting on the freight ramp at Baltimore-Washington International waiting to load and fly. Did you think we were going to burn them? We could ransom them many times."

"How?"

"You put one in a sale. People say, 'the Dillon collection, it is not burned.' You sell them back, a million here, five million there. Museums, governments fall all over themselves to be the one to save western culture. Fools."

"What about us?" Bialzac pleaded.

"Us? There is no us. There never was, you pathetic faggot. You were useful, now you are not."

Bialzac let the enormity of his betrayal sink in. He had come to believe with all his heart that the country that had nourished him and sheltered him all his life somehow deserved punishment, humbling, and like so many radicals turned revolutionaries, he had lost sight of the way reform got done. Now he sat and stared in disbelief as his whole credo crumbled like a stale cookie.

Samir strode toward the door. As he reached for the latch, he snapped upward. A second and then a third bullet tore into his back and heart. Bialzac emptied the chamber of the thirty-eight-caliber pistol into the now lifeless body of his lover and betrayer.

‹›‹›‹›

Ten miles south, Bialzac's contractors sat in the same stunned silence. Harry Grafton felt sweat trickle down his back. The room filled with the smell of fear, overwhelming the stale smoke and close air. He wondered if M. Armand Dillon realized that in his zeal to prevent the death and injury to innocent victims, he had signed the death warrant for at least two people, maybe more. The girl and boy could identify all four of them. At least the girl could. So here we are, he thought. What now?

Red removed a fat wallet from his hip pocket and placed it on the table next to his right hand. He drummed his stubby fingers and picked his teeth. Donati held out his hand to Angelo, who looked at him, hesitated a moment, then put his silenced Colt 1911 in it.

"Angelo," Donati said, his voice expressionless, eyes bleak, unreadable, like slate, "get our hostages."

Angelo left the room and went next door. A moment later he returned, pushing the boy and girl into the room ahead of him. He sat them on one of the beds. Donati murmured something to him. He left again, returned, went into the bathroom and a moment later came out. He carried all the remaining telephone cords from all the telephones. He disconnected the one on the phone between the beds, pulled out a pocketknife, opened it, cut the cords into pieces, and dumped them onto the empty bed.

"All of them not working?" asked Donati.

Angelo nodded.

"That's so none of you think you're going to be instant millionaires. Now, we have some decisions to make."

Red spoke, his voice very low. Harry was startled by its softness, the redneck accent gone, the inflection almost cultured. Red on the defensive was a very different person than on the attack.

"The kids go."

Donati nodded his agreement.

"Oh my God, why? What's happened?" the girl wailed, her voice a full octave higher than normal. She looked at Grafton. "You said that we would be okay. I believed you."

"I hoped, kid, I hoped, but it's gone sour."

"Shut up, Grafton."

"My God, Donati, they have a right to know why they have to die. The project fell through, Jennifer, and there is a reward hanging over us, a big reward. We are all going to die. Am I right, Donati, the two of them, me, Red, everyone, maybe even Angelo? All of us have to go, don't we?"

The boy shrieked. Angelo hit him on the temple. He rolled off the bed and onto the floor, his body wedged into the small space between the wall and the mattress.

They stared at each other in silence. Harry fumbled in his pocket for a cigarette, found only an empty package, and reached for his jacket. He remembered the right-hand pocket had a fresh pack. His fingers closed around it and he felt something else—the phone cord he had removed three days ago.

He slipped on the jacket, lit one of the cigarettes, and counted to twenty. He wanted to wait longer but he did not know how much time he had. He clutched at his stomach, and groaned.

"What's the matter with you, Grafton?"

"Cramps. I guess too much…no drinks. I don't know. I've got to use the john."

Donati stared at him, and then nodded. Harry, pain still etched onto his face, staggered past Red and into the bathroom. He kicked the door shut and moaned. He turned on the water in the sink and jerked out the telephone cord, connected its modular clips and punched in 9-1-1. Moan. Come on. Come on. Moan. To his surprise he found his diarrhea was real.

"Go ahead," the 9-1-1 operator said.

"Lee-Jackson Motel, room fourteen, art thieves, hurry," he rasped, his voice a whisper.

"Sir, where are you calling from?"

"Lee-Jackson Motel. The guys you are looking for are here but you have to hurry. Room fourteen." He moaned some more, hoping he covered the words. Harry hung up and disconnected the cord as Angelo pushed the door open. He reached for toilet paper, palmed the cord into a wad, used it, and flushed it away. For the first time in over a week, Harry saw Angelo smile.

"You that scared, yeah?"

"Yeah, I guess so," Harry answered, his voice somewhere between a moan and a croak.

"Vito wants you back now."

Harry nodded, pulled up his pants, and reentered the room. Stall for time, he thought, just stall for time.

The girl's eyes were as big as saucers. He tried to signal her, will her to hear his unspoken message, hang on, help is on the way, just hang on.

‹›‹›‹›

Dillon waited until the lights dimmed and turned to Ike.

"Well, what do you think?"

"Nice show, sir, forceful, sincere, believable. You could get elected to office on that speech."

"Not interested. You think it went well, then?"

"Yes, sir, very well. I just hope the hostages understand why they have to die."

"Can't be helped, son. Collateral damage, isn't that what you guys call it?"

"Not us guys, Mr. Dillon, government wonks, people like Kenny, military types who need to justify a misplaced bomb strike, industrialists like yourself, who close plants and lay off thousands to preserve stockholder profits, but not us, not me. No, sir."

Dillon bristled at Ike's tone. "What do you call it, then?"

"An avoidable tragedy."

"How avoidable? We were right on top of this. We had no way of knowing about those students."

"Avoidable, Mr. Dillon. Avoidable if my office had been called in as soon as the robbery was discovered, not six hours later. Avoidable if someone had the good sense or even just the common courtesy to inform me of the move in the first place. I would have put a patrol down at the bunker. A move like that is an open invitation for just what occurred. Avoidable if someone had taken the time to check out Loyal Parker before giving him a license to set up his personal peep show. There is no excuse for that Lover's Lane to exist, and both Parker and the hostages should be alive now. An avoidable tragedy created by academic and class conceit, by arrogance that assumes that out in the sticks, police are all bumbling rubes or Barney Fife. We can't cut it so we need the government or our betters from the big city to come in and solve our problems for us."

Dillon blanched under Ike's verbal onslaught.

"Sorry, Ike, I didn't know."

"You didn't want to know, Mr. Dillon, you assumed."

Dillon glared at Ike with a look that had melted more than one chief operating officer. Ike glared back. Dillon opened his mouth to say something just as Ike's cell phone twittered.

"Yeah?"

"Ike, 9-1-1 just called in an emergency. Listen." Ike listened to the recording.

"I'm on my way. Get Billy and Whaite on the road and call Scarlett's people—and no sirens."

"Sheriff?" Dillon asked.

"Got to go."

Ike raced out to the parking lot and within thirty seconds his car spun out of the parking lot, kicking gravel on several expensive corporate cars. It had happened fast, too fast. Real professionals would fence around for hours, days even, before one would break and run. It could be a crank call, or did someone get through? Why? Who? What's-his-name, the ex-Bureau guy, the locksmith, the one who bought the clothes; it had to be him. No matter what else happens to people, they never change, and according to Charlie, the man was a good, honest technician. He hoped that the message meant the hostages were still alive, that Grafton, that was the name, called in not only to save his own skin, but the kids as well. He hoped.

‹›‹›‹›

Harry talked, stalled, and tried to kill time. Donati stared at him, revealing nothing. Angelo maintained his state of apparent transcendence. Finally, Red interrupted.

"Stuff it, Grafton. You are not going to talk your way out of here. Fact—some of us have to go. First, we take those two out." He nodded at the girl and in the direction of the still unconscious boy. "Then, Rummy, it's you. Donati and the Italian sphinx over there, well, we go back a ways. I figure we'll just fade, fold this hand, and play another some other day, right, Donati?"

Donati continued to stare at a point midway between Harry and Red. He handed Angelo the Colt and in a barely audible voice said, "Angelo, do it."

Red picked up his wallet and had the Hi-Standard derringer out, cocked and aimed at Angelo in less than a second. He was not fast enough. The silenced Colt gave a gentle burp and sent a copper-jacketed slug between Red's eyes. Harry launched himself out of his chair toward Angelo, who stepped aside. Harry's momentum carried him past Angelo and to the girl. He collapsed on her, half protecting her. He braced himself for the shock of the bullet. Nothing happened. He turned to see what had happened, grateful for the respite, even if brief. Jennifer fainted.

Angelo faced Donati. "I am sorry, *Patrone*." He looked woebegone. "You see it is this way, the Giacomo family? Their youngest...you were contracted to eliminate. They put out a contract on you. You understand how it goes, yes?"

"Wait a minute. My contract also said Martelli would cover me. Angelo, there are always these contracts, but they go away when they need me again. This will be no different, you will see. Now take care of—"

"No, Vito, it is different this time. Martelli, he found out who contracted us. He wants no part of this new thing. He said he did not want anything to do with you now."

"There is no new thing. We are paid to do a certain job, that's all. What is so different about this one?"

"These people are with the ones who killed all the people in the World Trade Center. He says we don't do business with them."

"Since when has the Family made such a distinction? We run cocaine for South American dictators and heroin for the people he now says we cannot do business with. It's crazy."

"Even so, he told Giacomo to proceed. Giacomo has my mother and father in Sicily, you know, my sister, too, and they say if I do not do this, they will do terrible things and then kill them. They will. In Sicily, they are very true about those things, you know. Giacomo will see to that."

"*Si*, Angelo, I know. So now you must shoot me, and you would have to, no matter what, yes?"

"Yes, Vito, I must. I have no choice in this."

Donati looked at Angelo for a long time, saw the gun steady in his hand and sighed, "So shoot."

"Not me. This Red person, he will be the one who does it. First, he kills these three, then he tries to kill you and you shoot each other."

Angelo picked up the derringer and leveled it at Donati.

The door crashed open at the same instant the gun fired. Donati pitched backward into the dresser, the snub-nosed Smith and Wesson from his ankle holster halfway out. Angelo spun toward the door. Ike crouched, gun held two-handed and ready. For a split second, Angelo hesitated, unsure which gun to use. He lowered the derringer just as Ike's three fifty-seven magnum barked. Angelo, chest crushed, slammed into the wall and onto the floor.

Ike straightened up and looked at Harry.

"You called?"

Harry swallowed and nodded.

"You must be Grafton. Where's the other kid—is he okay?"

Harry motioned toward the wall. "I think so, knocked silly, and in shock. Doesn't know what happened to him. She," he pointed to Jennifer, "on the other hand, can give it all to you."

"But you called, right?"

"Right."

"Why?"

"Because I didn't want anyone hurt, because they were going to kill Jennifer, the girl, both of them. Me, I didn't care about. Hell, this just isn't my line of country."

"So I hear."

"What now?"

Ike studied Grafton, saw the pain, old pain, in his eyes, and recognized it. He looked at the girl, fainted. Just as well.

"Grafton, according to my information, you went camping up in the Adirondacks last week. And you have twenty seconds to get out of here, into that rental and away. If you are smart, you will lose that car in Richmond, go north for a day or two, camp out, and then go home. You are the one that got away.

"When you get back to your apartment, you will be contacted by some people who will want to talk to you about a job, a real job. You *will* talk to them, Grafton."

Harry read the implied threat in Ike's face, nodded and glanced at the girl, Ike, and the bodies on the floor.

"Thanks, I owe you."

"You sure'n hell do, Grafton."

Harry was driving out of the motel parking lot when Ike heard the sirens.

"I said no sirens."

The girl came to, her eyes focused, and she shuddered.

"You're the police."

"Right the first time. And you are Jennifer...somebody."

"Ames. Where's Har—the other one?"

Ike smiled. "What other one? Oh well, shoot, he managed to get away in the confusion."

"Get away? How? He really did?"

"Slick as a weasel."

"I'm glad. You know, he didn't belong in this."

"You're glad?" Ike asked, surprised and relieved.

"Yes."

"Then do me, and him, a favor. You never saw him, are we clear on that?"

"He wasn't here. The man who did the alarms was, ah...."

"Short and dark."

"Short and dark, and was called...."

"Hareem, Achmed Hareem. Sounds a little like Harry, doesn't it?"

"Hareem, yes, that is what they called him. Jack may remember Harry, but then he was in such a state, who'll believe him. Hareem."

"Hareem was Interpol's guess. They will be happy to find out they were right."

The sounds of sirens and screeching brakes announced the arrival of the state police. Ike winked at Jennifer. She winked back.

Chapter 30

Two hours passed before Ike could break away from the crowd. Dennis Kenny pestered him with questions and took Jennifer's statement. Asked her again about the man who got away. She lied smoothly and convincingly. Essie called to tell him about a shooting in Lexington. A witness said they saw a man leaving the area who might have been Bialzac. Later, a neighbor identified Bialzac as one of two men who rented the apartment where the shooting took place. They had not identified the victim yet but the neighbor thought they were "an item."

Ruth arrived as he finished filling in Scarlett's people. Kenny stared at him, a puzzled look on his round face.

"What happened here?" he asked.

"Agent Kenny, go home and tell them you lost your guy. How you're not even sure it was your guy."

"I'm not looking for anybody in particular. Why do you think that?"

"Because your plan to retrieve the paintings had nothing to do with them or the hostages. You wanted Harry Grafton and you were willing to sacrifice the rest to get him."

"You—"

"Don't even say it. I'm tired and I'm pretty sure they sent you in the hope you'd screw this up, so they won't mind much if you end up on extended sick leave for injuries received in the pursuit of your duty. I don't want to sound mean, but are you sure this is what you want to do the rest of your life?"

Kenny looked at his feet and sighed.

"Tell you what you do. Stick with the Achmed Hareem story. It's better for you and the Bureau. That way, they won't put you on permanent desk duty."

Kenny gave him a rueful smile and started to say something, then thought better of it and left.

"You could have been killed, Ike," Ruth said as she watched Kenny sidle away. "I was worried."

"All in a day's work, Ruth," Ike said, with more nonchalance than he felt. No doubt about that, he could have been killed. He guessed he was getting too old or, maybe old enough to realize that he did not need this kind of excitement anymore.

His cell phone summoned him again. Lee Henry's voice cut through the air like a mountain breeze.

"They told me I might could get you at this number, lover-boy. Remember you asked me to keep my ears open about some truckers or something? Well, my friend and some of his buddies was together last night at the Midway and I sort of primed them, you know, and one of them said something about a pair of high cubes, painted like Titan Moving vans, but they weren't because of the shape. Anyway, he saw them up and down I-81 for a couple of days, you know what I mean, Ike? Parked here, parked there, but looked like the same ones being shifted around. So I says 'Where're they at now' and he said 'They're over to the big Phillips 66 stop.' So there you are, Ike. Is that a help?"

"I hope so, Lee. I sure hope so, and thanks. I'll tell you how it comes out."

"You do that, honey, and you be careful, hear?"

"I'll do that. Thanks."

Ike snapped the phone closed. Ruth's eyebrows were making question marks on her forehead.

"We may have the paintings. There are two trailers still parked over at a truck stop ten miles north of here. I hope I can get there before Bialzac and his friends."

"Will it be dangerous, Ike?"

"No, no, just routine. Catch you later."

Ike strode across the parking lot and slipped behind the wheel of his car. Just as the motor caught, Ruth slid in beside him.

"Ruth, what do you think you're doing?"

"I'm going with you, Sheriff. See how the other half lives, so to speak. Be a nice change for me to ride in the front seat in one of these things."

"Ruth, you can't. It might be dangerous."

"Just routine, you said. Come on, you are wasting time. I'll be fine."

"No!"

"What? Why no? I'll stay out of the way."

Ike felt sick. The heat was oppressive, but he felt cold. He stared at Ruth—fear, panic, and memories, another time. Her words were the same.

"Ike," Ruth said, "this is not Zurich. Now go, or Bialzac will get there first."

Ike hesitated.

"Go! You've got to go now or it will never be over."

Ike put the car in gear.

There were fifty or sixty trailers parked in rows at the truck stop. Some, perhaps twenty, were attached to their tractors. The remainder stood alone, poised mantis-like on their stilt-like front props. Ike drove down one aisle, his eyes searching underneath, between, on the top of each. Halfway down the row he saw his man in the next row over.

"Hang on," he barked, and floored the accelerator. The police car leapt forward with a squeal of tires. A misplaced travel trailer blocked his entry to the aisle between the two rows of trailers. He jammed the car into reverse. It shot backward, fishtailing to the point where he had seen Bialzac. He was aware of the thump Ruth's forehead made as she was thrown forward against the dash.

"Seat belt on," Ike muttered.

"Thanks for the warning," Ruth retorted, rubbing her forehead and bracing her shoulders against the seat back in preparation for what she assumed would be an equally abrupt halt.

Ike braked and poured out the door in one disjointed but neatly executed motion. He tossed her his shoulder radio.

"Call for help," he said, his eyes glued on the figure between the two trailers, "And call the fire department."

Ike ran toward Bialzac.

"I don't know how to work these things."

"Just push the round button and talk," he shouted over his shoulder, "someone will hear you."

Bialzac teetered on an extension ladder placed against the brightly painted side of one of the trailers. He had climbed halfway up, his progress impeded by the plastic five-gallon can he was hoisting up with him. Ike saw three more at the foot of the ladder and another four containers in the back of the minivan parked at the far end of the passage created by the two rows of trailers.

He reached for his service revolver and then changed his mind.

"Bialzac," Ike called, his arms spread, hands held out, palms up. "Bialzac, stop. It's all over. Don't do it."

Sergei Bialzac paused in his climb and, owl-like, peered down at Ike. Ike didn't like the look in those eyes and decided the little professor no longer inhabited this world. His eyes were wild, taking in some other scene, some other time. He stopped and watched, waiting for the opportunity to step in and disengage the man from his mission.

"Bialzac, don't. It's over. Think of the paintings, what they mean to you. You told me...."

"No," Bialzac shouted, "they must be destroyed. The structure of a corrupt government must be attacked at its roots...betrayal....
" He paused and more quietly added, "He never intended to do this, he lied...."

As spoke, his left foot missed the next rung on the ladder. In his agitated state, distracted by the thought of imminent failure and, Ike guessed, the shooting earlier, and off balance, his other foot slipped and his one arm, the one not grasping the jerry can, could not hold the sudden weight of his falling body. He hung for a split second and then fell, arms outstretched to break his fall. The jerry can, released from his grip, fell into the other three a split second before Bialzac landed on all of them. His weight on the cans caused them to rupture, and their contents geysered up and over him.

Bialzac, stunned, sat like a small Buddha in the wreckage of cans. He shook his head like a wet dog. Droplets haloed his head and beard. He snorted in anger, frustration, and pain. Ike took a step forward and then stopped in horror.

"Don't do it, for God's sake....Freeze!" he screamed, with all the authority he could muster.

Bialzac struggled to free something from his belt and Ike recognized a cheap, nickel-plated revolver. Ike's next words were lost in the report as the hammer, caught in a fold of cloth, released and fired. Ike saw bright little sparks from the ricocheting bullet and then heard the whoomp as the gasoline fumes ignited. In that frozen moment, Ike saw the look of puzzled amazement on Bialzac's face, and then the little professor disappeared into a pillar of fire.

In the next few seconds, whatever passed for a soul in Sergei Bialzac made its transit into the next world. The heat from Bialzac's pyre was too intense to permit Ike to get within eight feet. He could only watch in horror. Ruth grabbed his arm and choked, "Oh my God," and buried her head in his shoulder as the remains of Bialzac toppled over in a shower of sparks.

Sirens screamed at them from every direction. State police, firemen, and Ike's deputies seemed everywhere.

He put his arm around Ruth and walked her back to the car. "Let's get out of here."

Chapter 31

Bells ringing.

He must be late for class. He held Ruth by the hand, urging her to hurry, not to be late. But she hesitated, afraid, and kept repeating something—how she could never pass the course anyway so why bother. Ike said she could, but she would have to try harder. He failed once himself, but knew he could pass this time. How hard could it be?

Other students scampered by. "Ikey's got a girlfriend, Ikey's got a girlfriend, nyah, nyah," they sing-songed at him. Margie Tice cartwheeled past in her cheerleader uniform. Charlie Garland, dressed in tweed short pants, appeared at his side, looking like Harry Potter, and said solemnly, "We've got to meet after class, Ike—at the secret clubhouse."

The room filled with people running, yelling, and then they were gone. Ike panicked. Someone was It and looking for him. He needed to hide—no, run to home base, be in free.

The bells were the fire alarm. The school was on fire and he had to get out.

"This way," he shouted at Ruth, "we've got to go to the roof and jump." She pulled away from him.

"No, I can't," she sobbed, "it hurt the last time. We all get hurt with you, when we go with you. Don't ask us to. You take us to the wrong places." Ike felt guilt without knowing why. When? I didn't know you then. "Ikey's got a girlfriend, Ikey's got a girlfriend."

Ruth's face dissolved, replaced by Eloise's.

"No!"

‹ › ‹ › ‹ ›

He woke with a start. His mouth was dry and sweat poured from his forehead and soaked the sheets between his shoulder blades. His heart raced. The phone kept up its insistent clamor. His heartbeat slowed and he recognized his surroundings, the familiar furniture of his bedroom outlined in the light that managed to filter through the blinds. He was home. Safe.

He reached for the phone. "Schwartz," he grunted.

"Ike? What have you been doing? I've been trying to get you all afternoon. I tried your office and filled your answering machine with a dozen messages." Ruth's voice was controlled, but Ike heard the worry in it.

"I'm fine, Ruth," he reassured her. "I came home after I dropped you off, took a shower, mixed myself a stiff drink, several stiff drinks in fact, and fell asleep. I guess I was out."

"Are you okay, Ike?" Ruth asked. "You sound, I don't know—strange."

"Bad dream, Ruth, about you and me, and secrets, and fire. I guess it got to me. But I'm fine."

"That's what happens when you sleep alone, Schwartz. No one there to make the dreams come out right. Now, do you want to ask me why I called, or do I have to blurt it out?"

"Why did you call?"

"To tell you that Mr. M. Armand Dillon is dancing around here like a girl who's just been named Miss America. He's thanking everybody and everything, giving interviews to the press, and asking me every ten minutes or so where you are. You are a hero, Ike Schwartz. The world is awaiting your appearance, wants to interview you, take your photograph, get your autograph!"

"Goody. They still there?"

"Well, no. When you didn't show up, they all left. They had deadlines to meet if the story was going to make the six o'clock news or the morning paper, but they'll be back tomorrow."

"Whoopee."

"And…are you listening?"

"I'm listening while I plan my escape to the border."

"M. Armand is having a party tonight, here at the college, and you're invited."

"Can't make it, Ruth. Give him my regrets."

"Ike, you've got to come. You're the guest of honor."

"You fill in for me. Tell everyone I have an acute case of low back pain and can't be there. Tell them anything."

"Ike, you have to. You can't hide anymore. Even if you wanted to, you can't, so why not come on out and get it over with? It's not so bad out here in the daylight. Besides," she added roguishly, "if you want a case of low back pain, I'll arrange for that, after everyone else leaves."

"Ruth, I don't want—"

"Ike," Ruth snapped, "if you ever want to get me in bed again, you'll haul your butt out here tonight at seven-thirty sharp."

"You are a hard woman. I'll be there, at eight, give or take."

"Be seeing you, Sheriff."

Ike replaced the receiver in the cradle and fumbled for his watch. Six-fifteen. He could just make it.

〈〉〈〉〈〉

The mayor and three members of the Town Council stood beaming in front of some television cameras. The local news channel, serving as the pickup for the network, was set up by the steps to the long porch and interviewed guests as they arrived. The mayor caught sight of Ike and signaled him over.

"Here's the man you want to interview," he brayed, "Sheriff Ike Schwartz, the man of the hour."

Ike groaned. No escape possible—he stepped in front of the cameras. Questions flew at him from every direction. He managed a few perfunctory replies and begged off. The mayor turned, still grinning like the trained chimpanzee Ike always thought him to be, and asked if there was anything the city could do for him.

"Well, yes, Mr. Mayor," Ike said, face serious. "I could use a position or two. The town has doubled in population in the past five years. There is a rumor that some major development is on its way here, and we are at the same staffing levels as ten years ago. Do you, does the Town Council, think they could manage some help in the Sheriff's Department?"

"Absolutely. Great idea, Sheriff," the mayor choked. His council members agreed, their smiles botoxed in place. "Absolutely."

"That's all, thanks," Ike said, his own smile sincere next to theirs.

The party had been set up in the large lobby of the main building. Guests filled plates, picked up drinks, and moved out on the wisteria-laden porch to see and be seen. Ike saw the Dillons, *père et fils*, near the fireplace. Colonel Scarlett and two of his minions stood, shuffling their feet, by one of three punch bowls. The fancy young man, the gallery owner from New York, drifted around the room, and there were others—faculty and spouses, a few law enforcement types, and what passed for society in Picketsville. Ike edged his way to the bar and asked the ancient waiter in a white jacket for a gin and tonic. M. Armand Dillon drew up in front of him.

"Well, Schwartz, I owe you a million. Five million, in fact."

"All in a day's work, Mad Dog."

"I mean it. I owe you five million dollars. I said on television that I would give five of the fifty million dollars to the person who caught the bastards. You did. You get it."

"I can't accept. I was on duty and it's in my job description. State law prohibits taking recompense or rewards for actions which the town pays me to do full-time. Give it to the college. Maybe it will help make up for the revenue loss they will suffer after the collection is moved. Or have you changed your mind about that?"

"No. The collection goes. But I have already taken care of the college. The other forty-five million will go to endow scholarships in the fine arts here. Forty-five million dollars buys a lot of financial security."

"Make it an even fifty then."

"You're sure?"

"I'm sure."

"You know, you're quite a guy. I was talking about you to your father just now."

"Abe's here?" Ike looked over the room. Sure enough, there was his father bending ears, pressing the flesh, working the room as though he were running for office again. You can take the boy out of politics, Ike thought, but you will never get the politics out of the boy.

"We had a nice chat about you and what you should be doing next."

"Now listen," Ike said, "I will decide what my future will be, not my father, not you."

"Of course, dear boy," Dillon said, "but you should know that when you're ready to run for attorney general, the backing will be there."

"Attorney general? You've got to be kidding."

"Not at all. You are a natural. And the seat will be open. Incumbent is retiring this year for personal reasons. An easy primary, a close general, and you're in," Dillon said, with the air of a man who had been there before, often, which he had, and for far higher stakes. Dillon had helped make presidents. The attorney general of Virginia would be pretty small potatoes to him.

"No, thanks," Ike said.

"Think about it, Sheriff. All I ask is that you think about it....Talk to you later." Dillon raised his glass and bestowed a crooked-toothed smile on Ike. He turned and moved back into the crowd. Ike's eyes followed him until his path intersected with Ike's view of Ruth. She was busy talking to Marge Tice. As if on cue, the two women looked at him, flashed him identical smiles, and turned back to their conversation.

His knees felt wobbly. He decided he needed another drink. His glass replenished, he made his way around the buffet. Between mouthfuls of cheese, chips, and dip, he fended off a conversation with his father—attorney general, my eye. He accepted congratulations from four or five couples, spoke with two faculty members, one who wanted his views on gun control and another from the English department, who told him he was going to write a book about the robbery and asked if he would mind being interviewed. Ike said he would be delighted.

Essie Falcao arrived on Billy Sutherlin's arm. The two had a quick, quiet argument that ended when Billy agreed to take off his cowboy hat. Essie waved at Ike. Ike waved back and smiled.

Sam the techno-geek arrived and walked, stork-like, toward Ike.

"About that job, Sheriff."

"It's yours if you want it. Everybody is so pumped tonight, I asked the mayor for a new position, and he said sure. He did that on national television so it's a done deal. It's yours if you want it."

"Just like that?"

"Just like that. You are now, or in the next few weeks will be, a real deputy sheriff with all the rights and privileges appertaining thereto, and all that. I leave it to you to break the news to your boss."

"Wow!"

"And put that piece away. This is a party, not a shootout."

"Yes, sir."

"Sam, there's something I wanted to ask you—"

"No. I did not play basketball in college. But I made alternate for the Olympic volleyball team. That answer you?"

"Pretty much."

He returned to the buffet and, left to his own devices, finished off half a plate of deviled eggs and was attacking a tub of Swedish meatballs when he sensed Ruth's presence at his elbow.

"Hello, hero," she said, twinkling. "I hear I owe you five million bucks. How can I ever pay you?"

"I'll take it out in trade," Ike said gruffly. "Let's see, at a hundred dollars a...um, I expect it'll take you about a thousand years working every day and most nights to pay me off. You interested?"

"I don't work cheap, Sheriff. Don't forget I'm a Ph.D. I'll be done with you in about two hundred years—if you can stand it, sooner."

Ike grinned and sipped his drink. "When can you start?"

"Tonight's fine with me, big spender. Just as soon as these folks eat up all the food and go home, you're on."

"You're a tough lady, Ruth."

"I only sound like a tough lady, Ike. You know me well enough by now to know that it's mostly show."

They stood in silence for a while admiring each other. Ruth cocked her head and gave him a quizzical look.

"Ike, how well do you know Marge Tice?"

"My first true love. I thought she was the most beautiful girl in the world and more than anything else I wanted to have her. That was a long time ago, high school."

"Did you? Have her, I mean? Hey it's none of my business…who am I to—"

"No, it never happened, much to my sorrow. Why ask about Marge?"

"Well, she said something strange about you. About billiards, I think."

"Billiards?"

"I think so. She said…let me see, 'If you ever get a chance to take him on in a pool hall,' I think that's right, 'If you ever get the chance to take him on in a pool room, grab it.' Does that mean anything to you?"

"Not a thing."

Chapter 32

The cab dropped Ike off in front of one of those old-fashioned apartment buildings located on the northern end of Connecticut Avenue. Built in the Twenties for Washington's young elite, they deteriorated in the Fifties and Sixties and then became fashionable again in the Nineties as condominiums and co-ops. Apartments that a few years before had rented for a few hundred dollars a month were renovated and sold for a quarter to a half million dollars apiece. Ike looked for Charlie's name next to the door buzzers. No Charlie. He had said 814. The name next to 814 was E. Farnham. Elwood again. Ike's eyebrows knotted in a frown. He wondered what Charlie was up to now. He rang and pushed through the foyer door as the electric lock buzzed him in. He rode the shiny new elevator to the eighth floor.

Charlie met him at the door of 814.

"Ike. Come on in. This is great! Look who's here, Peter. It's Ike."

Peter Hotchkiss lounged in a big recliner and waved a greeting to Ike. "Welcome back to the world of the living. It's been a long time."

"Hello, Peter. I guess you're right. I've been out of touch."

Charlie handed Ike a gin and tonic, then sprawled on the couch.

"Well, how does it feel to be a crime buster, Ike?"

"A what?"

"Crime-buster. That's what they used to call guys like you. You are all over the papers, 'Rural sheriff cracks art theft. Son of politically prominent former Virginia comptroller foils terrorist attempt to destroy five-hundred-million-dollar art collection.' Blah, blah, blah. You are a crime-buster, a hot property, as they say in show biz. Got any movie offers? People want to write your life story, stuff like that?"

Ike squirmed under the barrage. Peter smiled.

"Charlie's an unreconstructed P.R. flak. All he sees are headlines and chances to schedule press conferences."

"I'll tell you, Ike, Peter is almost right. We've had a run of bad press at the Agency—enough to drive a man to drink. Now, I am ready for a change. I need to do something about my sagging career and ego. It's obvious what you need is a good agent. Let me negotiate with the Hollywood scouts and book writers. Hell, I could even run your election campaign."

"I haven't decided to run for anything, Charlie. It's just talk. What makes you think I'd want to run for…whatever?"

"Ike, the nice thing about you is you're predictable. Put you in a certain situation, crank up the right physical and emotional stimuli, and you are as predictable as one of Pavlov's dogs. I can read you like a book, old man."

"And everybody else can, too?"

"Oh, absolutely. Easiest thing in the world."

"Then how did I survive so long in the field when I was with the Agency? If I'm so predictable, I'd have been wasted years ago."

"That's what's so nice about you, Schwartz. You do not know your strengths. You are predictable, yes, but also thorough, clever, resourceful, and very smart—those things, too. You do not make mistakes. And if the other side didn't know the plan—the stimulus—they could not predict the response. All they knew is you were the best we had, and they respected you. For them, the predictable part of you was that you could be trusted and you had integrity. No, they'd never, ever take you out, Ike. You were a good adversary—good at what you did, and even though you beat them more often than not, they'd rather be beaten by you than win with someone else."

"They miss you over there," Peter chimed in.

"You two are not here, by any chance, to talk me into coming back to work, are you?"

"Furthest thing from my mind," said Charlie. Peter studied Ike, assessing the possibilities, letting his computer mind sort through the stack of cards marked *Schwartz, Isaac*. At last, the flint in his eyes softened.

"No. Lord knows we could use you, but no, you are a public figure now and, well, I'm afraid we couldn't use you even if you wanted to return."

"There, you see? We don't want you, predictable or not, so just relax, drink your gin and we three old warhorses will tell lies to each other about the good old days."

"I still want to know why you think I'm so predictable."

"You miss my point, Ike. You were good. The predictable bit defines your personality—the way you read at a human level, not a professional level. For example, I am your friend. We go back fifteen years. I know a lot about you. You didn't tell me all of it. I know it because of the way you are—the kind of person you are. Before you left, I knew where you lived, what you did for fun, and I guessed that if I could talk Conrad Anton into escorting a beautiful blonde lady to my house, I could fix you up with someone."

"You're not going to tell me that you set it up so that Eloise and I—?"

"Not that simple. No, but I knew Eloise and I knew you and I knew you two were a fit. The rest was all chemistry or late-blooming adolescence or something. I had nothing to do with that."

"I'm that easy?"

"Right down to the gin and tonic, Ike. You didn't ask for that, did you? I just gave it to you. You never noticed.

"Now Peter, here…Peter is a different case entirely. He has those little flinty eyes that tell you nothing. Everybody knows you, but what do we know about Peter? Where does he live, what does he drink? Is he a Redskins fan? A Democrat? Does he hunt, read, or fool around? You two worked together for seven or eight years and I bet you cannot even tell me Peter's middle name—it's Carmichael, by the way. It's not that he's secretive, you know. It's just that when you're done talking, you discover that you've told Peter a lot about yourself, but you haven't found out anything about him. That's what makes him so good at what he does, I guess."

"Part of the job, Charlie. You can't do what I do and be obvious."

"Just my point. We need another round, Bloody Mary for me, gin and tonic for Ike, and what are you drinking, Peter?"

"Scotch, rocks, splash."

"See what I mean, Ike. He got his own and I never noticed, never have."

Charlie went to the kitchen to pour drinks. Peter turned to Ike and said, "It's true, you know."

"What's true, Peter? That you're anonymous, I'm predictable, or you drink Scotch?"

"No, never mind that bullshit. That's just Charlie. He doesn't have enough to do at the office, so after he's worked the crossword puzzle and had his three-hour coffee break, he turns what's left of his mind to jelly thinking about the rest of us. But it's true we miss you back at the Agency. When you walked out, you left the European section with nothing."

"There were others there—good men, young, eager, ambitious—still believing."

"Oh, they'll be all right. But they're not you."

"You'll survive."

Charlie returned, passed out the drinks, and, fixing Ike with a steady look, asked, "Peter telling you how Europe's gone to hell in a handcart since you left?"

"Something like that."

"Well, that's a funny thing, you know. We took a terrible beating in the press when the operation, that last one you were in on, failed. Lord love a duck, we couldn't hold the damned arms guy in and the next thing we knew, it was all over—Russians leaked we were providing arms to the Arabs. God, when the Israelis got hold of that one, there was no explaining anything to anybody. Biggest load of egg on our face since Castro's beard. But you were out of it then. Off hiding."

"I heard about it," said Ike. "Took a perverse pleasure in it for a while. But it didn't start when I left. We were having problems all along."

"Yeah, but you'd find out about the screw-ups and fix them, or pull out."

"Pull out is what we did, Charlie."

"Yeah. Well, anyway, Ike, it was a bitch."

The three sat silent for a moment, each lost in his own thoughts. Finally, Charlie asked, "Ike, how did you know the operation was blown?" Charlie still slouched on the sofa, but his eyes had narrowed, come alert, and his voice had changed subtly. He was serious now.

"I told Peter when I got back. I made a couple of phone calls and Kamarov said something. That clinched it."

"You could do that, Ike? Just check around and find out that easy?"

"It wasn't easy, but yes, I could do it if I had to."

"That's amazing. Don't you think that's amazing, Peter?"

"No, Ike worked the continent for twelve years. You get to know things, people. You do favors, look the other way, and after a while, you have a network."

"Uh huh," Charlie grunted, and then added, "you have anyone else in the field that can do that for you?"

"Oh, one or two, maybe, it's hard to say."

"Jeez, Peter, I thought you'd know that for sure. Hell's bells, anyone that good can save you a mess of trouble going into an operation."

"Yes, well, you rest assured, Mr. Special Assistant to the director, the soldiers in the trenches know what they're doing."

Peter's tone was lighthearted, but Ike thought he detected an agitated undercurrent.

"For example—" Charlie ignored Hotchkiss' remark—"could Ike here have stopped that mess from happening if he'd checked first?"

"Maybe, maybe not. It's hard to say. But that one was over a long time ago and Ike doesn't want to talk about it."

"Yes, I could have, Charlie," Ike interrupted, "but no one asked. All I got was a call from Peter to meet someone and bang."

"Peter called you?"

Charlie knew very well what happened. He read the reports. What game was he playing, Ike wondered.

"Yes. Peter called."

"Ike, I've never understood what happened that day and Lord knows I couldn't get you to talk about it. But it's just the three of us here—old buddies. I think it's time you got it out and over with once and for all."

"Not much to tell. We went to the meet, Eloise and I, and it went sour."

"Why in God's name did you take her, Ike? Nobody understands that. Why Eloise?"

"Why? Because Peter said 'a walk in the park,' because Peter said the drop had to identify me somehow, because Peter told me to. Why did I listen is the question."

"Peter said this?"

"Yes."

"Is that right, Peter? I read the reports and I didn't see anything in them about Eloise. There's lots of correspondence up and down the line about why Agent Schwartz took his wife on an operation, but I don't recall anything in there about the control telling him to."

"It was a suggestion." Hotchkiss looked uncomfortable. "We were rushed and I thought it'd be okay, and Ike went along."

"And you left it out of the report, slipped by it in the inquiries, so that you wouldn't look bad after the fact, right? No sense in compounding a tragedy."

"I…yes, something like that. Sorry, Ike, but you'd left and I figured the best thing to do was to let it die."

"So, let's see…you and Eloise went at Peter's request, and then what?"

"Charlie, I've been over this before. It's pointless."

"Maybe, but there are some things that still puzzle me, just can't leave them alone. What happened next?"

"Forget it, there's nothing to tell."

"I want to hear it, Ike." Charlie's voice had a steely quality Ike had never heard before. He did not just want information. He was giving orders. Ike studied his face, tried to read his eyes. Charlie was onto something and he wanted Ike's help. "Play along with me," the eyes said. "It's important."

Ike began to describe the scene, the placement of the table, cups, saucers, the pot of chocolate, the man, and the shots.

"Wait a minute, Ike. How many shots?"

"Two."

"From a what?"

"An AK47 or SKS, more likely an SKS with a scope."

"You can tell that from the sound?"

"On those two, yes. Most rifles sound pretty much alike, but those two have a very distinctive crack. In Vietnam, some of the Marine snipers used them instead of the M-16. But they always told the rest of their platoon or patrol where they were, afraid one of their guys would put a mortar round down their pants, just on the basis of the rifle's sound."

"So there are two shots. One hit Eloise, one hit the other guy and…what hit the coffee pot?"

"Chocolate pot. First one, I guess, and it ricocheted off and hit Eloise."

"Wait a minute, Ike. Let me understand this. One, the pot blows up. Two, you see Eloise is shot. Where?"

"Just left of the midline, second intercostal space, clean."

Something did not fit. Ike remembered the feeling he had before, after he told Ruth. But that had to be the way it happened. Two shots. Ike got up and walked to the French doors that opened out on a tiny balcony, putting distance between him, Charlie, and the awful snake-like thoughts that started to slither into his mind. He looked back. Charlie's eyes were closed. He raised his forearm and he held up one finger, then two, shook his head, and then a third.

Chapter 33

Ike stood on the postage-stamp sized balcony and stared out over the treetops toward the National Cathedral. June in the District. He took a couple of deep breaths of humidity-laden air and turned back toward the room. Charlie sat up and looked at him from the couch. Peter stared at a small print on the wall, eyebrows knotted in concentration.

"Ike, come back. We are almost there."

Almost where? Ike did not know if he wanted to go "there," wherever it might be. It could involve some pain, and he had managed for the past three, no, three and a half years without it. Why risk it now? He did not need this. He walked back into the living room and poured himself another drink, a weak one.

"Picture perfect, you might say. Eloise is shot. She is sitting on your left. You're at the corner, so she's facing the east-west street and the Russian is across from you, catty-corner to the north-south that intersects at your back, right?"

"Right. Charlie?"

"Not now, Ike, I'm on a roll. So that means the shot came from across the street. It hits the pot and ricochets up and kills Eloise. Then a second shot gets the Russian, who falls at your feet. It won't work."

"What do you mean, it won't work?"

"Peter, tell him why it won't work."

"Me? Charlie, you are the one who can't see it. The shooter misses, reloads, fires and hits—it's in the report."

"Charlie, it had to be that way—Kamarov said the man was new, nervous. He missed." Ike sat rigid in his chair, hands clenched into fists, the muscles in his neck like cords. He felt something ugly hanging in the air.

"Kamarov said. You didn't tell me about that."

"Well, it was after, later. He said he was sorry and he wanted me to know they didn't plan it that way and he was sorry."

"He was a sort of friend?"

"Yes, I suppose you could say that. We respected each other as professionals, as adversaries, and yes, I guess you could say that in that crazy world, we were friends."

"That's another thing. Kamarov's disappeared."

"What do you mean, disappeared?" Fear joined apprehension and Ike stood up.

"I mean two weeks after the shooting, he just dropped out of sight—no trace."

"Well, maybe he was pulled back to an office job or retired or something."

"Maybe. Peter, you have a line on him yet? It's been three years. Has he surfaced anywhere?"

Peter stared at Charlie for a moment. He uncrossed his legs and sat forward, hands limp between his knees but eyes alert, searching. "No, but then that doesn't mean much. We don't put much effort in headquarters types. We keep tabs on their field people."

"Right. Well, anyway, the nervous shooter, with the scoped SKS, hits a chocolate pot in a way that bounces the slug neat as a whistle and it gets Eloise. Sorry, Ike, but stay with me, it's important. You want to compute the probabilities of that for me? And then, the Russian stands up, turns around, and as he's turning right to left, he gets shot, spins on around and falls down next to you on the deck."

"He didn't stand up, Charlie. He just sort of crumpled out of his chair and then pitched forward on me."

"Think, Ike, think—what's wrong?" Charlie's eyes pleaded with him. "You said the back of his head was blown away...."

Ike collapsed back into his chair, nearly spilling his drink.

"Ike?"

"My God, oh dear God, Charlie, it can't be...."

"Has to be."

"I'm missing something. You two care to fill me in?" Hotchkiss' voice seemed to come from another room.

"Oh, well, it's this way, Peter." Charlie leaned back with a faraway look. "Ike says the Russian fell out of his chair."

"So? What the hell does that mean?"

"It means," Ike recited, in a soft dead voice, "that he was shot from the north-south street. The back of his head was a mess. That's an exit wound, Peter. The entrance would be clean. Eloise was shot from the east-west street. Her wound was in her chest. She never moved. Neither of them moved. Two shooters, Peter, there were two shooters."

"I still don't see what that has to do with anything. So there were two shooters. They wanted to be sure they got their man. Snipers often work in pairs."

"Kamarov said, *he*—singular—*he* was new, *he* was nervous, not 'one of them,' or 'they,' but *he*. And Kamarov is missing. He told me he did not understand. He started asking questions—I would have if I had been him—and then he disappears, no protest from the Russians, nothing. He just disappears."

"It happens."

"Oh yes, it happens. It happens when the poor son-of-a-bitch in the field is kept in the dark about stuff going on higher up. By the time he digs it out, he finds that knowing can screw up everyone else, so he is removed. The Russians are very direct. Kamarov knew too much, so Kamarov disappeared."

"So there were two, and he found out and maybe he would have told you. So what, he made a mistake."

Charlie broke in, his eyes still faraway, but his voice firm. "Not a mistake, a discovery. Remember, Ike said two shots, but we have three hits. Eloise, the Russian, and the pot."

"A ricochet. One was a ricochet."

"Not likely. The pot exploded, Ike said, so we cannot be sure where the shot came from, but it's a fair bet it came from the same direction as the one that took out the Russian. And that means it would have to ricochet backward. The chances a slug, a jacketed slug, would have taken the pot, reversed direction and gone in clean are—slim to none."

"Well, maybe there were three shots after all."

"Could have been, but Ike remembers two and the pot going up first."

"Yes, the pot, then Eloise, then a small space of time and then the Russian."

"There. You see, Peter, it can't be a spent bullet. It's not likely a ricochet, so where does that leave us?"

"I don't know, Charlie. I could use a drink though, Scotch, rocks—"

"—and splash. I remember."

Charlie fixed another round of drinks while Peter and Ike sat in silence. Then Charlie settled himself and began.

"It's this way. Ike hears two shots but sees three hits. Ike is good at his job and under any other circumstances, would have figured this one out. But Ike is too wrapped up in this one to see straight, to think straight—to do anything but suppress it. So we have to wait three years to get back to it—to finish the job. Three long years, Ike—we needed you, buddy, but you weren't playing. So what happened? The fact you do not hear three shots does not mean there aren't three shots. We have two shooters, one has a silencer, and one does not. One is shooting from close range, to correct for the silencer, and one is not. One is new and nervous and hits a chocolate pot with his first shot. The other hits the first time. One shooter is a Russian, one is not. One is aiming at the Russian double agent and the other is aiming at Eloise."

"Eloise?" Peter rasped. "Who would want to shoot Eloise?"

"That, my friend, is the proverbial sixty-four thousand dollar question. Who indeed? She was the target, Ike. All along, she was the target. If you just put it out of your mind that you were involved in some kind of an operational screw-up, an accident, and accept what your eyes saw, you would know that to be true. Eloise was shot and the hit was textbook perfect."

Ike nodded. It had to be. There was no other explanation. And Kamarov's disappearance had to be accounted for.

"Charlie, why do you think it happened?" Ike asked.

"It's a long story, Ike. For a couple of years, we knew we had a sleeper in the Agency. We just couldn't find him. We knew he was there and we knew he was in the European section, but that is as far as we got. So we set up an operation—one that could not work but would sucker the Russians in and get, we hoped, our man out in the open. We decided we would run guns to the Arabs against the State Department's—hell, the country's Israel policy. That would be too juicy for them to miss. We had Schwartz over there. If he were the traitor, we would soon find out. You would let it go down. If you were not, you would be on the line within hours screaming your bloody Semitic head off. If not you, then it had to be someone else and we thought we knew who."

"But it didn't happen that way. I didn't know anything until much later."

"Yes, that blew the whole game. We sent down the order to Peter to set the thing in motion, and then you go off and get married and become a tourist. We do not know if you knew, and pulled the slickest cover imaginable, or what. We decided to ride it for a while—see what happened.

The next thing we know, you are back in, and all hell breaks loose. The job is a botch and you quit. But if you were our guy, you would not have left the Agency. And then again, maybe leaving is your way of getting back for Eloise's death—no, getting back at us, at them. They lose their mole. That is why it was so important we talk.

"Still, you looked like the one. And the fact that you refused to talk, and everything stopped about that time, supported the idea.

Then about two months ago, it started up again. We couldn't be sure if it was a new plant or the old one or both.

"What made you change your mind—or did you?"

"Oh, well, because you survived for three years in rural Virginia without any protection. As near as we can tell, you were never even contacted, and Kamarov disappeared."

"So you're saying I'm not It."

"We don't think you are, Ike. We never ruled you out until you told me about the shots last week."

Not 'It'—all-ee, all-ee outs in free.

"Last week? You two were talking about this last week?" Peter looked nervous.

"Oh, well yes. Ike here needed some help with his robbery, so we chatted a bit about things. A little of this, a little of that.... You see, Ike, once you get it into your head that Eloise was a target, not an accident, then you are led to the reason for things, to a name, a person. That is what happened to Kamarov. He found our sleeper for us. He didn't know he had, of course. He only knew that his people didn't shoot Eloise, so he figured one of ours did, and he was ready to tell you who, if he could find you, that is. But you were not around, so he couldn't. And by then, our man found him and he disappeared. The reason was the hard part. I thought I knew, but wasn't sure until today. Just now."

"What happened today?"

"Two things. I handed you a gin and tonic without asking, and I found out Peter told you to take Eloise. He is the only one on our side who knew she was going to be there."

Hotchkiss uncoiled from his chair and was halfway to the door when Charlie swung his arm in a lazy arc and caught him in midair with a classic karate chop. By the sound of the snapping, Ike guessed the second cervical vertebra was shattered. Hotchkiss hit the floor with a crash. Charlie got up and went to the door, propped it open, and returned to drag Hotchkiss to the elevator. He pried the doors open and dropped him down the elevator shaft.

"Funny thing about elevators, Ike. Years ago, before we all got safety conscious, folks used to fall down elevator shafts all the time. Then it got so it was damned near impossible to do that—a great inconvenience for the folks who made their living arranging accidents. Then we got these new computer-controlled jobs, and they are nothing but trouble. Program goes wrong and the elevator stops at nine, door opens at eight. I reckon Peter must not have looked this afternoon—old building like this with a shiny new elevator. It's a real shame."

Ike had not moved from his chair. It happened so quickly.

"Charlie, it was Hotchkiss?"

"Had to be, Ike. Remember, I told you earlier, you were predictable and you were good. You were a threat to him. When he got his orders to set up that operation, he saw the trap and knew we were getting close. You were the answer to his prayers. First, you pull yourself out of Europe, and then put yourself back in as a visitor. You will be there but you will not be there, if you follow me. So he gets you your passports, everything, and quick as a wink, you are on the spot, ready to be party to an all-time screw-up. He knows you will take the assignment—you are loyal. He also knows that he has got to get you out of Europe forever, and so Eloise is killed. You might find out about the scheme, but you are not going to be thinking straight enough to see it all. And you did what anyone who knows you would expect you'd do—walk out without talking."

"But if he was the sleeper, their guy, the operation cost them three dozen of their agents. Would they allow that?"

"Collateral damage, Ike."

"Good Lord. Charlie, why didn't he just kill me instead?"

"Because if he had, it would have meant that you weren't our man and because we, that is, our side, the other guys, and that network of yours, would want to know why and we'd find out. Someone would."

"So he has Eloise killed and I pick up the gin and tonic as predicted."

"Exactly."

Ike let the facts sink in. He had been set up, and one way or another, Eloise and he, the whole business, were doomed. Once he became an attacking piece on Hotchkiss' board, he, no, both of them were goners.

"Charlie?"

"Yeah, Ike."

"Did you have to kill him?"

"Well, to tell you the truth, Ike, I was supposed to cuff him and use him in a trade later. But you know us deskbound types get a little rusty after awhile. I must have hit him too hard. I'll catch hell for that. Come on, let's get out of here. Peter's watch says he fell down that shaft an hour from now, so let's get out of here and make sure the Super sees us leave."

In the lobby, Charlie talked to the superintendent about rental availability and gave him his card. On the way out, Charlie peeled the E. Farnham label off the mailbox. Underneath, the name read *Peter Hotchkiss*.

"Oh yeah, this was his place. I thought I'd see if you lost a step," Charlie said with a grin.

"Charlie…one more thing."

Charlie turned.

"Who was the other shooter, the one who killed Eloise?"

"I don't know for sure, Ike, but I think it was Peter."

"Peter?" Ike said, amazed. "He couldn't. He called me from Washington that day. The call came through Call Central."

"Don't think so, Ike. Peter had his phone rigged to forward or receive calls from anywhere—variation on call forwarding. Hell, Ike, my dad used a bookie in Baltimore named Lefty. He had a thing called a cheese box that could do it, and that was forty-five, maybe fifty years ago.

"My guess is Peter checked in the hotel across the street from the café. He called you, patched through his phone at the Agency, and set it up. It is not the sort of thing you check, you know. You said he called, he said he called. Unless you took the trouble to look at the sign-in sheets to see if he was in that night, you would never know, all very vague.

"Charlie?" Ike's voice was quiet. "Is that why you killed him?"

"Like I said, Ike, I'm losing my touch."

"Charlie, I'll never understand you. You must be—"

"Ike, do yourself a favor. Do not even think what you were about to ask. Forget about today. It's over. Do not make me have to come after you, too. You understand?"

Ike looked at Charlie, nondescript in baggy tweed coat, khaki slacks, frayed blue button-down shirt, rep tie, horn-rimmed glasses askew and taped together where he'd lost a screw at the hinge. "You must be a very important person, Charlie."

"Ike," Charlie said, his voice a warning.

"I mean, how the hell do you get away with it? You get paid to be the worst public relations man I've ever met, and your only accomplishment seems to be working the *New York Times* crossword puzzle every day."

Charlie grinned, relieved. "But in ink, Ike, I do it in ink."

Ike watched as he disappeared into the crowd.

Epilogue

Jennifer Ames snapped her purse shut, waved to Archie Boyer, and headed toward the revolving door.

"Have a good weekend," Archie called out after her.

"You too," she replied over her shoulder. She stepped out into the August heat and bounced down the broad steps in front of the Art Institute, toward Michigan Avenue. The street filled with people like herself, leaving offices, leaving work, and heading for bus stops, the El, or parking lots, on their way home.

She almost missed them. A gesture, a raised hand of greeting, caught out of the corner of her eye, made her turn and look at the three figures at the foot of the steps. She saw the girls first, miniatures of their father, but different, darker. And then she saw him. He looked younger, taller. The lines that once etched his face, the roadmap of his pain, were smoothed and softened. He smiled and she realized with a start that she had never seen him smile before.

She looked down at the children, their eyes wide with wonder.

"You must be Karen and Julie," she said to them, and then to him, "Hello, Harry," and made no attempt to stop the tears that began to fill her eyes.

To receive a free catalog of Poisoned Pen Press titles, please contact us in one of the following ways:

Phone: 1-800-421-3976
Facsimile: 1-480-949-1707
Email: info@poisonedpenpress.com
Website: www.poisonedpenpress.com

Poisoned Pen Press
6962 E. First Ave. Ste. 103
Scottsdale, AZ 85251